Sunrise Ridge

Redemption Mountain

Historical Western Romance Series

SHIRLEEN DAVIES

Book Three in the Redemption Mountain

Historical Western Romance Series

Cover design by Kim Killion, The Killion Group

ISBN: 978-1-941786-18-5
Library of Congress: 2015907712

I care about quality, so if you find something in error, please contact me via email at shirleen@shirleendavies.com.

Description

Sunrise Ridge – Book Three
Redemption Mountain Historical Western
Romance Series

"The author has a talent for bringing the historical west to life, realistically and vividly, and doesn't shy away from some of the harder aspects of frontier life, even though it's fiction. Recommended to readers who like sweeping western historical romances that are grounded with memorable, likeable characters and a strong sense of place."

Noah Brandt is a successful blacksmith and businessman in Splendor, Montana, with few ties to his past as an ex-Union Army major and sharpshooter. Quiet and hardworking, his biggest challenge is controlling his strong desire for a woman he believes is beyond his reach.

Abigail Tolbert is tired of being under her father's thumb while at the same time, being pushed away by the one man she desires. Determined to build a new life outside the control of her wealthy father, she finds work and sets out to shape a life on her own terms.

Noah has made too many mistakes with Abby to have any hope of getting her back. Even with the changes in her life, including the distance she's built with her father, he can't keep himself from believing he'll never be good enough to claim her.

Unexpected dangers, including a twist of fate for Abby, change both their lives, making the tentative steps they've taken to build a relationship a distant hope. As Noah battles his past as well as the threats to Abby, she fights for a future with the only man she will ever love.

Visit my website for a list of characters for each series.
http://www.shirleendavies.com/character-list.html

Dedication

This book is dedicated to all of my friends and family who continue to encourage me and spread the word about my writing. Your support means more to me than you know.

Thanks so much!

Acknowledgements

Thanks also to my editor, Kim Young, proofreader, Alicia Carmical, and all of my beta readers. Your insights and suggestions are greatly appreciated.

As always, many thanks to my wonderful resources, including Diane Lebow, who has been a whiz at guiding my social media endeavors, my cover designer, Kim Killion, and Joseph Murray who is a whiz at formatting my books for both print and electronic versions.

Sunrise

Ridge

Prologue

Gettysburg, July 1863

Major Noah Brandt peered down the long barrel of his Sharps rifle, sighting his target, adjusting for the wind. As a Union Army sharpshooter, orders to kill a specific threat to the North's cause had become commonplace. His battlefield promotion to major didn't excuse him from raising the rifle to his shoulder and carrying out the command.

That morning, he'd received orders to send forward a detachment of one hundred sharpshooters to determine enemy positions. Posting his men on a hill past Emmitsburg Road, it didn't take long for them to engage a heavy force of Confederate troops.

Noah took a breath, ignoring the smoke already impeding his vision. He sighted down the barrel once more, then squeezed the trigger, watching as the man clutched his chest and toppled from his horse. Another Confederate officer leaving this earth to stand before his maker, and another piece of Noah leaving with him.

Over the course of nearly six hours, Noah sighted again and again, dispatching more Johnny Rebs, including several officers. He walked up and down the line of sharpshooters, encouraging them, and watching as each advancement of southern troops was held at bay...sometimes retreating, occasionally advancing. He estimated for every ten casualties the enemy sustained, the sharpshooters sustained one. He expected nothing less. His troops were the best at what they did, having passed rigorous skill tests to be accepted into Berdan's First United States Sharpshooters Regiment.

"Major, we're running low on ammunition. What's your order?" Captain Norquist came up beside him, crouching low as enemy fire spewed overhead. Noah had met Tom Norquist within a month of volunteering. They'd followed each other through the ranks, from battle to battle, and became close friends. Noah trusted him implicitly, valuing his instincts on the battlefield.

"How much longer can we sustain the effort?" Noah asked, noticing enemy movement on both flanks.

"Not long. Perhaps ten, fifteen minutes."

"Call the men back. We'll report our findings to the commander." As Noah shouted the last order over the thundering explosions and screaming troops, he saw Tom spin, pull his revolver, and fire toward a group of rebels fighting their way over the hilltop.

Noah dropped to a knee, aimed his rifle and fired, dropping one rebel as he pulled his Remington .44, then killing two more, watching as the remaining troops turned and ran.

"Good work, Tom. If you hadn't..." Noah's words died on his lips as he looked to his side, finding Tom prone and bleeding from wounds to his chest and arm. "Tom!" Noah's anguished cry could be heard over the gunfire as he dropped to the ground, placing his hands over the wound in Tom's chest, several of his men forming a circle around them, providing cover.

"Major, we must move out. The rebels are advancing and we're out of ammunition." One of Noah's lieutenants kneeled beside them, checking Tom's pulse and shaking his head. "He's gone, sir. There's nothing we can do for him." His urgent voice pierced the pain Noah felt deep in his gut.

He nodded, then stood, signaling his men to retreat, knowing he needed to report the large number of Confederate forces to his division commander.

"Take the captain's rifle and lead the men to the encampment, Lieutenant. I'll follow behind. Do not wait for me." Noah handed the man his own rifle and knelt down, shoving his arms under Tom's body and lifting.

"Sir, we can't leave without—"

"I gave an order and I expect you to carry it out. Understood?" Noah growled as he held Tom close to his chest.

"Yes, sir." He recognized the stern expression, accepting there'd be no changing the major's mind.

Noah barely noticed his men move out or the continuing sound of the battle behind him. His expression grim, he concentrated on the man in his arms, his heart aching to a point he found it hard to breathe. It would be up to Noah to write a letter to Tom's widow, a woman he'd never met, but felt as if he knew. She'd break the news to their young son and somehow find a way to move on. They all had to.

Noah trudged into camp as the sun dropped behind the low ridge to the west. No one disturbed him as he passed men cleaning their weapons, cooks ladling supper to the hungry troops, and the chaos inside the medical tent.

He hesitated outside the makeshift hospital, looked at Tom's face, and leaned down to whisper in his ear, "I won't forget you, my friend."

A nurse saw the action, touched his arm, and indicated a cot a few feet away. "We'll take care of him."

Noah placed him on the cot and glanced at her, his face a mask. "He's gone."

"I know, Major." Her soft words drifted over him as he took one last look and turned away, making his way to his tent and solitude.

Noah lowered himself to his cot, leaning forward and resting his elbows on his knees, burying his face in both hands. He had until the end of the month, then his commitment would be over.

Even his promotion to major a few months before did nothing to change Noah's mind. He'd come into the Sharpshooters as a volunteer, and he'd made the decision to voluntarily leave. After three years, he'd done his duty, performing beyond his commander's expectations. But each kill took a piece of his soul.

He was proud of his accomplishments, would have made the decision to volunteer again, but he was through. By the end of July, Major Noah Brandt would transform himself into a private citizen, leaving military life behind and creating a new direction for his life—if he survived until then.

When the day came, all he had to do was change into civilian clothes, fold his uniform, grab his gear, and mount Tempest, the gelding he'd entrusted with his life more than once. If their plans held true, he'd meet his lifelong friend and they'd ride west, away from the battlefields, carnage, and command. He had no idea where he'd end up but, after today, anywhere would be better than here.

Chapter One

Splendor, Montana 1867

"Damn it, Noah. You've got to find a way to pull yourself out of this hole you're in and figure out what you want." Gabe Evans, the sheriff in Splendor and Noah's closest friend, watched him stand by the forge, sweat thick on his face and arms, heating the metal until he'd be able to pound it into another useful tool.

Noah ignored him, turning the metal, trying not to think of the events of the past week. He felt the burning sensation from the moisture dripping into his eyes, but he didn't care. Nor did the scorching heat of the forge irritate or slow him down. Instead, the pain served as motivation to work harder, push the loss from his mind.

Gabe placed his hands on his hips and shook his head, following Noah as he set the burning metal on the anvil, picked up a hammer, and began to pound.

"You can't ignore what happened forever."

Noah stood and squared his shoulders, glaring at the man he'd known since they were both shorter than the height of his workbench. "Why?"

"Because it will eat you up inside." Gabe's voice took on a hard edge. "And because she'll be back someday and you'll have to face her."

Noah glanced outside, seeing the sun peek through the darkening clouds, and wiped an arm across his brow. He swallowed the lump lodged at the back of his throat. "She'll belong to someone by then."

"If you believe that, you're a bigger fool than I thought." Gabe grabbed a ladle, dipped it into the water trough, and poured the contents over his head and neck, shaking his head from side-to-side. "For whatever reason, the woman sees you as quite the prize—one she's determined to win. There's still time to go after her."

Noah spun toward Gabe, tossing the hammer aside. "For what? To live with me in a cabin not as big as her father's study? Do you believe for one minute I'd want her to live that way?"

"How do you know she doesn't *want* to live that way? Did you ever take her to see the cabin, talk to her about your plans?"

He held his arms out, palms up. "Don't you see? I have nothing to offer her. Look around, Gabe. I'm a blacksmith—"

"With a growing store and more business than you can handle. People wait weeks for your work." He leaned against a nearby post, crossing his arms. "And I happen to know you have a sizeable sum put aside in the local bank."

"Sizeable by whose standards?" Noah snorted.

"Most anyone in this town. Other than Tolbert or the Pelletiers, there are just a handful of successful businessmen, and you're one of them."

"I'm a smithy, not a businessman," Noah grumbled, wiping his hands down his apron. "Besides, Tolbert could've sent her anywhere, even though he mentioned Philadelphia."

"It is Philadelphia."

Noah paused, turning a dark look at Gabe. "How do you know that?"

"I sent a telegram to Sheriff Sterling in Big Pine. Tolbert rode that far with Abby, then sent her on to Philadelphia with an escort to live with some distant relation." He pushed away from the post, eyeing Noah. "It wouldn't be hard to find out where she's living. I'm heading to the boardinghouse for some grub." Gabe took a few steps, then turned back. "Think about what I said."

Noah stared at his retreating back and slumped onto a bench, leaning forward to rest his arms on his knees. He looked at his dirt-encrusted hands, turning them over to finger the calluses. His arms were marked with burns from the forge and the sparks that flew when he hammered the hot metal. He scrubbed his hands over his stubbled face and stood, walking to a small back room where he kept his necessities for when he had no time to ride to his cabin. The small mirror he'd had since the war lay on a shelf. Picking it up, he studied his face, noting the lines around his mouth and eyes had grown deeper, more pronounced since he'd arrived in Splendor.

No, he was nobody's prize, especially Abby's. His dark blonde hair was still thick, and although Suzanne Briar, owner of the local boardinghouse, trimmed it on occasion in trade for a new pot for her restaurant, he still kept it shaggy. He'd slicked it back for Luke Pelletier's marriage to Ginny Sorensen the week before, slipping into his one suit and polished boots.

The thought of the wedding and the reception following had him resting on a nearby chair, closing his eyes, wishing he could have that day back.

Luke and Ginny's reception...

The wedding had been beautiful, and Ginny was nothing short of stunning. The Pelletiers knew how to throw a shindig and the reception proved it. He'd stayed in town instead of riding to his cabin, closing his mining supply and tack store so his young helper, Toby, could attend.

He'd hoped to see Abigail Tolbert, the woman he'd been in love with since the first time he spotted her getting out of her father's buggy. Her father, King Tolbert, owned the largest cattle spread in the area, plus more land and businesses in the territorial capital of Big Pine, which was a good day's ride from Splendor. There was little love lost between Tolbert and most of the townspeople, yet few would slight him by withholding an invitation to a wedding, especially when it involved another prominent ranching family, the Pelletiers.

His gaze had caught hers the moment they entered the church. Tolbert escorted her to seats near the front, taking what he felt was his rightful place where all could see him. Abby tried to hide it, but Noah noticed each glance over her shoulder toward him and returned her smile, seeing her blush in return. He'd sought her out at the reception, glad for a few moments alone in conversation before a group of women pulled her away.

An hour into the festivities, she walked straight toward him, laced an arm through his, and pulled him with her, asking if he'd ever had a tour of the church. He'd told her no, not imagining there was much more to see than the main chapel. To his surprise, the building included a kitchen, two small offices, and a storage room in the back. She drew him into the pastor's office, letting the door close behind them.

Noah reached his hand toward the door, saying it was improper for them to be alone. Both knew Abby's father would punish her and skin him if he found them together. She'd smiled and placed her hand on his, bringing it to her mouth, brushing her lips across his knuckles. He remembered thinking Abby Tolbert might just kill him before her father had a chance.

She looked into his face and smiled as her hands moved up his arms to rest on his shoulders, giving her enough leverage to lean up and kiss his cheek. She let her lips travel to his jaw, not quite claiming what they both wanted. His fragile willpower slipped as his arms circled her waist, pulling her close enough for one taste. That's all he wanted. One taste and he'd set her aside.

He knew she had little experience, yet the one brief kiss caused a fire to flash through him, stronger than anything he'd ever felt with another woman. The thought caught him off guard, stilling his actions as he lifted his head and set her aside—at the same instant the office door flew open, an angry King Tolbert standing on the other side.

"What the hell have you done to my daughter?" King yelled, storming into the room as Noah moved in front of her. "I'll have you hung for this."

"Father, nothing happ—"

"This is between the men, Abigail."

"But, Father…"

"What's going on back here?" Luke Pelletier stopped in the doorway as his brother, Dax, and Gabe Evans walked up behind him.

"I want this man arrested, Sheriff." Tolbert's face glowed red, his eyes sparking.

"Father," Abby protested, placing herself between the two men glaring at each other.

"And why would I arrest Noah?" Gabe asked as he glanced between the three people.

"He attempted to attack my daughter—"

"Noah did no such thing, and I won't have you accusing him of it." Abby moved closer to her father, her back to Noah.

"It's all right, Abby—" Noah started.

"No, it isn't all right. He's trying to make a scene and I won't have it." She rested her fisted hands on her hips and glared at her father. "Tell Sheriff Evans you made a mistake."

"I made no mistake, Abigail. I saw his hands on you."

"I kissed him. All he did was try to set me aside."

Noah winced at the image she painted. If they'd been someplace else, he didn't believe he would have been able to show much restraint. He would've dragged her up to him, kissing her senseless.

"Abigail." Tolbert's hard, cold voice did nothing to cool her anger.

"It's true." She turned to Noah. "Tell him."

Noah's jaw worked as he tried to clear his mind. He couldn't blame her for something he'd wanted for a long time. "It's my fault, Mr. Tolbert. We never should've come back here."

"Noah…" Abby's response died on her lips as King grabbed her arm, escorting her from the room.

"You'll hear from me, Brandt," Tolbert said as he disappeared with Abby.

Noah cursed, dragging a shaky hand through his hair.

Gabe rested a hand on his shoulder. "It'll blow over. In a few days, Tolbert will forget all about it."

Noah's gaze snapped to his friend. "Somehow, I don't believe he will."

The men began to leave when Rachel, Dax's wife, came storming toward them. "What happened in here?" she asked, a look of alarm on her face.

"It wasn't anything, Rachel," Dax said.

"It must have been something. King stormed past us with Abby, saying he'd had enough. He said he'd made up his mind and would be taking her to Big Pine, then putting her on the first train to Philadelphia."

Noah slowly opened his eyes, the memory of that afternoon draining the life from him. Each day since she'd boarded the stage, he'd told himself it was the best thing for her. She needed to meet a respectable man, someone with a future, money, and social status—none of which he could provide. No matter the truth of his words or the logic in his thinking, he slipped deeper into a hole of his own making each day.

Chapter Two

St. Louis, Missouri

"I won't be long." Abby glanced at the escort her father had provided for the trip to Philadelphia. She could only guess how he'd found someone on such short notice. For months, King Tolbert traveled to Big Pine each week to oversee his businesses and other property—at least, that's what he said. Abby had heard rumors about a woman he'd been seeing. After several days of traveling with the woman, she felt certain her companion was her father's mistress.

"I'll wait on the train," the woman called as Abby dashed into the depot, running out the front door, not once looking over her shoulder.

After the incident at Luke and Ginny's reception, her father had almost killed the horses harnessed to their buggy in his haste to get home. Not even a day later, he'd told her to pack her belongings, then bundled her into the wagon for the trip to Big Pine. Luckily, she'd anticipated his actions.

Abby had been forthright about her feelings for Noah. Her father's response had been to forbid her from spending any time with him outside the livery—no dinners, suppers, or conversing with him at church or other social gatherings. In her heart, she knew threats wouldn't be enough to keep her away from Noah.

Her father didn't know she'd saved the spending money he'd sent to her while she was at school in Philadelphia. Each month, the headmistress would provide funds sent to the girls from their families, and Abby would hide almost every cent in an old tin. She'd amassed a sizable sum over all those years. It had been the first item she packed while her father raged that evening in the parlor.

As the sound of the train pulling from the station caught her attention, she slowed her pace, trying to calm her racing heart. She'd done it.

Glancing around, she spotted a hotel and restaurant across the street. She raised her skirts, stepping cautiously through the dense muck, dodging numerous horses and buggies. She'd almost made it when she felt a shove at her back, causing her to pitch forward, saving a face-first disaster by bracing her arms in front of her.

"May I help you, miss?"

She glanced up to see a strong hand reach down toward her. Grasping it, she found herself being hauled up by a man almost as tall and broad as Noah, with deep-set eyes, long hair pulled into a queue, and weather-beaten skin. His eyes crinkled as he took in the sight of her.

"Thank you, sir. I must be a sight." Abby tried to brush the mud from her traveling outfit, doing nothing but creating a bigger mess. She looked up at the low chuckle, then began laughing herself. "I suppose I should find a hotel and get cleaned up."

"You're standing in front of a good one. Let me escort you inside." He held out his arm, taking her bag in his other hand. "I'm Beau Davis."

"Abigail Tolbert, Mr. Davis. I'm pleased to make your acquaintance."

Abby glanced around the small hotel room, noting the canopied bed, beautiful quilt folded across the bedspread, and vase filled with a

single flower. It was a place she'd feel comfortable staying in for a night or a week. The exact length of time was up to her.

Beau Davis had insisted she dine with him. She'd learned little about him, other than he'd fought for the North during the war, now making his living hunting those outside the law. He'd refrained from using the term "bounty hunter", although Abby felt certain that was his profession.

"And you, Miss Tolbert...what is a lovely young woman such as yourself doing in St. Louis alone?"

She blinked a couple times, deciding how much she wanted to divulge.

"The answer, Mr. Davis, is not simple."

He sat back, holding up his cup of coffee, the corners of his mouth tilting upward. "I have plenty of time."

"To be quite truthful, I deserted my traveling companion, who is still on the train for Philadelphia."

"Was he not to your liking?"

"My companion was a woman my father arranged to escort me to my aunt's home. You see, he sent me away in an attempt to separate me from, well...from someone he didn't approve of."

"A scoundrel?"

Abby's eyes blazed at the insult to Noah. "Absolutely not. He is the kindest, most humble, sincere man I've ever met. But my father can see none of that." Realizing her voice had risen, she took a breath to calm her temper. "All my father cares about is money, social standing, and..." She glanced away, trying to find the right words.

"Making a good marriage for you?"

She blew out a breath. "Yes. At least *his* idea of a good marriage."

"I take it the men he would choose aren't acceptable to you?"

She locked eyes with him. "I know perfectly well who I want, Mr. Davis, and it's not some stuffy banker or lawyer from Big Pine."

He couldn't hide his soft chuckle at the determination she showed. Most young women, especially those of means, would go along with the wishes of their father. The more she spoke, the more intrigued he became.

"Big Pine. That's in Montana, correct?"

"It's the territorial capital, a day's ride from my home."

"Which would be…?"

She pursed her lips, then moistened them. "Splendor."

Beau tilted his head. "I've heard of it. It's near Redemption Mountain, right?"

Her eyes widened. "Why yes, it is."

"I may have reason to go that way on business in the near future. Will you be returning to Splendor?"

"I haven't quite decided." An image of Noah crossed her mind. Her anger at the way he acted at the church hadn't subsided. She didn't understand why he felt the need to shield her from her father's anger, taking all the blame on himself. But what hurt most was that he hadn't come after her, ridden to the ranch or followed them to Big Pine. He'd given up without a fight.

Each time she'd thought through his actions, the unavoidable conclusion hurt. He simply didn't love her.

Abby had always believed Noah cared much more than he let on. Her feelings for him were no secret. She'd grown tired of waiting for him to make a move and had taken matters into her own hands at Luke and Ginny's reception. The outcome had been wonderful and awful at the same time. Being held by Noah and kissing him had been all she'd thought it would be. She hadn't wanted him to stop, yet he'd seemed unmoved by the experience. His calm detachment told her more than she wanted to believe.

If she made the decision to return to Splendor, she had to accept it wouldn't be into Noah's waiting arms. She'd go because it was her home and nothing more.

"Good morning, Sheriff. Something I can do for you?" Bernie Griggs, manager of the Western Union and mail office, asked as Gabe strode inside.

"I'm riding out to see King Tolbert, then going by the Pelletier ranch. Thought I'd see if you needed anything delivered."

"A telegram for Tolbert came in an hour ago. I'd be obliged if you'd take it and his mail to him. There are a couple letters for the Pelletiers. I believe one is from Rachel's parents."

Gabe slid the documents into his coat pocket. "I'll see they get these."

The road heading north out of Splendor split outside the town. Right would take him to the Tolbert ranch, left would lead him to the Pelletier ranch, where Dax's wife, Rachel, had invited him and Noah for supper—a common occurrence both men enjoyed. He reined his horse right, wanting to get the less pleasurable part of his trip finished first.

Less than an hour later, the Tolbert ranch house came into view. Getting no response to his knocking, he headed toward the shouts from the barn.

King Tolbert stood inside a circle of men, staring down at a cowhand who lay sprawled on the ground, attempting to sit up. As he got traction, a kick of Tolbert's boot had him on his back once more. He wiped blood from his already bruising face and looked up.

"All I did was what you told me, Boss. Took the horse out to see how he'd do. Wasn't my fault he broke his leg in a hole." The cowhand rolled to his side, this time pushing to stand up a few feet from Tolbert.

"He's right, Boss. There's nothing he could've done. It was an accident." Another of his hired men stepped forward, attempting to get between the two men.

Tolbert turned toward the second man. "What I know is that man was responsible for bringing the horse back in one piece. How it happened doesn't concern me. If you feel different, you can pack your gear and ride out with him."

They stared for a long moment before the man nodded. "You're right. We have a different way of working than you. We'll be collecting our pay, then be off your ranch."

The two men walked out, passing Gabe without a glance, heading toward the bunkhouse.

Tolbert's eyes widened at the sight of the sheriff before a hooded expression crossed his face.

"Didn't know you were back there. What can I do for you?" Tolbert asked, walking up to Gabe as the other ranch hands returned to their duties.

"I received a complaint of more missing cattle from ranchers on your eastern border. Not a great number, but enough to cause concern. Thought I'd check with you." Tolbert had been implicated in cattle rustling in the past, although there'd been no evidence to prove he'd been involved. Instead, the blame had been placed on a few of his men who'd left the territory when suspicions turned toward them.

"Thanks for the warning, but I haven't experienced losses. Trust me, I'd know." He turned toward the house, Gabe moving alongside him.

"If you *do* lose cattle, I expect you'll send someone to let me know and not take action on your own."

Tolbert had a reputation of handling issues directly, using his own men. In his opinion, the law helped people of lesser means, not those of his status. When something happened on his land, to his property, he took action without a second thought, excluding Gabe or anyone else with a badge.

"You'll be notified," Tolbert replied. "Anything else?"

Gabe reached into a pocket, handing him the telegram and mail. "Griggs asked me to deliver these to you."

Tolbert shuffled through the messages, stopping when he saw the telegram and unfolding it. He read through it, cursing in a loud voice, then read it once more.

"Bad news?" Gabe asked.

"Abigail. She missed the train when they stopped in St. Louis. Her companion didn't realize it until the train was miles away. She had to wait until the next stop to notify me."

"How long ago?"

"I don't know. Several days."

"And you've heard nothing from her?"

Tolbert scrunched the telegram in a hand and threw it to the ground. "Not a damn word." He turned and stomped toward the house, letting out a string of curses before slamming the door shut behind him.

Gabe opened the door and followed him inside, watching as Tolbert strapped his gun belt around his waist and grabbed a hat.

"Where do you think you're going?"

"To find my daughter," he growled, trying to push past Gabe.

"She could be anywhere, King. Maybe still in St. Louis, but she may also have taken the next train east. There are other ways to handle this."

Tolbert glared at him. "And what would those be?"

"I'll send telegrams to the sheriffs in the towns between Splendor and Philadelphia, provide her description, and ask them to look for her, check to see if anyone has seen her. You may want to contact Allan Pinkerton, bring his agency into this."

"Perhaps I could convince Luke Pelletier to search for her. He used to work for Pinkerton," Tolbert said.

"Maybe, but he's married now. I'm riding over to see them when I leave here. I'll talk to him."

"I'm her father. I should start a search."

"What if she shows up here looking for you? Or sends a telegram to let you know where she's staying? You need to be here if that happens, at least for a while—until we've had responses to my requests."

"You know I don't work that way. I'm not used to letting others handle what I consider my job."

"Give me some time, see what we learn." Gabe scrubbed a hand over his face. "You know, she didn't leave under the best of circumstances."

"And whose fault was that? I'll tell you. Your friend, Noah Brandt." He turned away, pacing toward the window.

"If that's what you believe, I won't try to change your mind. But the way it looked, you forced her to leave. Did she thank you when she got on the stage in Big Pine?"

"That's none of your damn business, Sheriff."

"I'm making it my business because Abigail may have run off. She may be trying to get away from you."

Tolbert spun toward him. "She'd never disappear like this."

Gabe rested his hands on his hips, glaring at the other man. "Are you sure?"

"Of course. She's a good girl. Willful, headstrong, with her own ideas, but I don't believe she'd run off."

"Even if she felt angry and humiliated by the way you sent her away against her wishes?" Gabe asked.

"You have no idea how she felt."

"You left her with Suzanne Briar while you made arrangements to leave town. Trust me, King. She told Suzanne plenty."

Tolbert's shoulders slumped at the news. He'd been so angry, he hadn't realized how much his actions upset Abby, perhaps pushing her into the decision to run.

"But she has no money, no place to go," he ground out. "A single, young woman alone. She's smarter than that."

"Are you certain she has no money? From what I've seen, she's resourceful. She may have harbored more secrets besides how she feels about Noah."

"I won't discuss her feelings for Brandt. He's not good enough for her and never will be. And I believe he knows it."

Gabe's jaw worked, but he remained silent. He knew Noah Brandt better than anyone, knew him to be one of the best men he'd ever met, and felt proud to call him a friend.

"My guess is she took money with her, jumped off the train, and is deciding what to do next. She may return here, or consider building a new life elsewhere."

"You don't believe she was abducted?"

"No, I don't." Gabe turned to leave. "I'll send out telegrams and let you know what I learn."

As he rode toward the Pelletier ranch, he considered Abby's disappearance and what he'd tell Noah. His friend would be frantic and want to ride out, the same as Tolbert. Gabe had been surprised at his success in convincing

Tolbert to stay, although he didn't know how long the man would wait.

Gabe spotted a fire a mile from the ranch and reined his horse toward it, recognizing the ranch hands Tolbert fired. They stood when he approached—one tall and lean, the other of medium height with broad shoulders.

"Gentleman, I'm Gabe Evans, sheriff of Splendor. Is it all right if I share your fire for a spell?"

"I'm Jeb. This is my cousin, Robert. You want some coffee?" the taller of the two asked.

"Thank you." Gabe looked around. Although the sun shown overhead, the day had turned chilly. "You going to camp here tonight?"

"Is there a problem with that?" Jeb leaned forward, handing a cup to Gabe.

"Nope. Just asking."

"Truth is, we don't know where we'll go from here. Most of the ranches have all the hands they need right now. We'll probably ride south toward Wyoming, then maybe Colorado. We need to find something." Robert lowered his gaze, staring into the fire.

"Do you know the Pelletiers?" Gabe sipped his coffee, his eyes glancing over the rim.

"Never met them. We hear they own the spread next to Tolbert." Jeb tossed out the last of his coffee, setting the cup on the ground.

"You're a mile from their place. I'm riding there now. Why don't you pack up and go with me? They're always looking for good men."

Chapter Three

Abby counted her money one more time, making the decision to purchase a ticket and travel back to Splendor on the next train. She felt certain the companion she'd left behind would've notified her father by now, who'd be frantic and already searching. Abby believed she had three choices.

One, she could use her ticket to continue west to her aunt's place, a woman who didn't want her, but who would do whatever King Tolbert requested. Abby would live a quiet life, find work as a companion or teacher until a suitable match could be found, then slip away into oblivion.

Two, she could stay in St. Louis and seek work, returning to Splendor if she ran out of funds. The problem with this solution would be to find something suitable, which she assumed would be quite difficult in a town where no one knew her.

Living with her father, the skills she'd acquired in bookkeeping were wasted.

Numerous times he'd turned down her offer to help with the business aspects of the ranch, seeing her as only fit to act as hostess and direct the activities inside the home. She groaned. Even if she did try to return home, she thought it doubtful her father would accept her. He'd put her on the first stage out of Splendor, but this time he'd send at least one of his men with her.

Three, she could take the train home, obtain a room at Suzanne's boardinghouse, and look for work. She grew up in Splendor, knew most everyone, and felt she could find something suitable. Her father didn't know that Horace Clausen, president of the Splendor bank, had mentioned several times how valuable her skills would be to him. She didn't know if he meant in a bookkeeping role or as one of the tellers, but it didn't matter. He'd be her first stop.

Redemption's Edge Ranch, Splendor

"Glad you brought those two men with you, Gabe. We can always use more help." Dax

Pelletier, the older of the two brothers, poured drinks and nodded toward a chair.

"I can't vouch for them. All I can tell you is they didn't hesitate to take their pay and leave Tolbert when he became abusive." He brought the whiskey to his lips, then stopped at the sound of the office door opening.

"Noah's here." Rachel, Dax's wife, poked her head in the office, then swung the door open. "Luke, Ginny, and Mary are putting the wagon away. Supper will be ready in a bit."

"How'd it go with Tolbert?" Noah asked Gabe, taking a chair next to him.

"As you'd expect. He said none of his cattle are missing. Luke and Dax aren't missing any, either. Right now, the rustling seems to be confined to the east of Tolbert's property. He said he'll notify me if he discovers any cattle have disappeared."

Noah snorted. "I don't believe that for a minute. He'll gather his men and go after whomever he suspects—and there'll be no trial."

"Good evening, gentlemen." Luke Pelletier walked straight toward the bottle of whiskey and a glass. "I miss anything?"

"Gabe says Tolbert hasn't lost any cattle," Dax replied.

"Neither have we, but I'm posting more men at night, keeping the herd together. I figure it's only a matter of time before we're hit." Luke settled a hip against Dax's desk, sipping his drink.

Gabe leaned forward, rolling the glass between his hands. "There's another issue. I don't want to talk about it at supper with the children present, but there's no reason the adults shouldn't know." He glanced at Noah, holding his friend's gaze.

"What is it? News about Abby?" Noah asked, his chest tightening. He'd seen the look in Gabe's eyes before, indicating whatever he had to say wasn't good.

"In a way, yes. She jumped off the train in St. Louis—"

"What the hell?" Noah slammed his hand on the chair arm, trying to make sense of her doing anything so irresponsible.

"The companion Tolbert sent along didn't realize Abby hadn't returned until the train was miles from the depot. Tolbert wanted to go after her right away, but I convinced him to wait. I'm going to send some messages to people I know in towns between Splendor and St. Louis. Someone must have seen her."

"To hell with that, Gabe. I'm going after her." Noah set his glass on the desk and stood.

"Sit down. We need to talk this through before any of us react too early and waste time."

Noah sat down, crossing his arms over his chest. "Go on," he ground out, his eyes hooded.

"Think about it. Abby's stubborn and willful. She hates being controlled by her father, and she loves you."

Noah cursed softly, nodding toward Gabe to continue.

"I don't believe your woman has been taken. My guess is she had money stashed away and will return to Splendor, probably to find work. I've had time to think through this and I believe her first stop will be Suzanne's boardinghouse. She trusts her, knows she can be honest with her. I think your girl is going to do what Ginny did—find work and become independent of her father."

Luke's wife, Ginny, became the sole support of her and her younger sister, Mary, when their parents died. She worked as a server in a saloon and cleaned rooms at the boardinghouse before going to work at the Pelletier ranch and, eventually, marrying Luke.

"What are you suggesting? That I sit around and hope she'll return and no one's abducted her?" Noah didn't like the idea of biding his time, hoping no one had taken Abby.

"The same as I said to Tolbert. I'll send telegrams, see if I can learn anything." He looked at Dax and Luke. "I'd be obliged if you two would notify anyone you know between here and St. Louis. Someone will have seen a beautiful young woman traveling alone. Her red hair is distinctive, and her clothes identify her as someone from wealth. I doubt she went east. All my instincts tell me she plans to come home."

"But not to her father." Noah agreed with Gabe, at least on that point.

"Where would she find work?" Luke asked, remembering how hard it had been for Ginny to earn enough to support her and Mary.

"She can do bookkeeping. She learned it in school back east, but Tolbert would never allow her to help with ranch business. Horace Clausen at the bank told her he'd hire her if he could, but she never told her father." Noah recalled their one formal meal together at

Suzanne's restaurant. Abby had shared much about herself and her dreams. When Tolbert found out about their meeting, he'd forbidden her from spending time with Noah again.

"Abby may go straight to you, Noah," Dax added.

"I want to believe it, but doubt it's true. The look she gave me when Tolbert pulled her from the church, well...I hurt her by not standing up to her father."

"You had good reasons. Nothing would've been gained by pushing Tolbert. He was beyond being able to have a rational conversation about you and Abby," Luke said.

"He mentioned speaking with you about mounting a search." Gabe looked at Luke.

"I'm glad to help, if that's what's decided, but it would be better for him to contact Allan Pinkerton directly. He has the resources for a search such as this one."

"I told him the same thing, but also said I'd mention it to you."

A soft knock preceded Rachel entering the room. "Everyone is here and supper's on the table." She glanced around, knowing right away something wasn't right. "What's going on?"

Dax walked around his desk and put an arm around her. "Abby is missing."

Rachel gasped, covering her mouth with a hand. "But...how?"

"We don't know and we don't want to worry the others. I'll tell you all about it when we're alone." He leaned down, placing a kiss on her temple.

Rachel and the men followed the sound of laughter to the dining room. A few months before, several of the men tracked what they believed to be thieves to a hidden cave in Redemption Mountain. Inside, they found five orphans ranging in age from seven to nineteen. They'd run from their Crow captors, stealing food, doing whatever they could to survive. Four now lived with the Pelletiers, taking on chores and finishing their studies. Fifteen-year-old Billy had opted to live with two widowed brothers who owned a ranch south of Redemption's Edge.

Two ranch hands sat at the table. Bull Mason, one of their main men, and Travis Dixon, Luke's right-hand man in their horse breeding business. Noah took a seat next to Bull, noticing nineteen-year-old Lydia, the eldest of the orphans, on Bull's other side.

From what he could see, Bull's feelings for Lydia mirrored how Noah felt about Abby. And, the same as Noah, Bull had yet to say anything to Lydia. It took Abby's disappearance to make him realize his mistake in not being honest about his love for her.

Noah spent supper only half listening to the conversation moving from one topic to another, his mind consumed with thoughts of Abby. He had to fight the urge to ride back to town, pack what he needed, and leave for St. Louis. What Gabe suggested made sense, except Noah had never been one to sit around and wait when a job needed doing.

He chewed his food in slow, measured bites, nodding as people spoke to him while deciding what he needed to do before leaving town. Toby, his helper at the tack and supply store, could keep watch on the livery, letting people know Noah had gone on a trip. Closing his cabin on Sunrise Ridge wouldn't take long.

His first stop would be Big Pine, then each town between there and St. Louis. He couldn't wait for word to trickle back to Gabe from the various lawmen he knew, and he did not want Abby's father to find her first. Even though Tolbert indicated he'd wait before starting his own search, Noah didn't believe it. Past actions showed the man to be arrogant, handling situations without involving the law.

If Noah was going to locate Abby before Tolbert's men did, his search needed to begin right away. He'd find her, acknowledge his feelings, doing whatever he could to undo any harm created by his actions, and pray he could still make it right.

"Good morning, Miss Tolbert. Are you waiting for the train?" Beau Davis set his bag on the boardwalk outside the depot.

She looked up from her bench seat, smiling at Beau, hoping he might also be heading west. They'd shared a nice meal a few nights before and he'd been a complete gentlemen.

"Yes, I am. Will you also be taking the train?"

"West, then taking the stage to Big Pine. And you?" He sat down beside her, removing his hat and setting it on the bench.

"The same. Except I plan to go on to Splendor. It's a day's ride by stagecoach from Big Pine."

"I hope you'll allow me to accompany you. It's a long trip by yourself, and from what I understand, quite boring." His mouth tipped into a smile and she could swear she saw a slight twinkle in his eyes.

"It would be wonderful to have someone join me on the journey." She pulled out an embroidered handkerchief, dabbing at the moisture on her face. "Are you chasing someone, Mr. Davis?"

He chuckled softly. "No, Miss Tolbert. I'm not chasing anyone. Although I do plan to meet with my partner in Big Pine. He's following men he believes to be cattle rustlers and has requested my help. I'll make my decision once I speak with him. And you? Are you returning to the man you hope to marry?"

She hesitated a moment, feeling somewhat uncomfortable having this discussion with a man she barely knew. His manner, however, put her at ease, making her feel like she confided in a friend. "I don't believe so. You see, I learned he may not share my feelings."

"Perhaps he keeps his thoughts to himself."

"No, Mr. Davis. His actions were quite clear the last time we saw each other. Besides, if he cared for me, he would've made some effort to stop my father from sending me away. He's a wonderful man. I'm simply not the woman he wants."

"Train's on its way." The railroad attendant walked outside, then paced back and forth. "Not too many getting on here. You two and another couple. I hear the weather's pretty good going west." He stopped and looked down the tracks as the train rounded a bend and headed toward them. He looked at Abby's bag. "Is that all you have, miss?"

"Yes. Just the one."

He reached down to grab it, but Beau beat him to it. "I'll take care of it." He took her bag in one hand and his in the other as the train pulled to a stop. "After you, Miss Tolbert."

Although numerous passengers exited the train, it took them several minutes to find adjoining seats.

"Appears we won't lack for company on the trip." He pulled out a small bottle from his inside coat pocket, opened the top, wiped the top, and offered it to Abby. "Would you care for a drink?"

She stared at the bottle, surprised he offered. She'd never had whiskey, and brandy on only one occasion.

"I don't think—"

"It may help you relax."

She shifted in her seat as the train started forward. "Well, perhaps one sip." She took the bottle, put it to her lips, and swallowed a small amount, wincing at the strong, burning sensation, then choking as it went down.

"Never had whiskey?"

She choked again, then cleared her throat. "How could you tell?"

Beau laughed, took the bottle, then a long swallow, letting it trickle down his throat. "Ah, that does taste good." He winked at Abby, then closed the bottle and slipped it back inside his coat. "Would you mind if I took a brief nap?"

"Not at all. I believe I'll enjoy the scenery for a while."

Abby rested her head against the seat and watched as the miles passed by, the combination of whiskey and the rolling railroad car relaxing her. An image of Noah crossed her mind. Tall, broad-shouldered, and so incredibly handsome. Her heart squeezed as she closed her eyes and drifted off.

Chapter Four

"I'm not surprised, Gabe. King went too far by sending her away without giving himself time to calm down and think through what happened." Suzanne Briar sat in the kitchen of her boardinghouse with Gabe, drinking coffee as he explained Abby's disappearance.

"You don't believe she may have been abducted?"

Suzanne thought of Abby as a young girl after her mother died. She'd follow Suzanne around, clinging to her apron, asking questions, almost begging for the attention unattainable from her father.

"You know, King never gave her much of what mattered. She attended boarding and finishing schools in the east, seldom making trips back to Splendor, except at Christmas. She refused to return to Philadelphia after she graduated and came home. It was the first time I'd ever seen her stand up to King. She did it again when he threatened to send her away if she continued to see Noah. Do you know what she did? Explained to him what a good man Noah is, how much people respect him, and reminded her father of what he did to save Rachel and the others from those outlaws. She told him she had no intention of avoiding him." She sipped her coffee, focusing her gaze on Gage. "So do I think someone abducted her? Of course not. She had no intention of reaching Philadelphia and never seeing Noah again. Now, I'm not a betting woman, but if I were, I'd wager we'll see Abby back in Splendor in no more than three weeks."

"You seem to know her better than anyone. What do you think she'll do once she comes back?"

"Well, she won't go back to the ranch. I hope she'll come here. Beyond that, I don't know."

"Guess I'd better check with Griggs to see if I've received any responses to my telegrams. I don't know how much longer I'll be able to hold back Tolbert or Noah from going after her."

"You don't know?" Suzanne asked, surprised at the confused look Gabe flashed her.

"Know what?"

"Noah packed up and left early this morning."

"Damn that man," he swore, then looked at Suzanne. "My apologies."

"It's quite all right. What I don't understand is why he didn't tell you."

"Because I asked him not to leave, at least until I got replies to my telegrams. He knew I'd try to talk him out of it so he took off before I could stop him. How'd you find out?"

"He came by to pick up some food for the trip. Told me he was on his way to Big Pine."

"Thanks, Suzanne. I need to send another telegram to Sheriff Sterling in Big Pine. He'll be the first person Noah will go see."

It took Noah longer than he'd thought to finish the jobs he'd committed to at the livery, make sure Toby had what he needed during Noah's absence, and close the cabin. His worry grew with each passing day until he'd finally tied his saddlebags onto Tempest and rode out.

Halfway to Big Pine, he spotted a Crow hunting party, which forced him to detour further south, losing precious time. It had taken him almost two days to reach the territorial capital.

The sun had set by the time he dragged himself into Sheriff Sterling's office.

"Sheriff, I'm Noah Brandt. I rode in from Splendor and am looking for a woman who came through here about two weeks ago. Abigail Tolbert. Any chance you saw her?"

"Have a seat, Mr. Brandt. Coffee?"

"I'd appreciate it." Noah slumped into a nearby chair, tossed his hat on the desk, and dragged a hand over his face.

"I got a telegram from Sheriff Evans asking the same question. I did see her and her father when they arrived. He planned to put her on the stage. She and her companion were to take the train to Philadelphia, if I remember right. I haven't seen her since."

"She left the train in St. Louis."

"Evans said that in his telegram and asked me to keep watch for her. I guess he expects she'll head back this way."

"That's what we're hoping." Noah drained his cup, then set it on Sterling's desk.

"I've spoken to my deputies, asked them to watch for her. Unless she's on a horse, she'll have to take the stage through Moosejaw, then on to here. Someone will see her."

"I appreciate your help." He stood, picking up his hat. "I can't wait around."

"Didn't believe you would."

"I'll be heading to Moosejaw in the morning, then follow the route until I find Abigail."

"Hope you find her." Sterling reached his hand out to clasp Noah's.

"So do I."

"A couple more days and we'll be in Moosejaw, then on to Big Pine. I know I'm ready to get off this stage." Beau shifted in the seat as the coach bumped over a bad stretch of trail.

The stage served as the major means of transportation between the frontier towns not yet serviced by a railroad. Some thought the train might reach Big Pine within a few years. For now, travel occurred by horseback, wagon, or stagecoach.

"I agree with you, Mr. Davis." The stage bounced along and Abby's voice jerked with it. "I'll have one more day in this contraption before reaching Splendor. Afterwards, I may never step into a stage again.”

Beau grinned. She’d been a good travel companion, never complained, asked few questions, and enjoyed the changing scenery as if she’d never seen it before. Abby had traveled this same route many times, yet she still seemed to find joy in the land.

“What will you do when you reach Splendor?”

“Visit my friend who owns the boardinghouse, then look for work.”

“And your father?”

“I’m certain he’ll learn of my return within a day or two, but I won’t return to the ranch.”

“And if you can’t find work?”

She glanced over at him, then shifted her gaze back outside. The same question had repeated in Abby’s mind over and over since leaving St. Louis. She’d finally decided not to think about the possibility she may not find work. She would, and that was the end of it.

“I’ll find work, even if it’s washing dishes or sweeping floors.”

"I appreciate you riding out with the news." King Tolbert turned away from Gabe, signaling for his foreman and a few ranch hands to join them.

"What are your intentions now that you know the sheriff in St. Louis learned Abigail took the train west?" Gabe asked. His gut told him Tolbert would send men for her. If they encountered Noah searching for Abby—or worse, found him with her—Gabe wasn't sure they wouldn't shoot first, not caring about an explanation.

"I'm going to send my men to intercept Abigail and return her to me."

"Would it not be more prudent to wait until she arrives in Splendor? Why work shorthanded when it appears she's on her way home without a formal escort?"

"Because she's willful and I can't depend on her coming here. Her feelings for Brandt may cause her to make yet another bad decision, perhaps even going to him instead of returning to the ranch. I can't allow that to happen."

"If she's as willful as you claim, your actions may cause her to refuse the help you send. She is a grown woman and does have the right to turn your men away."

"She's still a child, Sheriff. Her judgment is impaired and I'll not have her on her own, perhaps ruining any chance for an appropriate match. Now, if you'll excuse me."

Gabe swung up on Blackheart, deciding to return to town and send word to Noah. He'd said his peace, warned Tolbert of the consequences of his actions. Now he needed to get a message to his friend and hope it reached Noah in time.

He'd made it as far as the fork in the road leading to the Pelletier ranch when a group of riders, Dax out front, intercepted him.

"We were coming to see you. Luke spoke with Frank and Hiram Frey. They're missing cattle. Discovered it when they consolidated their herd. Hiram sent word to us this morning and asked we pass it along to you."

The Frey brothers owned a large spread southwest of the Pelletier ranch and a half-day's ride to Splendor. It wasn't unusual for them to send word to Dax or Luke, then ask it be sent on.

"They have any idea when it happened?" Gabe asked.

"Luke didn't mention it. We've doubled our men. Any ideas who might be doing this?" Dax shifted in his saddle, looking behind him at his men.

"None. I'd feel better if Tolbert were missing cattle. At least I could rule him out."

"You think he could be behind this?" Dax held no love for Tolbert after some actions ordered by him when the Pelletiers took over the ranch. The property passed to them when fellow Texas Ranger, Pat Hanes, died chasing a gang of bank robbers in Texas. Tolbert wanted the land for himself and did whatever he could to drive the brothers out. None of his actions dissuaded Dax and Luke from continuing the ranch Pat had started.

Gabe took off his hat and swiped an arm across his forehead. "No, I don't. He'd have nothing to gain by setting up a gang of rustlers. Besides, he already has enough problems with Abigail."

"Any word on where she might be?"

"The sheriff in St. Louis found out she left on a train heading west. Seems she's decided to come home. Tolbert's sending men after her."

"I'd do the same in his situation," Dax said. He and Rachel were expecting their first child and he already felt a strong measure of protectiveness toward the baby.

"Except Noah took off after her. I sure don't want Tolbert's men confronting him, especially if he has Abby." Gabe settled his hat on his head and reined Blackheart toward town. "Looks as if I'll need to find a few men to deputize, see if we can find out who's stealing the cattle. First, I've got to send telegrams out, try to reach Noah."

"Best decision he could make is to marry Abby as soon as he finds her. Nothing else will stop Tolbert from getting between them," Dax said.

"That's about the most sensible suggestion I've heard in a long time. I believe I'll put that in the telegram."

"Sorry, Brandt. I don't recall seeing the young woman you describe. The stage is due in tomorrow. Why don't you wait around to see if she's on it?" The sheriff of Moosejaw had also received a telegram from Gabe and been prepared for Noah's arrival.

Noah took a deep breath and nodded. "I believe I'll get a room and wait. If she's not on the stage, I'll continue to follow the trail until I reach St. Louis. I've got to find her, Sheriff."

"Good luck to you."

Noah headed toward the one hotel, spotting the telegraph office across the muddy main street. He changed directions, deciding to send a message to Gabe first.

"Can I help you?"

"I want to send a message to the sheriff in Splendor."

"Write it out and I'll send it right off."

Noah wrote a few words and handed the paper back to the clerk, who quoted a price and sent the message.

"You're Noah Brandt?" the clerk asked.

"I am."

"I've got a telegram for you. Came in yesterday."

Noah read it through, cursing as he set the paper down.

"Add that I got his telegram to the one you're sending." He dropped another coin on the counter and walked out. The one bit of good news from Gabe's message was Tolbert believed the same as everyone else—Abby had decided to come home.

He arranged for a room, then located the nearest saloon. Nursing a drink, he thought of what he'd say to Abby, how he'd convince her to marry him and return to Splendor as his wife. Gabe's idea had merit. Marrying her would be the only way Tolbert would leave them alone. Of course, the fact he loved her would be his most compelling argument.

The strongest argument against their marriage, and the one he'd used over and over to convince himself to hide his feelings, had nothing to do with his love for her.

He'd had success in Splendor, building his livery and blacksmith trade, then opening a shop catering to miners and those who needed tack. Frugal by nature, he'd saved enough to build his cabin and buy a couple vacant shacks behind the livery, renting them to travelers who decided to make Splendor their home. Few, except Gabe and Horace Clausen at the bank, knew how well he'd done. Still, he had nowhere near the means to support Abby in the way she deserved. There'd be money for them and their children, but little for extras, such as fancy dresses or travel. He wanted so much more for her than what he could provide.

"Another drink, mister?"

Noah glanced up to see a young, tired-looking woman staring down at him. He could see desolation and resignation on a face which seemed much older than her years.

"One more."

She moved closer, brushing her hip against his arm. "Is there anything else you want?"

"Just the whiskey, ma'am."

A look of regret passed over her face. Noah knew it had nothing to do with him and more to do with the loss of money from not enticing him upstairs.

"Let me know if you change your mind." She moved to the next table, where he heard the same conversation repeat itself.

Sipping his drink, he thought of Tolbert's men. Their first stop would be Big Pine. Sheriff Sterling might or might not tell them Noah had already come by. As with many, Sterling held no respect for a man who took the law into his own hands and cared little for anyone other than himself. Even Abby suffered from his selfish ways.

Perhaps he'd get lucky and the men would wait for the stage to arrive in Big Pine and not travel to Moosejaw. Assuming Abby arrived tomorrow, he'd convince her to leave with him, bypassing Big Pine and following a trail to Splendor few knew about. They'd be home by the time Tolbert and his men realized what had happened.

Chapter Five

The wind flared around him, lifting his hat off his head, forcing Noah to stay hunkered down on a chair outside the stage station. The stationmaster expected the coach to arrive within the hour. Soon, he'd know if his search would take him home, with Abby, or on to St. Louis, alone.

"Mind if I sit with you?"

Noah glanced up to see the sheriff grab a chair. "Suit yourself."

The sheriff leaned back while rolling a cigarette, then lit it.

"I got a message from Sterling in Big Pine. A group of men rode in looking for Abigail Tolbert. He thought you'd want to know."

Now he knew he'd be taking the long way home. "Thanks. I expected as much."

Both men looked up at the sound of horses to see the stage some distance away. Noah's pulse quickened and he said a short prayer, hoping she'd be inside.

The minutes passed at a slow rate, the tension inside Noah building until he wanted to jump on Tempest and ride out to meet them.

"Guess you'll know in a minute," the sheriff said, noting him shift in the chair.

Noah exhaled a slow breath. "Guess so."

The stage pulled to a stop, the horses snorting as the driver jumped down and opened the door.

"This is Moosejaw. You may want to stretch before we leave for Big Pine."

Noah's breath caught at the sound of a familiar voice.

"Sounds wonderful. Will we have time for a meal before leaving?"

"We leave in three hours, Miss Tolbert."

Noah watched as the woman he loved emerged from the coach, setting her hand in the driver's for balance, then taking a few steps forward. She brushed her hands down her skirt and looked up, the expression on her face turning from relief to surprise.

"Noah," she whispered, not making any attempt to move toward him. "What are you doing here?"

He took a step forward, reaching out a hand, which she ignored. "I came for you."

She glanced at the stage, seeing Beau step down and stop by her side. He looked from her to the man standing a few feet away, then tilted his head.

"Miss Tolbert, do you know this gentleman?" Beau asked, noting the look of caution pass across Abby's face.

She cleared her throat. "Why, yes, Mr. Davis. This is Mr. Noah Brandt. He lives in Splendor. Mr. Brandt, this is Mr. Beauregard Davis. He accompanied me from St. Louis."

Noah should've been glad Abby had someone to protect her on the journey. Instead, all he could feel was a twisting in his chest and a slow burn in his gut.

"Mr. Brandt, it's a pleasure."

Noah clasped Beau's hand, his gaze never leaving Abby. "Mr. Davis."

The air became thick as silence reigned between the three until Beau felt the need to break the spell. "I believe I'll grab a meal. Would either of you care to join me?"

Noah opened his mouth to decline when Abby spoke up. "That's a lovely idea." She slid her hand through Beau's arm, letting him guide her past Noah and down the street.

Noah's heart sank. He'd been so certain she'd be glad to see him, even if she still felt anger at his behavior the last time they'd seen each other.

The sheriff, who'd held back, placed a hand on Noah's shoulder. "Women are a fickle bunch, son. You follow along, take a meal with them. I believe this will all work out."

Noah nodded, then looked away, confused and feeling a powerful blow to his pride. Ahead of him walked the woman who'd stood up to her father weeks before, defending Noah while letting her feelings be clear to those in the room. He'd been the one to miss the opportunity to set his intentions straight, not only in front of King Tolbert, but his friends, as well. Yes, he'd taken the blame for their actions while, at the same time, not giving any indication of his deep feelings for Abby.

"Will this be suitable, Mr. Brandt?" Beau asked as he escorted Abby inside the first restaurant he saw.

"Yes, fine." Noah followed them, taking a seat across from Abby, ordering the first item the server mentioned. He stared across the table, waiting for her to acknowledge his presence, but her gaze wandered everywhere except at him.

"What brings you to Moosejaw, Mr. Brandt?" Beau asked.

"To escort Miss Tolbert home."

"Do you work for her father?"

Abby couldn't hide a soft snort at the question.

"No. I'm a blacksmith and own a livery."

"And a successful shop," Abby added, unable to continue her silence. She looked at Beau. "He sells supplies to miners and tack to ranchers. Noah does quite well."

"Sounds as if you're a good businessman, Mr. Brandt."

"I do all right. And you, Mr. Davis? What do you do?" Noah relaxed. At least Abby had spoken a few words, even if they weren't directed at him.

"I'm a bounty hunter."

Noah's eyes widened, never expecting the well-spoken man accompanying Abby to be someone who sought men and brought them in, dead or alive.

"What brings you to Moosejaw?"

"I'm going on to Big Pine, the same as Miss Tolbert. I'll be meeting a friend there."

"Another bounty hunter?" Noah asked as he brought a cup of coffee to his lips.

"A man I partner with—Cash Coulter."

Noah set down the cup as he choked on the hot brew.

"Are you all right?" Abby asked, jumping up to thump him on the back.

"Yeah, fine." He coughed once more. "You did say Cash Coulter?"

"Yes. Do you know him?"

"I do. He's been to Splendor, helped mutual friends with a problem, then took off after some men who used to work for King Tolbert."

Abby looked at Noah, her brows knitting together. "What men?"

"Parnell Drake and two others."

"I remember Mr. Drake. He was father's foreman for a while. Father fired him, or was about to when Drake disappeared."

"He ran when Gabe came to your ranch to arrest him. No one's seen him since."

"That's not quite true," Beau interrupted. "Drake and his men are wanted for cattle rustling in Colorado, possibly Wyoming, and now it appears they're working in Montana. Cash is on his way to Big Pine so we can go after them."

"Where do you think they're working?"

"The ranches between Big Pine and Splendor."

"I must send a telegram. I'll meet you at the stagecoach, Miss Tolbert. It was a pleasure, Mr. Brandt. I'm certain we'll see each other again."

"Mr. Davis," Noah shook his hand, then turned to Abby. "I don't want you going to Big Pine on the stage. I want you to ride with me back to Splendor."

"There's no reason to—"

"Abby, your father's men are waiting for you. They're to take you to the ranch as soon as you get off the stage."

"No," she whispered. "How did they know I'd be coming back?"

"The same way I did. The sheriff in St. Louis learned you boarded the train west. It wasn't hard to figure out where you were headed. Even Suzanne believes you'll return to Splendor."

"I'm not going back to the ranch...ever. The days of my father controlling every decision I make, how I live, are over."

"If that's true, go back with me. I know a trail home few know about. By the time they realize you aren't coming, we'll be home." He reached out to touch her shoulder, but she backed away. "Abby, come with me, please. I promise to get you back to Splendor without your father's men knowing."

She squared her shoulders, steeling herself as she looked up at him. "If I go with you, it will be to live at Suzanne's. I'll find work, support myself." She hesitated a moment before continuing. "I've thought much about what happened at Ginny and Luke's wedding, how I handled myself, and your reaction. I realize now you were a fantasy—a beautiful one, but a fantasy nonetheless. I threw myself at you and—"

"Abby—"

"Please, let me finish." She swallowed the growing lump in her throat, taking an unsteady breath. "You tried to let me know numerous times you had no feelings for me, but I refused to listen. I'll always remember how you've been a perfect gentleman, one who treated me as a lady, no matter how foolish my actions may have seemed to you. I now know my feelings were nothing more than youth and inexperience. I'm embarrassed by the way my actions must have been perceived by you."

"Abby, please, let me explain." Noah's stomach twisted.

"There's no need, truly. I've acted as a foolish, rich girl, trying to have what I thought I wanted. When I return to Splendor, I'll be making my own way, figuring out what it is I *do* want. I hope you understand and accept my apologies for how I've behaved."

Her words cut as if a sword had sliced clear through him. She'd changed her mind, no longer wanted him or a future together. He should be glad and not feeling as if his world had come crashing down. In his heart, he knew Abby deserved better. She'd just made it clear her conclusions were the same as his.

"I'll take you to Splendor, help you in any way possible to build your dream, but I will not accept your apology." He turned, walking toward his horse.

"But, Noah…" She ran after him, touching his arm, trying to get him to stop.

"I won't accept it because there's no need for one. You've made your decision, which is how it should be." He settled his hands on his hips and took a slow breath. "I need to get more supplies. We can buy a horse and saddle for you, or you can ride with me, whatever you prefer, but we need to leave soon."

Abby flinched at his cold voice and hard expression. She'd seen him angry, attentive, relaxed, laughing, but never the look of indifference he offered now.

"I'll ride behind you."

He nodded. "Then be ready to leave within the hour. It will be hard riding with few stops as we need to cover as much ground as possible. Do you understand?"

"Yes."

Without another word, he grabbed Tempest's reins and walked to the general store. She watched his retreating back, wishing a life with Noah had been possible. All she had to do was get through the next few days. Perhaps by the time they reached Splendor, she would begin to believe the words she'd spoken, leave her feelings for Noah behind, and start a new life.

"I'm sorry to lose your company, but understand Mr. Brandt's concerns," Beau said, preparing to enter the coach for the final part of his trip.

"I have the same concerns. If my father's men find me, I'll have no choice but to return to the ranch. If that happens, I fear I'll never be free to make my own decisions."

"It seems you've made the right choice. I hope to see you in Splendor, Miss Tolbert, and wish you a safe trip."

"You, as well, Mr. Davis." She waited for him to board the stage, watching as the driver slapped the reins. She raised her hand to wave before covering her face from the dust, hoping she would see him again.

"Are you ready?"

She'd been so focused on Beau, she hadn't noticed Noah standing beside her, an impatient hand on his hip.

"I wanted to tell him my plans. I'm ready now."

He swung up on Tempest, then steadied him as Abby placed her foot in the stirrup and mounted.

"Hold tight, Abby. I don't want you falling off."

It didn't take long for Abby to realize her mistake in riding behind Noah with her arms wrapped around his waist, her chest tight against his back. She could feel each shift, every constriction of his muscles, every breath. When she'd try to ease back, he'd grab her arms and pull her closer, then rest one large, calloused palm on her joined hands.

She didn't know how long they rode, turning south a few miles, then west before veering north. By stage, it took several hours to reach Big Pine from Moosejaw. On horseback, it should take less. When the sun fell behind the western horizon, she leaned forward, close to his ear.

"How long?"

He glanced over his shoulder. "How long what?"

"Until we stop."

Noah had been so focused on ignoring the woman whose body aligned perfectly with his that he'd lost track of time. He winced at the discomfort she must feel.

"We'll stop up there." He reined Tempest toward a stand of trees, then pulled to a stop, letting her slide off before he dismounted. Reaching into a saddlebag, he pulled out a water sack and small pouch, handing them to Abby. "I'll set up camp."

"We're staying here?" She looked around, seeing nothing for miles.

"Did you expect a hotel?" he shot back, then walked away, leaving her standing alone.

Abby didn't try to reply. Instead, she took a drink of water, then opened the pouch, biting into the hardtack and retrieving a section of jerky. She watched him walk several yards before descending a slope. His head bobbed up and down as he bent, then straightened, loading his arms with stray bits of broken branches and anything else they could burn. Setting down the water and hardtack, she walked toward him, mimicking his efforts at rounding up enough wood for a fire.

"I can handle this. Why don't you pull down the bedrolls?" Noah asked, not looking at her, doing his best to calm his agitated body.

She tried to do the same as she walked back toward Tempest, dumped a few branches on the ground, and pulled the ties on the bedrolls. She shook them out, placing them side by side under the trees, then sat down, tucking her legs beneath her.

Noah came over the rise and stopped when he saw how she'd laid out the bedding. Lying so close to her wouldn't work, at least not for him. He'd take care of Tempest, start a fire, then move his bedroll a safe distance away from hers.

He untied the saddlebags, tossing them to her. "I didn't bring much besides the hardtack, jerky, and some dried fruit Suzanne packed for me." He tossed her the pouch full of apples. "There's another one, so eat as much as you want. We'll get an early start tomorrow and be in Splendor by midday."

Once the fire glowed and Tempest grazed several yards away, Noah grabbed his saddle and bedroll, moving both to the other side of the fire and away from Abby. Although almost dark, enough of a moon remained for him to scan the hills. In country this wide open, it would be hard for anyone to sneak up on them, but he wouldn't take chances. He sat, then propped himself against the saddle, stretching out his legs and crossing his arms, facing away from Abby.

It had been harder than he thought to ride all afternoon with her tucked behind him, trying to reconcile what he believed to be right with what he wanted. For so long he'd told himself he wasn't the man for her and he'd finally thought he believed it—until she'd told him what she felt had never been real. Maybe it hadn't been real for her, but it sure as hell felt real to him.

Knowing he wasn't right for her meant little when the ache in his chest grew with each mile. He'd be glad to get to Splendor, leave her with Suzanne, and vanish to his cabin. Toby would be fine running the store, and the smithy work would just have to wait.

Chapter Six

The rain started a mile before Splendor, sheets of water blowing toward them and slowing their progress. Noah pulled out his duster several miles back, wrapping it around Abby. Even so, he knew she'd be drenched by the time they reached Suzanne's.

Black clouds turned the sky dark when he reined Tempest to a stop. Letting Abby go would be much tougher than he imagined. Having her arms wrapped around him for hours, holding tight, had been both heaven and hell. Cursing under his breath the entire ride, he'd shifted in the saddle several times to relieve his discomfort.

The reality of the unexpected change in her feelings hit hard. He'd still see her in town, but it wouldn't be the same. She'd find work, meet someone, and build a life without him. Noah experienced worse setbacks in his life, although he couldn't recall what they were at the moment.

"Good heavens." Suzanne ran outside as Abby slid to the ground and ducked under the shelter of the building's overhang. Engulfed in

Suzanne's waiting embrace, they dashed inside where a fire burned in the parlor.

Noah debated what to do next. First, he'd grab the small leather satchel Abby used for her personal belongings. He'd drop it inside, then ride off—leave for the cabin before the storm got worse. Grabbing the bag, he stepped up to the boardinghouse door as Suzanne pulled it open.

"I wondered if you were coming in." She motioned him inside. "How about coffee?"

"Another time. I'll leave this and be on my way." He held out the bag, then turned to leave.

"Absolutely not. You aren't going anywhere until you've had a decent meal. Now, follow me to the kitchen."

He groaned, but did as she asked, finding Abby seated at the table Suzanne reserved for herself and close friends who visited.

They'd spoken just a few words since starting the last part of the journey at sunup and Noah didn't want to start a conversation now. He'd eat and then leave, knowing all would go well now that Abby had been safely delivered to Suzanne's.

Abby stood next to Suzanne washing dishes, trying to hide the misery she felt at Noah riding away. He'd kept his promise—getting her home without running into her father's men. She'd thanked him as he walked out the door. He held her gaze for a moment, then left without a word.

With any luck at all, her father wouldn't learn of her return until she'd had a chance to speak with a few people about work, starting with Horace Clausen at the bank.

"Did you and Noah talk?" Suzanne dried the last plate, wiped her hands, and turned toward Abby.

"Of course we talked." She tossed the dish towel on the counter without looking up.

Suzanne crossed her arms and leaned against the counter. "I mean about the two of you."

Abby slid her hands down the front of the apron, then turned her gaze to Suzanne. "I told him the truth."

"Which is?"

She sat down at the table, repeating the discussion she had with Noah in Moosejaw, leaving nothing out.

Suzanne let out a breath, not saying anything for several moments as she absorbed Abby's words. She knew Abby had strong feelings for Noah that had nothing to do with her age. By twenty, most women in the frontier were married, many already having children. Abby was past that age, even if not by much, and knew her mind.

"Why did you lie to him?" The desolate expression on Abby's face broke Suzanne's heart.

"Because I had to let him go. I'm not what he wants or he would have made his intentions clear long ago. He had a chance to tell me at the church. Instead, he set me aside, acting as if…as if…" She stumbled over the words as her voice shook. "He just doesn't want me." She rocked to and fro as her voice broke.

Suzanne placed a comforting hand on Abby's arm. She knew enough about Noah to understand his feelings for Abby ran deep, suspecting he didn't feel worthy of her. She supposed his misgivings were understandable given the way King Tolbert treated him, as if he were too far beneath Abby to even consider courting her. However, she also blamed Noah.

At this point, the two were at an impasse. If Abby found a job, a way to support herself and stay in town, the two might find a way back to each other. They could also find that what they felt for each other wasn't deep enough to forge a lifetime bond. For now, Suzanne comforted herself with the knowledge Abby was safe and Tolbert would no longer be able to control her every action.

"Abby, I saw Horace go into the bank. You might want to head over and talk to him now." Suzanne stood at the base of the stairs, tossing a towel over her shoulder as she stepped back into the kitchen to finish the preparations for breakfast. The boardinghouse restaurant opened early, and her boarders and customers would start walking in and filling tables any minute.

"How do I look?" Abby stood still, nervous tension radiating through her body.

"Well, for wearing a dress one of the boarders left behind, you look good. As little as people have these days, it still surprises me to find what they've forgotten."

"Or didn't want in the first place," Abby added, her tentative grin widening.

Eagerness mixed with fear coursed through her as she thought of meeting with Mr. Clausen. She knew he thought well of her, although his comments about a job may have come from courtesy rather than a genuine interest in her training. She reminded herself her father hadn't cared a whit about the time she spent studying mathematics and bookkeeping. He'd seen her fit to act as his hostess and nothing more.

"Wish me luck, Suzanne." Abby slid her reticule over her arm, grabbed a parasol, and stepped outside.

The storm passed during the night, leaving the street ankle deep in mud, even though the sun shown bright in the eastern sky. The bank stood at the opposite end of the main street, which posed a small problem. Abby hoped no one would recognize her during her brief walk, then send a rider to her father's ranch. Her bonnet covered her hair, and she did her best to hide her face behind the parasol until she lowered it at the bank entrance. Glancing around, she opened the door and stepped inside, spotting Horace Clausen talking to his secretary.

"Good morning, Mr. Clausen." She did her best to plaster a smile on her face, even as her stomach rolled with nervous tension.

"Hello, Miss Tolbert. I didn't know you had returned to Splendor." Clausen's right brow raised a fraction.

"I wonder if I might have a word with you in private."

"Of course. Please, come into my office." He gestured to a chair before walking behind his desk. "I saw your father yesterday. I'm surprised he didn't mention you were back in town."

"He doesn't know." She cleared her throat, sliding her damp hands down the skirt of her dress.

"I see." Clausen had known King Tolbert for years. As one of the bank's largest depositors, he often spent several hours a month going over accounts with him. Even so, he detested the way Tolbert treated his daughter and others in town.

"I'm hopeful he won't find out until I've found employment."

Clausen folded his hands on the desk and leaned forward, beginning to understand her visit. If he were right, fate must be with both of them as one of his employees had left a week before and he'd been unable to replace him.

"When did you return?"

"Last night. I'm staying at Mrs. Briar's."

"I take it, other than Suzanne, I'm the first person you've spoken to about this?"

"One other person knows I'm in town, but he doesn't know I've come to speak with you."

"Would that be Mr. Brandt?"

"Yes, but please don't ever tell my father. There's already so much bitterness between them..." Her voice trailed off as she thought of what her father would do if he knew she'd spent two days and a night with Noah.

"I quite understand. Now, tell me why you're here."

She squared her shoulders and pulled out a small bundle of bills from her reticule. Placing it on the desk, she sat up straight, raising her gaze to his.

"For two reasons. First, I have a small sum of money. Not much, you understand, but enough to open an account." She slid the bills toward him.

He counted them out, surprised at the sum. It was more than many of the smaller ranchers and shopkeepers were able to save.

"All right. And the second reason?"

"You once mentioned my bookkeeping skills might prove beneficial at the bank. What I need is a job, Mr. Clausen. I don't care what, although I am trained to do books and have a gift for mathematics."

He slowly stood, his thoughts hidden behind a neutral expression. Walking to the front of his desk, he crossed his arms and leaned against the edge. "You know, of course, what your father will say if he finds out you're working?"

"Yes, I do, and I'm quite prepared to have words with him."

His mouth twisted into a wry grin. "I see you understand your father quite well."

"He can be formidable and controlling. But I'm a grown woman, Mr. Clausen, and am ready to move out on my own."

"Most young women live at home until they marry. Few leave as you want to, unless their circumstances require it. Are you certain you're ready for such a big change?"

"Yes, sir, I am." She tilted her chin up in a small measure of defiance. "I've known it might come to this for a long time, although I hoped it wouldn't."

He dropped his arms to his sides, gripping the edge of the desk as he thought over her words. If Abigail came to work at the bank, Tolbert might be incensed enough to withdraw all his funds in retaliation. The bank had grown at a significant rate with the new people moving to Splendor and opening businesses or expanding their ranches, similar to the Pelletiers. Still, the loss of Tolbert's money would be a blow.

"This may not be the smartest decision I've ever made, but I'm willing to hire you for a trial period. I lost my head teller and haven't found a replacement. You have to be a quick learner—"

"I am, Mr. Clausen." Abby's heart pounded so hard she could almost hear it.

Clausen stifled a chuckle at her enthusiasm. "Yes, I'm certain you are, Miss Tolbert." He returned to his chair, opened a drawer, and pulled out a piece of paper, sliding it across the desk. "This explains your duties. I pay once a week. When would you care to start?"

Abby glanced up from the paper she held in shaky hands. "Tomorrow."

"Aren't you going to ask about the pay?"

Her eyes widened at the question. She'd been so focused on getting a job, she hadn't thought of how much she would earn.

"I suppose whatever you paid the last person will be sufficient."

Clausen cleared his throat, feeling his face blanch. His last teller had been a man who'd worked in a bank before traveling to Splendor. He wanted to be fair, although paying her the same was out of the question.

"I'll do what I can, but I assure you, it will be fair." He stood, grabbing her money for the deposit. "Welcome to the Bank of Splendor, Miss Tolbert. I look forward to seeing you bright and early tomorrow."

Noah finished installing the door on the work shed he'd started before leaving on his search for Abby. With this task complete, he had no other excuses for his absence from town.

A week had passed since leaving her at Suzanne's and coming to his cabin—a long time for a man to be away from his businesses. He wiped his dirty sleeve across his forehead, glancing at the sun as it dropped behind the nearby mountain range. Various shades of yellow, orange, and pink danced across the sky as the last rays shot skyward. He never grew tired of the sight.

Grabbing his empty coffee cup and rifle, he made his way into the cabin to eat the last of the stew warming on the wood stove.

Gabe had ridden out the day before to check on him and offer help with the tool shed. At least that's what he'd said. Noah suspected his visit had more to do with his friend letting him know Clausen had hired Abby. No one had yet seen Tolbert, although Gabe expected fireworks when the rancher heard the news.

"You've seen her?" Noah asked, filling Gabe's cup once more.

"I did. Spoke to her when I had supper at Suzanne's."

Noah waited for Gabe to continue, hoping he didn't have to push him for more information.

"She started yesterday." Gabe sipped the coffee and shook his head. "She couldn't contain her excitement and can't wait to go back on Monday. Who would've thought a job in a bank would mean so much to a woman who doesn't need the work."

Pride swelled within Noah. On more than one occasion, Abby had told him of her desire to use her skills in some fashion, and now she'd found the opportunity.

"Your woman wouldn't be home and working if you hadn't gone after her." Gabe finished his coffee and stood.

"She's not my woman," Noah growled.

"And whose fault is that? You're gonna be one sorry son of a bitch if you let someone else step in and take her away."

Noah knew that, but he had no choice, not after learning she no longer cared for him.

"She made it clear her feelings for me have changed. It's best for both of us." He tossed the last of his coffee out onto the dirt and shot a pained look at Gabe. "Don't you have work back in town?"

He didn't respond before stepping off the porch, grabbing Blackheart's reins, and swinging into the saddle. "You ever think she may have said that for *your* benefit?"

Noah's startled expression swung to Gabe. "What are you talking about?"

"Think about it. You might come to a different conclusion." Gabe settled his hat firmly on his head and left, leaving Noah to try to make sense of his words.

While continuing work on the shed, Noah pondered Gabe's parting comments, wondering what his friend had meant. In his mind, Abby had been clear, letting him know she no longer found him to be the man she wanted. The pain at her declaration had been intense, ripping through his heart, never letting up on their ride to Splendor or during his time at the cabin. He'd cut boards, pounded nails, and done everything he knew to purge himself of her, yet nothing worked. And Gabe's words made it worse, stirring up hope where none existed.

He scraped the last of the stew from the plate, shoveling it into his mouth in a stabbing motion more out of frustration than hunger. He'd planned to get a good night's sleep and ride to Splendor in the morning, but the agitation he felt told him sleep wouldn't come soon and he might as well head out tonight. The moon shone bright and Tempest knew the way through the trees. He'd stop at the Wild Rose, have a couple drinks, then return to the small sleeping quarters at the back of his livery.

Saturday nights were good at the Rose. Perhaps he'd see the boys from the Pelletier ranch, swap stories, and listen to the new piano Amos brought in from the east—his response to the entertainment at the new saloon, the Dixie, which opened a few months before.

As he finished tying the saddlebags on Tempest and swung into the saddle, a night at the Rose started to sound better and better. Maybe he'd even have more than two drinks and break his standing rule of not partaking in the offers by the women in the saloon. A grim smile played across his face at the thought. Perhaps tonight he'd start a new path, pushing Abigail Tolbert from his mind and heart altogether.

Chapter Seven

"Hey, Noah. I heard you were back." Bull Mason, one of the top hands at the Pelletier ranch, held out his hand. "Also heard you brought Miss Tolbert back with you."

Noah pulled out a chair next to Bull, signaling for a drink.

"She'd decided to come home anyway. I just accompanied her, nothing more." He sipped the whiskey and settled back. "Haven't seen her since I dropped her off at Suzanne's."

Bull narrowed his eyes and studied Noah. The whole town knew how the two felt about each other and figured they'd soon start courting openly. "That right?" he asked, trying to get Noah to talk.

Noah ignored Bull's scrutiny. He didn't want to discuss Abby, her father, or anything having to do with the past. "I've been at my cabin."

Bull took the hint, glancing around the table at the other ranch hands who'd remained silent. "You in?" he asked Noah, referring to the ongoing card game.

"Yeah, I'm in."

"Dax saw Miss Tolbert working in the bank when he came to town yesterday." Travis Dixon, another of the Pelletier men and one who rarely came out on a Saturday night, tossed down a couple cards and leaned back. "You think her pa knows?"

"I believe we'd all have heard about it if Tolbert knew." Noah tossed back the last of his whiskey, then fell silent.

"Well, look who's returned." Dinah, one of the newest women at the Rose, placed a hand on Noah's shoulder. "Thought you'd left the territory."

"Not yet," Noah answered, glancing at her rouged cheeks and painted lips. He'd heard she was a favorite of the men at Tolbert's ranch. Until tonight, he'd never considered visiting with her or any of Amos' women. Somehow, trekking up the stairs held little appeal as he relaxed with his friends.

"You want to celebrate your return with something special?" She squeezed Noah's shoulder, hoping to entice him to her bed.

The men around the table shot looks between themselves, knowing Noah's aversion to taking his pleasure so everyone would know. Of all the men in Splendor, he kept his life private, sharing little of his past, even with those who'd known him since he first set foot in town.

"Not now, Dinah. Maybe later."

"You let me know, honey. I'll be waiting." She flashed a smile around the table before moving on.

"Guess I may want to stick around for this," Bull quipped, earning a scowl from Noah and chuckles from the others.

"Anyone been in the Dixie lately?" Travis leaned forward and settled his arms on the table.

"Heard from Luke the other owner is coming to town on next week's stage to join Nick," Bull answered.

Nick Barnett and his partner owned the other saloon in Splendor. The Dixie offered entertainment, including the occasional singer or actress from back east. Most of the girls had been brought in from the south, where the owners started in the saloon business years before. People respected Nick, even when the Dixie began to take business away from the Wild Rose.

"Luke would be the one to know," one of the other men said.

Before they were married, Luke's wife, Ginny, had caused a minor confrontation between Nick and Luke. After the anger had cleared, Luke had finally seen his way to ask Ginny to marry him. The two men had settled their differences, and Luke even stopped at the Dixie for a drink on occasion.

"Stage is coming in again Tuesday, so guess we'll get to meet him." Noah pushed back from the table. "I believe I'll head out."

"And miss out on Dinah's special celebration?" Bull said with a straight face.

Noah spotted Dinah walking up the stairs, one of the Tolbert men behind her.

"Don't believe that will be a problem."

He pushed out the doors and into the bright, moonlit night, a slight breeze blowing. He glanced up and down the street, noticing the Dixie's lights blazing as music wafted outside. He moved his gaze to Suzanne's boardinghouse, not surprised to see every light out, and found himself wondering in which room Abby slept.

Shoving his hands into his pockets, he walked the short distance to the livery. It and the tack shop stood directly across the street from the boardinghouse. If he chose, he could pretty much keep track of the town happenings by who went in and out. His stomach lurched, knowing he'd be seeing Abby every day, at least from a distance. The realization both taunted and comforted him as he slipped through the back door of the livery.

Abby sat at her window, looking out at the main street and listening to the noises from the two saloons. She'd never stayed in town overnight, had no idea what went on after the stores closed and most slept. The activity surprised her.

Saturday proved to be difficult. With the bank closed, she made a brief visit to the general store, purchasing a dress and pair of gloves. She stopped to let Sheriff Evans know she'd returned to Splendor against her father's wishes, but the jail had been locked tight.

On a normal visit to town, she'd make sure to see Noah and spend as much time around him as he'd allow. Today, she'd walked by the closed blacksmith shop, then wandered into his mining supply and tack shop to see Toby cleaning the shelves. They'd visited for a few minutes, neither mentioning Noah, before she returned to the boardinghouse, keeping Suzanne company in the kitchen. Suzanne refused her help with supper, instead asking if Abby might take on the responsibility of keeping the books for her. She jumped at the chance, working into the night until her eyes crossed.

She'd climbed under the covers, tucking them beneath her chin to ward off a slight chill, thinking sleep would claim her within minutes. An hour later, she lay in the same position, staring at the ceiling. Frustrated, she threw off the covers and slipped into her wrapper before taking a seat at the window to watch the moonlight create images from the passing clouds. Drawing her knees up, she wrapped her arms around them and leaned against the window frame. Abby let her eyes drift shut, allowing herself to think of Noah.

It had been a hard decision to tell him she no longer cared. Lies never came easily to Abby. After many hours of reflection, she'd accepted it had been her mistake to push Noah for something he couldn't offer. He must have believed her to be one of the brashest women he'd ever met, yet he'd always been a gentlemen, never suggesting he thought her actions impetuous given how little they knew about each other.

She wrapped her arms around herself and, closing her eyes, remembered the first time she'd meet Noah.

Abby had come home from Philadelphia the summer before what she thought would be her last year back east. She didn't want to leave the ranch when her father first mentioned boarding school, but he'd ignored all her protests and pleading. A rigid and controlling man, King Tolbert disregarded Abby's objections, believing she had little common sense and approached all issues with emotion. The assumption had no basis in fact. In many ways, Abby took after him more than her mother.

Smart, brash, and energetic like her father, she also held qualities Tolbert lacked- —compassion, empathy, and an infectious personality. All had been traits of her mother, who'd passed away years before, leaving Abby to fend for herself in a world surrounded by men.

Within minutes of her arrival on the stage, her father visited Noah. Tolbert ordered tools, picked up a horse Noah tended, and made arrangements for repairs to their buggy.

Abby shifted on the window seat, remembering how she'd let her gaze roam over the man who towered above her father. His broad shoulders, muscular arms, and piercing blue eyes cut straight through her, unnerving and exciting her at the same time. His shirt stretched taut over an expansive chest, a hint of golden-colored hair peeking out. She drew in a breath and tried to look away, but couldn't. He intrigued her, even though he made no attempt to introduce himself or include her in the conversation with her father.

After several minutes of being ignored, Abby stepped forward and wrapped her hand through her father's arm. "Aren't you going to introduce me, Father?"

Both men glanced at her—King Tolbert in irritation, and Noah with what she thought resembled amusement.

"Abigail, this is Mr. Brandt. Brandt, my daughter, Abigail Tolbert." His exasperation at having to include her didn't surprise Abby or discourage her from dropping her arm from his and walking forward.

"Ma'am." Noah nodded as she came to a halt within a couple feet of him.

"Mr. Brandt. It's a pleasure to meet you. I just arrived on the stage from Philadelphia."

"Is that so?" Noah asked, the deep rumble of his voice washing over her, igniting a warm sensation in her stomach that traveled to her toes.

"Oh, yes. I've been at boarding school for so long, I sometimes forget how much I miss Splendor. Do you like it here, Mr. Brandt?"

"Yes, ma'am, I do."

"Have you—"

"That's enough, Abby," her father cut in, settling a hand on her elbow and pulling her back toward him. "I'll be back in a week for the order, Brandt."

"It'll be ready," Noah answered, never taking his eyes off Abby.

As her father escorted her away, Abby remembered glancing over her shoulder at Noah, flattered to see his gaze still fixed on her. She knew nothing of love or courtship, or even much about what happened between a man and a woman. However, at that instant, she knew Noah Brandt would be someone important in her life.

Abby opened her eyes and yawned, feeling as if she might now be able to claim sleep. She pulled back the curtain, took one more look outside, then shifted away when she spotted a man walk out of the swinging doors of the Wild Rose. He stepped into the moonlight and her breath caught. Noah. She dropped the curtain, continuing to stare.

Even from her vantage point a floor above and across the street didn't diminish his tall, muscular form. She watched as he glanced down the street, then moved his gaze to the boardinghouse, his head tipping up until he appeared to be looking straight at her. She flinched away before realizing he wouldn't be able to see into her dark room through the dust-covered glass and sheer curtains.

Noah seemed to be searching. Abby wondered if he might be trying to guess which room was hers, then shook her head at the silly thought. He shoved his hands into his pockets and turned toward the livery. Abby didn't move as he disappeared inside. Even then, her gaze stayed locked on the door to his private quarters.

For a brief, impetuous moment, she thought of slipping into her coat and shoes and dashing across the street, pounding on his door and admitting she'd lied. She wanted to explain her true feelings and hope he might admit to returning her affections. Thankfully, she reined in her impulsive actions and turned toward her bed, slipping under the covers and shutting her eyes tight.

"What do you mean you don't have her?" Tolbert roared at the hired hand who'd returned with several other men from Big Pine.

The man took a step back, fingering the brim of the hat he held in both hands. He knew if they returned without Miss Tolbert, there'd be hell to pay. Their boss wasn't the type of man who listened to reason.

"We watched three stages come and go, as you ordered, and when she didn't appear, we rode back. The stage master told us a young woman got off the coach in Moosejaw, but he didn't have a name. We could ride to Moosejaw—"

"No," Tolbert interrupted, slamming his fist on his desk. He had to think. "Get out," he ordered, lowering himself into a chair, wondering where she'd gone.

She'd always been stubborn, having her own ideas and opinions, which often conflicted with his own. Until Noah Brandt entered her life, she'd never been defiant.

Tolbert believed Abigail thought she loved Brandt, but he knew otherwise. He believed Brandt to be nothing more than a tool she selected to get back at him for sending her away and controlling the direction of her life. By offering herself to Brandt, she'd found the one instrument of complete retaliation.

The blacksmith represented everything she knew her father scorned—people in trade who used their hands to make a living. They lacked social standing and wealth and, therefore, were beneath him and Abigail.

He stood, paced to a table, and grabbed a bottle of whiskey. Pouring a good amount into a glass, he took a sip, trying to put himself in Abby's place. Where would she go, and whom would she turn to for help? Several names came to mind, but only one made complete sense—Noah Brandt.

Tolbert tossed back the last of the whiskey, buckled his gun belt in place, and charged outside, yelling to some of his men to saddle his horse and follow him. They'd ride to town, find Noah Brandt, and force him to tell Tolbert what he wanted to know.

Chapter Eight

Sunday passed in a pleasant blur. Abby attended church with Suzanne, not caring who learned she'd returned to Splendor. She had a job and a place to live. Her father could no longer compel her to return to the ranch to live under his expectations of her.

After church, Suzanne prepared food for her boarders, then packed a picnic for her and Abby. They borrowed Doc Worthington's wagon, heading east toward a small hill overlooking the town. Abby tried to conceal her interest as they passed the livery, then felt a stab of disappointment to see it closed with no smoke coming from the forge.

Noah often worked Sundays to keep up with the increasing demand for his services. She knew he hoped to hire help at some point, perhaps training one of the new arrivals needing work. It appeared he'd decided to ride to his cabin, or perhaps visit the Pelletiers.

Within no time, they'd arrived at a special spot Suzanne loved, then ate their meal. Abby stretched on a blanket afterwards, closing her eyes and summoning up an image of Noah walking down the street to his livery the night before. Before she knew it, Suzanne's voice called to her and she sat up with a jerk.

"You've slept for almost an hour." Suzanne smiled as she set the basket back in the wagon. "As lovely as the day is, we need to start back. Those boarders of mine get grumpy when their supper is late."

Her leisurely Sunday ended as they made small talk on the ride back to town. After helping Suzanne with a few chores, she fell into bed, anticipating the following day.

She'd woken up Monday and jumped out of bed, excited to return to work. Mr. Clausen had praised her on Friday, handing her a small amount for her one day of employment, which she immediately deposited into her new account.

By noon, her feet ached, yet she felt a strong sense of accomplishment.

"Miss Tolbert, why don't you take your lunch now? You can finish what you're doing this afternoon," Horace said, then turned at the sound of the front door opening. Nick

Barnett, part owner of the Dixie Saloon, entered and walked toward him.

"Good afternoon, Mr. Clausen. I wonder if you might have a moment," Nick asked, glancing at Abby and offering her his best smile. "Hello, Miss Tolbert. Are you working here now?"

She beamed at his lack of judgment that King Tolbert's daughter would be paying her own way by working in a bank.

"Yes, Mr. Barnett, I am. My first day was Friday."

"And she's doing quite well," Clausen added before turning back to Nick. "Why don't we go into my office, Mr. Barnett?"

Abby grabbed her reticule and the lunch Suzanne packed earlier, and stepped into the bright sunlight. Selecting one of the four chairs lined against the outside wall, she opened the lunch and took small bites of the biscuit stuffed with ham as she watched the activity in town.

The bank sat at the opposite end of the street from the boardinghouse, across from the church and the Dixie. To the outrage of the minister and congregation, the city had gone ahead and allowed the saloon to open within thirty yards of the church. In truth, city leadership consisted of five key citizens…Mr. Clausen, Stan Petermann, owner of the general store, Amos Henderson, owner of the Wild Rose, Bernie Griggs, who ran the telegraph office, and King Tolbert, who generally sent one of his men to town with instructions on the way he wanted the town to proceed. The vote on the new saloon had been four to one, with Amos the one dissenting member.

Abby watched as wagons filled with supplies moved past, and people walked along the wooden boardwalk. From her spot, she could see the north end of town, which led to the Pelletier and Tolbert ranches, but she couldn't see the livery, which stood back from the main street.

Abby finished her lunch and turned to grab her reticule when she recognized a rider entering town from the north. Several ranch hands accompanied her father, all making a sharp turn toward the livery. Abby's senses went on immediate alert. She dashed toward the livery, almost passing the jail before dashing inside.

"Sheriff Evans, please, you must go down to the livery," she gasped, trying to breathe.

Gabe Evans looked up from his desk, then stood when he saw the look of despair on Abby's face. "What's going on?"

"My father. He and some of his men are headed for the livery. I don't know why, but I'm afraid he's going after Noah. Please, can you go there with me?"

He grabbed his hat and escorted Abby down the street, hearing shouts as they rounded the corner. Both stopped at the sight before them.

Three of Tolbert's men had Noah pinned, while another landed blows to his face. Gabe pulled out his gun and fired into the air.

"Let him go. Now!" Gabe pointed the gun at the men restraining Noah.

Tolbert turned, his face red with anger, then spotted Abby.

Gabe fired another shot in the air, then one in the dirt at the men's feet before they dropped their hold and stepped away.

Abby barely noticed her father walking toward her. Seeing Noah bloodied—and at her father's orders—jolted her, forcing her to look at him in a different way.

"Abby, where have you been?" His voice didn't soften as he approached. If anything, his rage seemed to refocus on her.

She backed away as Tolbert reached for her. "Don't touch me."

"You don't understand what happened here." His gaze flickered between her and

Noah, who wiped a sleeve across his bloodied face.

"I understand more than you think, Father. What you did here is despicable. What did you hope to accomplish by beating up Noah?" Her voice rose as her anger increased. "Did he tell you he accompanied me to town safely, or did you even ask before setting your men on him?"

"You are my daughter—"

"Not any longer." She ran past him, stopping inches from Noah, who splashed water on his face and arms, then grabbed a rag. Her gut clenched at the bruises and swelling. "I'm sorry, Noah."

He dropped the rag and turned toward her. "Your father's been looking for an excuse to do this since you and I first met. Bringing you back to town, behind his back, was all he needed. It's not your fault."

"You four...to the jail."

They turned at Gabe's command, watching as he trained his gun on Tolbert's men.

"You can't take my men to jail. They've broken no laws."

"What do you call assault, Tolbert? I have room for you, also."

"I didn't lay a hand on Brandt."

"Maybe not, but *you* gave the order."

"Is that what my men said?" he smirked, knowing none of these men would turn on him.

"Not yet, but several nights in jail can change a story."

"You can't hold them that long," Tolbert complained, his earlier bravado fading.

Gabe ignored him, marching the men to the jail and into cells.

"Are you all right?" Abby asked Noah after Gabe disappeared.

"Yes, I'm fine. You can go on now. I know you have a job and I'm sure Mr. Clausen isn't aware of what happened."

Her eyes widened in surprise. "How did you know?"

He tilted his head, a warm smile lighting his eyes. "It's a small town, Abby."

She didn't want to leave, especially with her father still hovering in the background, but she needed to return to the bank. "Perhaps I'll see you in the bank."

"Perhaps."

She nodded, then turned to leave, walking past her father without sparing him a glance.

"Abigail, I want to speak with you."

"I can't now, Father. I have to return to work."

Tolbert's jaw flapped, but nothing came out. Instead, he followed her, watching as she stepped into the bank. His anger returning, he pushed open the door to see Abby take her place behind one of the teller windows. He stormed inside, letting the door slam behind him.

Horace Clausen had been on his way to speak with Abby when Tolbert marched up to him, stabbing a finger into his chest.

"What is my daughter doing working at this bank?"

"Good afternoon, King. Would you care to come into my office?" Clausen worked to keep a straight face as Tolbert's eyes bulged from their sockets. After a customer rushed into the bank moments before, telling everyone how Tolbert's men roughed up Noah, the banker knew this moment would come.

"I want to know why you hired Abigail. We both know she doesn't need the money. Her place is at home, taking care of the house and—"

"We'll talk about this in private." Clausen's tone cut through Tolbert's outburst. He quieted, but only until the door to the office closed. "Have a seat."

"I don't want a seat. I want answers."

"My main teller quit and Abigail asked for the job. Since her education supported it, I hired her. So far, she's doing remarkably well."

"And where is she living? In the back of the bank? Or with the blacksmith?"

Clausen held his temper at the insult to Tolbert's own daughter. "I don't think she'd be too pleased if you spread rumors about her, especially ones that besmirch her reputation. Now, sit down and I'll tell you what I know."

"You certain you don't want to press charges?" Gabe sat across the desk from Noah, studying the bruises, swelling, and cuts adorning his face.

"You said yourself the circuit judge won't be through for a few more weeks. That means you'd have four mouths to feed and clean up after them. They're not worth your time."

"And the damage to you?"

"These?" Noah touched his face. "Scratches."

Gabe choked out a laugh. "If you're sure...I'll keep them overnight, then set them loose in the morning. Did you see where Tolbert went?"

Noah folded his arms across his chest and looked away. "The last I saw, he followed Abby to the bank."

"You didn't follow him, make sure he didn't cause another scene?"

"She's not my concern, Gabe. Not any longer." Noah dropped his arms and stood, defeat and regret written on his face. "I'd best get back to work."

Gabe checked on the prisoners before making the decision to visit the bank. He didn't know how Tolbert would react to Abby working, but wanted to be close in case he pulled any more of his antics, hurting others in the process. A few feet from the bank, Tolbert burst outside, mumbling to himself and passing Gabe without acknowledging him.

"You all right, Tolbert?" Gabe asked, but the man ignored him.

After a few steps, he stopped, then swung back toward Gabe. "I want my men released."

"Not today. They'll spend the night in jail, then I'll make a decision."

Tolbert glared at Gabe, then swore, turning toward his horse. Gabe didn't move until the dust settled behind Tolbert as he rode out of town.

"That wasn't so bad." Horace placed a hand on Abby's shoulder as her father stormed out. "He didn't disown you or close his accounts." He dropped his hand, trying to make his comment sound light to relieve her tension, but the words sounded flat, stilted.

"Today anyway. You're right, though. It could've been so much worse."

Clausen looked over her work and smiled. "You've done well, Miss Tolbert. To be honest, you've caught on much faster than I anticipated. Do you have any questions?"

Abby allowed herself a tentative grin, although she beamed inside at her boss' praise. After living with her father's constant badgering, any encouragement felt wonderful.

"No. It all seems quite clear."

"That's good." He checked his pocket watch. "I have a meeting and won't be back before closing. I'll see you in the morning."

"Yes, sir." Abby looked at the longcase clock across the lobby. She hoped her father had already left for the ranch. Even though he'd been angry, he hadn't exploded the way she expected. His clenched teeth and barely concealed fury when he told her he disapproved of her working might have been uncomfortable, but at least he hadn't shouted. To appease him, she'd agreed to spend Sunday supper at the ranch.

Abby finished the last of her work and grabbed her light coat. She planned to work on the boardinghouse books when she got to her room, then help in the kitchen—if Suzanne let her. Perhaps she'd take supper with Suzanne instead of sitting in the dining room where she'd be forced to eat alone.

Crossing the street, she passed the Dixie Saloon where piano music already drifted outside. Abby tried to keep her gaze straight ahead and not let it wander toward the livery, but her efforts were wasted. The bright glow of the forge drew her attention. She stopped in the shadows outside the boardinghouse, watching Noah move toward the anvil with a burning piece of metal in his tongs. He picked up a hammer and pounded the softened material. Long, hard strokes at first, followed by short precise raps to form whatever he worked to produce.

He raised the hammer, gripping it with strong fingers, the muscles in his back and arm taut, revealing the strength in his powerful body. She suspected there were no soft spots anywhere on him, as beads of sweat glistened on his sun-browned skin. Clutching her hands together, she fantasized about running them down his arms and chest, feeling the knotted cords of muscle and crisp hair.

Without warning, he stopped the hammer in midair and turned, looking straight at the spot where she stood. Abby shifted further back against the wall, hoping he hadn't discovered her watching him. She couldn't bear to embarrass herself in front of Noah again.

After a moment, he lowered the hammer and grabbed a rag, dragging it across his forehead before tossing it aside. He didn't look back, just picked up his hammer and continued to pound the cooling metal.

Abby scooted along the outside wall, pushed open the door of the boardinghouse, and slipped inside. She exhaled a deep breath and shrugged out of her coat before passing the dining room on her way to the kitchen. She'd been lucky. He hadn't seen her staring, admiring him and imagining how it would feel to touch him. Abby took a moment to calm her racing heart before stepping into the kitchen, inhaling the rich aroma of roast meat.

"Just in time for supper," Suzanne said without turning from the counter where she piled roast, potatoes, and gravy on a plate, setting it aside, and doing the same with another. "Sit down and I'll prepare one for you."

Abby hung her coat on a hook and walked to the stove, inhaling deeply. "I'd rather wait and eat with you, unless you have other plans."

Suzanne snorted. "The only plans I have are to clean up and get off my feet when all the customers leave."

"Good, I can help. Who are these for?" Abby grabbed the two plates brimming with food.

"The couple next to where Nick is seated."

Abby nodded. She'd seen Nick Barnett in the bank earlier and knew the saloon owner rented a room from Suzanne so he wouldn't be forced to stay upstairs night after night, listening to the sounds of the soiled doves and their customers in adjoining rooms. She smiled at him as she passed his table, setting the food down in front of a man and woman she'd never met.

"Please let me know if you need anything else." Abby glanced around, noting everyone else seemed deep in conversation or content to eat in silence.

"How is your job going, Miss Tolbert?" Nick asked as his gaze caught hers.

"Very well, Mr. Barnett. Of course, I've only been there two days."

Nick found her self-effacing nature in sharp contrast to her father, although she'd never be considered a wallflower or timid.

"Clausen seems to be a fair man. I'm certain you'll do well."

She bent closer, as if sharing a secret. "Yes, he is somewhat unusual. I believe I might be the first female he's hired to handle money."

Nick's laugh drew the attention of other diners, causing Abby to straighten, a light blush creeping up her face. "That's certainly good news, Miss Tolbert." His laugh settled into a warm smile.

"Well...I'd best get back to the kitchen and help Suzanne." She could feel her heated cheeks all the way to the kitchen. She didn't know why her openness bothered her. He'd never say a word to Mr. Clausen, she felt certain of that, but Abby hadn't expected her comment to spark such an amused reaction. Of course, Nick seemed to be a little more understanding of the few choices open for women. Gossip was he made sure any woman who worked in his saloon wanted to be there and already had experience. He turned away any female who came to him with her virginity intact—at least those were the rumors.

After the last diner left and Nick returned to his saloon, Abby and Suzanne shared a quiet meal, neither feeling the need to fill the silence. Abby's thoughts shifted between Noah, her father, and her job, still not quite reconciling the changes in her life over the past few weeks.

Her father had contained his anger at her new living arrangements and job while inside the bank. She held no illusions about what to expect when she visited him for Sunday supper. He'd push to bring her home with the purpose of sending her away again, this time under the watchful eyes of his men. She would be as resolute in her right to choose. Although necessary, it would be a miserable encounter. It was time King Tolbert learned his daughter had dreams of her own and would no longer be controlled by a domineering father.

Chapter Nine

"Whoa."

Gabe watched from outside the jail as the stagecoach pulled to a stop near the livery. Seemed as if every stage coming through required Noah's expertise to repair a problem before they could head out. He had to hand it to his friend—Noah picked the right business and right town to ply his trade.

Gabe ambled down the boardwalk, passing the Wild Rose and stage office before stopping to watch the passengers debark. A woman and two small children stepped off first, the boy and girl running into the arms of a man Gabe recognized as the new owner of a ranch south of town. Similar to many others, he and his family had been uprooted by the war. Rather than rebuild, they'd chosen to travel west, see what the frontier held for them.

He was about to turn back to the jail when a gloved hand settled on the stage door, followed by a flowing dark blue traveling skirt.

"I'll help you down, ma'am." The driver held out his hand. The woman grasped it in hers and, holding a parasol in the other, stepped onto the uneven street, her face turned away from Gabe.

He strained to get a look at her as she thanked the driver and tried to tip him. He waved off the money, looking a tad insulted, then turned to speak with Noah, who stared at the woman the way a man does when he's spotted something beautiful. Gabe could see him touch a finger to his forehead in salute.

"Ma'am," Noah said in a low drawl before turning his attention to the stage driver.

The woman bent to pick up her bag, looking over her shoulder before making a complete turn and walking toward Gabe. Thinking back, he'd realize his whole world shifted at that moment. She was tall with ample curves and an olive complexion enhanced by rich auburn hair. As she stepped closer, he could see her brilliant blue eyes. When he took a step forward, a familiar voice came from behind him.

"Lena, *ma chére.*" Nick Barnett pulled her into a warm embrace before grabbing the bag from her hand. "How was your trip?"

She slipped her hand through his arm. "Ah, *mon cher.* It is always the same," she laughed. "Long, dusty, and bumpy."

Nick started toward the saloon before spotting Gabe. "Sheriff Evans, may I present my business partner, Magdelena Campanel. Lena, our sheriff, Gabe Evans."

"Miss Campanel, it's a pleasure." Gabe tipped his hat, finding it difficult to shift his gaze away.

"Thank you, Sheriff. I've been looking forward to this visit for quite some time."

"Come, Lena. I'll show you the saloon, then take you to your room at the boardinghouse." Nick nodded at Gabe as they strode away, a knowing smile tilting his mouth upward.

Gabe tipped his hat as they left, letting a whoosh of air escape his lungs.

"Stunning. I don't believe I've seen anyone quite like her."

Gabe's head swiveled to see Noah standing beside him. He'd been so absorbed in watching Miss Campanel, he hadn't heard him walk up.

"Who is she?"

"Nick introduced her as his business partner." Gabe stood in one spot, unable to move until the two disappeared into the Dixie.

"I'll be darned. Never thought his partner would be a woman."

"Neither did I." Gabe's words rasped out, as if something had caught in his throat.

Noah's narrowed gaze took in his friend. He had more self-control around beautiful women than any man Noah had ever known. It was obvious Miss Campanel sparked something in Gabe he'd never felt before.

"Don't you have someplace to go, someone to arrest?" Noah joked, slapping him on the back in open amusement.

"What? Uh...yeah. Guess I'd better get back to the jail."

Gabe forced his feet to move until he tossed his hat on the desk and slumped into a chair. As soon as she'd turned toward him, it felt as if someone had landed a heavy blow to his gut, knocking the wind from his lungs. He couldn't remember ever being this affected by one glance from a woman.

He scrubbed a hand over his face, deciding the edgy feeling had more to do with missing lunch than the beautiful Miss Campanel. It could also be due to the fact he hadn't had a woman since he'd accepted the position as Splendor's sheriff. He smiled at the thought of Dolly, the saloon girl in Big Pine, who'd taken care of him before he'd ridden to Splendor. He grabbed his hat and headed toward the new restaurant a few doors away, deciding a quick trip to Big Pine might be just what he needed.

"You gotta do something, Sheriff. We're missing another twenty head." Hiram Frey and his brother, Frank, had spotted Gabe as he'd left the restaurant and followed him into the jail. They and several ranchers east of them had already lost several head to rustlers over the last month, even though all posted extra men.

"Have you or your men seen anything to help figure out where they might be taking the cattle or how they're getting to them?" Gabe knew there was little he could do as one man, but he'd be willing to deputize others if they had some idea where to start looking.

"They'd be foolish to head west and get caught in the mountains. North is the Pelletier ranch, and east the cattle would have to travel past Splendor. My guess is south, down past the smaller ranches." Frank Frey leaned against a wall and pulled out one of his cheroots, twisting it between his fingers.

"Don't know about that," Hiram said. "The mountains might be the right place to hide cattle until you could get enough to herd them south to Denver. There are so many places to hide in those mountains, it would take a hundred men to ferret them out."

Gabe scratched his chin as the brothers continued to debate where the rustlers might be keeping the stolen cattle. He required more men for this type of search and that meant approaching the local ranchers, such as the Pelletiers and King Tolbert. What he needed was someone like Cash Coulter, an expert tracker. A close friend of Dax and Luke Pelletier, the bounty hunter left Splendor almost a year before, chasing men he believed responsible for the deaths of family members. It might be time for Gabe to send out some telegrams, see if he could locate Coulter and convince him to return.

"I need more men for this. At first light tomorrow, I'll speak with Dax and Luke, then Tolbert to see if they'll provide some men. We need to get an idea where the rustlers are holding the cattle before gathering a large enough herd to drive to Denver. You two have any men you can spare?"

"Maybe two, but no more than that. We're always short of men." Hiram glanced at

Frank, who nodded. "Frank and I've been discussing going to Big Pine, bringing back some men who'd be willing to work for room and board, maybe a little pay, and help us locate this gang. What do you think, Sheriff?"

He didn't believe they'd get many interested in making the day's ride to Splendor, but he'd be willing to try. "Keep your men posted. I'll talk to Tolbert and the Pelletiers tomorrow, then ride to Big Pine. I need to speak with Sheriff Sterling about this and some other matters. Maybe I'll be able to persuade a few men to ride back with me. Any chance you'd be able to keep any of them on afterwards?"

"Might be able to do that," Frank answered. They lived further out than most ranchers and always had a hard time keeping good help.

"All right. I'll let you know what I learn."

Gabe spent the evening packing what he needed for the trip, speaking to Clausen and a couple others to let them know he'd be gone a few days, then had supper with Noah. Whenever Gabe left town, Noah became the official substitute sheriff, which kept the city leadership happy, even if Noah held no great love for the position. At least there'd be someone to go to if trouble started.

As the sun rose over the eastern mountains the following day, Gabe rode out of town, figuring how best to find the rustlers while looking forward to some personal time at a certain saloon in Big Pine.

Abby stashed her lunch under the work counter and counted the money in the drawer. Sally Phelps, Mr. Clausen's longtime secretary, grabbed her keys and prepared to open the doors. She was an older widow, perhaps the age of Abby's father, and had worked at the bank since Abby was little. Most days at least one customer stood outside, waiting to meet with Mr. Clausen or handle bank business. Today, a group of four men milled about outside, causing Sally to hesitate.

"Abby, would you mind coming over here a moment?"

She walked out from behind the teller counter to peek through the window where Sally stood, watching the group outside. Wiping dirt from the glass, she gasped at the sight of one man who looked familiar.

"Do you recognize any of those men?" she asked Abby.

"One looks like a man who used to work for my father. I can't be certain until I get a better look, but I wouldn't be comfortable letting him in the bank until Mr. Clausen returns."

Sally hesitated. They'd never missed opening the bank on time. She glanced at the clock, then back at Abby.

"Why don't you go get Mr. Brandt? Mr. Clausen told me he's taking Sheriff Evan's place while he goes to Big Pine for a few days. Perhaps he can be inside when we open, keep an eye on them."

Abby had no desire to pull Noah into whatever this might be, but had little choice. They needed to open the bank, yet both women felt unsafe given Abby's concerns about who might be standing outside.

"All right, Mrs. Phelps. Please, do not open the doors until we return."

"Hurry, Abby," she nodded, watching as Abby dashed out the back.

She turned toward the livery, knowing Noah would already be working. At least the men outside the bank wouldn't be able to see her going for help. In some ways, she felt foolish. What if they were nothing more than newcomers wanting to open accounts? Except the one looked so similar to the man her father intended to fire and Sheriff Evans wanted to arrest before he and two of his men left the ranch. They'd never been spotted again around Splendor and, as far as Abby knew, had no reason to return.

She continued to run, kicking up dust, until she spotted Noah shoeing a horse. He dropped the foreleg and stood as she approached, noticing a look close to panic on her face.

"What is it?" he asked, reaching out to grip her shoulders.

She took a breath and looked up at him. "There are four men outside the bank. Mr. Clausen hasn't arrived, and neither Mrs. Phelps nor I recognize them...except one. He might be..." Abby's voice trailed off as she thought once more about the former ranch foreman, Parnell Drake.

"Might be who, Abby?" Noah prompted.

"Do you remember Parnell Drake?"

"You mean your father's man who took off?"

"Yes."

"I remember him. Why?"

"I think he may be one of the men waiting for the bank to open."

Noah didn't hesitate. He grabbed his gun belt and buckled it around his waist before reaching for his rifle. "Let's go."

"It's best to go through the back." Abby took off the way she came, Noah following.

Entering the bank, Noah took a position between Sally and Abby, his rifle cocked and resting in his arms. He'd forgotten how much a part of him this rifle had been for so many years. Even now, it felt like an extension of his body rather than a tool he used when needed. He nodded at Sally to go ahead and open the doors.

The men shuffled in, all four noticing Noah right away. The man Abby recognized as Parnell Drake walked up to her, no hint of recognition on his face. She glanced at Noah and nodded once, her signal it was the man she suspected.

Noah took a step closer, shifting his stance and readying his hands.

"I want to deposit some money," he drawled, his eyes darting between hers and Noah's.

"Of course. Do you have an account with us, Mr...?"

"Drake. Parnell Drake."

Her heart slammed in her chest as her face stilled in an attempt not to show her reaction.

"Let me get your information, Mr. Drake," she said, proud her voice didn't betray how she felt. She checked through a file, pulling out his account information, then wrote out a receipt.

"Here you are, Mr. Drake."

"Thank you." He slipped the paper in his pocket, then shot another look at her. "Have we met?"

"No. I don't believe we have."

His eyes narrowed on her a moment before he motioned for his men to follow him out.

Noah paced to the door and looked out, noting the four gather their horses and ride south, away from town. As he turned, the door flew open. Clausen stopped at the sight of Noah holding a rifle and wearing a gun belt. He glanced at Sally, her face white as a sheet, and Abby, standing rigid behind the teller bars.

"What's going on?"

"Just a customer who made the women uneasy," Noah replied. "Let's go into your office and I'll explain."

"I'm so glad you were able to get Mr. Brandt to come here. I didn't like the look of any of those men, Abby." Sally wrung her hands in front of her, looking toward the door as if she expected them to return at any moment.

"Parnell Drake, the man who made the deposit, has always frightened me. He worked as a foreman for my father for several months before strange activities began—accidents, injuries, cattle stampedes. All of it directed at Pelletier men. Thank goodness no one was killed. At first, the sheriff thought the actions were done on orders from my father." Abby's gaze darted to Mr. Clausen's office, wondering when Noah would reappear. She wanted to thank him, let him know how much his presence meant to her and Mrs. Phelps. "It seems Mr. Drake may have been behind it all. He took off with two of his men before the sheriff had a chance to question him."

"Well, it's good you recognized him. I still have a bad feeling about this."

"So do I, Mrs. Phelps."

Abby's head turned at the sound of Noah walking out of the office. His eyes locked with hers, his face devoid of expression as he strolled past her toward the door.

"Mr. Brandt."

He turned, the corners of his mouth tilting upward. "Noah, remember?"

She bit her bottom lip, her eyes lighting up. "Thank you, Noah."

He walked to within a foot of her, never breaking eye contact as he lifted her chin with a finger. "Anytime, Abby. If you ever need help, all you have to do is ask." He continued to stare a moment longer before dropping his hand and walking out.

Noah lay awake, tossing and turning, unable to get images of Abby out of his mind. No matter how he tried, everything about her—her unique smell, the way she talked, her mannerisms—couldn't be erased, as if they were branded on his skin. He threw off the covers and paced to the window, looking out on a clear sky lit with a partial moon.

It had taken every bit of willpower he possessed not to reach out and pull her to him before leaving the bank. Her lips trembled when she came to ask his help, and he knew it had taken courage to face him. When he'd left her with Suzanne, their parting had been awkward, strained, neither knowing what else to say. Two weeks later, after mulling over Gabe's words, he knew precisely what he should have said.

"Damn fool," he muttered to himself as he stoked the fire in his small stove and started coffee. Deciding he might as well work, Noah pulled on pants and slipped into a flannel shirt.

Noah heated the metal needed for a tool one of the ranchers ordered, then began to pound. With each downward thrust, he ticked off all the reasons he should ignore his doubts and go after Abby. Court her, do everything any man would do if he wanted a woman.

In the past, his hesitation in voicing his intentions had been due to several reasons, the main one being her wealth. Raised to believe the man supported his family, Noah's pride had never allowed him to accept marrying a woman worth many times more than him. Nor someone used to social status and well-placed friends, neither of which he could offer.

Separating herself from her father changed everything. Abby had made it clear, more than once, she wanted a life independent of him and his wealth. She held no love for his manipulations or behavior toward those he believed to be beneath him. Her decision to make her own way altered Noah's previous uncertainties about pursuing her. Over the past weeks, he'd thought of her declaration in Moosejaw and had come to the conclusion it didn't make sense. He'd stake his life on the belief she still loved him.

This time he didn't have to worry about Tolbert objecting. All that need concern him was Abby. If she agreed to let him court her, all her former protests would amount to nothing. If she didn't, he'd be no worse off.

He set the hammer down and straightened. She wasn't going anywhere, not with her job and room at the boardinghouse. He let out a breath, knowing he had time to decide the best approach, maybe even talk with Dax or Luke and get some ideas on how to do it right. He chuckled at the thought. Neither would be considered a stellar example on how to court a woman, but at least they had more experience than him. He crossed his arms and stepped away from the anvil, feeling a reprieve from the depression plaguing him the past few weeks. A slow grin spread across his face. Perhaps his future wasn't as bleak as he first believed.

Chapter Ten

Big Pine

"I've got two fellas in town looking into the cattle rustling around here." Sheriff Parker Sterling sat forward, leaning his arms on his desk.

"Deputies? U.S. Marshals?" Gabe asked, rocking his chair back on two legs.

"Nope. Best I can tell, they're bounty hunters looking for one man in particular—Parnell Drake."

Gabe's chair slammed forward. "Drake? You certain?"

"Yep. That's the name Coulter gave me."

"Cash Coulter is the bounty hunter?"

"Him and Beau Davis. Got here close to two weeks ago and have been talking to every rancher with missing cattle. They stopped in yesterday to see if I've had any more reports. Appears the rustling seems to have stopped—at least for now. Coulter thinks they may have moved on." Sterling sat back and crossed his arms. "I believe he may be looking for Drake for more than rustling. You know anything about that?"

Gabe *did* know more about Cash and Drake's history, but he wasn't prepared to share it with the sheriff.

"You'll have to ask him. Do you know where they're staying?"

"Up the street at The Imperial Hotel. Best place in town."

Gabe took off toward the hotel. He needed a place to stay, and where better than the same hotel as Cash and his partner. Besides, the hotel stood a block away from the saloon where Dolly worked. He'd leave a message for Cash, grab supper, then go for a few drinks and whatever else struck his fancy.

"Nothing more out here. I'm telling you, Cash. The rustlers have moved on, probably taking the cattle with them." Beau swung into the saddle and turned toward town. "It's time to move on."

"West?" Cash asked.

"From the tracks, yes. I'm guessing they have at least a hundred head and more than a week's head start."

"Seems it would be hard to hide a hundred head." Cash pulled off his hat, shaking his overlong blonde hair, then settled the hat back down.

Beau looked around, focusing on the mountains to the west. "Not with all the open land surrounded by mountains. We'd need a lot more men to find them in this vast territory. I'd head south if it weren't for these tracks. Clearly, someone's moving cattle and they're not going in the direction local ranchers drive their herds."

A circle, Cash thought as he looked in the direction of Splendor. Somehow, he always knew he'd be heading back to the small town where his friends owned a ranch. He just didn't think it would be so soon.

"Let's get cleaned up and have supper. We'll head out at first light."

The sun had set by the time they put up their horses and entered the hotel. Both were dusty, tired, and hungry, but neither would turn down a drink or a game of cards.

"Message for you, Mr. Coulter." The desk clerk held out a piece of paper. "The gentleman is staying in the hotel."

Cash read the message quickly, then looked up. "Is he in now?"

"I don't believe so. He mentioned having supper, then going to the saloon—in case you came looking for him."

"Someone you know?" Beau asked.

"Gabe Evans, a friend. He's the sheriff in Splendor."

"He say why he's in Big Pine?"

"No. He'll be at the saloon down the street. We can meet up with him after supper."

"It's been a long time, Gabe." Dolly slid a hand along his shoulders, purring in his ear as he tried to focus on the cards he held.

He glanced over his shoulder, a smile breaking across his typically stoic face. "Too long, Dolly."

She let her fingers trace a path along his neck, feeling him stiffen slightly and shift in his seat. The signs were clear. He'd come to spend time with her. Gabe had always been different from her other customers. Kind and thoughtful, he rushed nothing, including taking time to talk as if they were friends. He never spoke of anything personal, such as his past or family. They talked of their futures and their dreams—simple topics with no fear of their thoughts ever going beyond the walls of her room.

"I'll be at the bar when you're ready," she cooed in a soft voice.

Gabe nodded, not taking his eyes from the table. He played a few more hands, winning one and losing the others.

"I'm done, boys." He grabbed his hat and joined Dolly at the bar, slipping an arm around her waist and drawing her close. "You ready?"

"Of course."

He grabbed a bottle and two glasses, following behind as she ascended the stairs. When he reached the landing, something prickled the back of his neck and he turned, trying to see what caused the warning. His gaze lit on two men as they entered the saloon.

"Shit," he mumbled to himself, recognizing Cash. "I'll be right up, Dolly. There's someone I need to speak with first."

She took the bottle and glasses, giving him a soft kiss on the cheek before disappearing through a door.

Cash spotted Gabe coming down the stairs, his eyes crinkling in understanding. He held out his hand, then slapped Gabe on the back.

"It's good to see you again." Cash turned toward Beau. "This is Beau Davis. We're working together."

Gabe shook Beau's hand. "Sheriff Sterling told me you were in town. Looking for Drake?"

Cash shook his head as they took seats at a nearby table. "News travels fast."

"So it's true? Drake may be back in this area?"

"Appears that way. We believe he and his men rustled cattle in Colorado before moving to Montana. We spotted tracks indicating a large number of cattle. They're heading in the direction of Splendor."

Gabe leaned forward, his voice low. "I believe Drake and some of his men are already in Splendor. Neither the Pelletiers nor Tolbert are missing cattle, but others are. Seems whoever is doing this knows who to go after and who to avoid."

"For now," Beau grumbled. "At some point they will rustle from the bigger ranchers. That will be their last job, then they'll move the cattle out."

"We're leaving for Splendor tomorrow." Cash glanced up the stairs to see Dolly leaning against the rail. "Appears you have unfinished business. We'll meet you at dawn in front of the hotel."

Gabe clasped his shoulder. "I'll be there." He hustled up the stairs, ignoring the sounds of chuckles coming from behind him. At least he'd have one good night before what he knew would be another long dry spell.

"Good morning, Abby."

Abigail looked up to see her friend and Dax's wife, Rachel Pelletier, standing on the other side of the teller window, a broad smile lighting her face.

"Hello, Rachel. It's so good to see you. How are you feeling?"

"Wonderful. The first few months were a little rough, so I'm thankful that part is over." Rachel and Dax were expecting their first child in a few months. "I heard Mr. Clausen hired you. I always knew him to be a smart man."

Abby grinned at the comment. "He and Mrs. Phelps have been wonderful. What can I do for you today?"

"I've come to draw money for this week's pay at the ranch." Rachel handed Abby a piece of paper with a total of what she needed. "I also heard you're staying at the boardinghouse."

"I am." She lowered her voice so none of the other customers could hear. "It's been different living in town instead of coming in once or twice a week with Father or one of his hands. I feel as if I belong and less like a visitor. I hope that makes some sense."

"It does. After living with Uncle Charles and working in his clinic, moving to the ranch has been an adjustment. It's been better since Luke married Ginny. Of course, we have the orphans living on the ranch, and I do come to town as often as possible to help at the clinic." Rachel's uncle, Doctor Charles Worthington, ran the clinic where she worked as a nurse. Her experience during the Civil War, working in field hospitals for the Union Army, had provided a good background for working in a frontier clinic.

"Did you work today?" Abby counted out the money for the Pelletier payroll and slipped it into a bag Rachel had placed on the counter.

"I almost didn't ride in today, but I'm glad I did. Noah had an accident at the livery."

Abby stopped counting, her eyes widening. "What happened? Is he all right?"

Rachel reached across the counter and touched Abby's hand. "He'll be fine. Somehow, he lost his grip on a tool he was heating at the forge. When it slipped, he tried to grab it without thinking and burned his hand. I don't think he would've come to the clinic if his helper, Toby, hadn't been there when it happened and told him he'd fetch my uncle if Noah didn't get it tended."

A stream of air rushed from Abby's lungs as she slid the money bag to Rachel. "How bad is it?" Her voice shook, as did her hands.

"He should heal fast. I applied some salve and wrapped the burn. He might not be able to do much for a couple days which, of course, he didn't want to hear. Truth is it could've been much worse." Rachel rolled the bag tight and placed it into her reticule. "If you don't have plans, why don't you come to the ranch for supper tomorrow?"

"I'd love to, but I don't have a horse or buggy. I'm hoping to be able to purchase a horse soon, boarding it at Noah's livery."

"My uncle is coming out, too. Why don't you ride with him? He'd love the company."

"If you're sure he won't mind, then I'd love to."

"Good. I'll let him know before I leave town."

"Thank you, Rachel. I'll see you tomorrow."

Abby finished with the last few customers as she thought about the invitation. She didn't realize a simple request to join a friend for supper would make her feel so good. Since she'd been back, all her time had been spent at either the boardinghouse or the bank. It would be a welcome change to sit with friends and catch up on everything.

"We're almost ready to close, Abby." Sally pulled out her keys and walked toward the front entrance. "I'm certainly glad it's Friday."

"So am I, Mrs. Phelps." Abby finished closing her money drawer and locked it in the safe. "May I help you with anything before I leave?"

"No, dear. You go on home. I'll see you Monday morning."

Abby slipped into her coat before stepping into the evening air, the door closing behind her. She took her time, strolling past the general store, the noise and lights from the Dixie across the street catching her attention. She'd met Magdelena Campanel at the boardinghouse where she had a room.

Even though Nick told Suzanne his relationship with Magdelena was business only, few thought it as platonic as he made it sound.

Magdalena's rich, dark auburn hair and olive complexion gave her an exotic, sophisticated look. One of the girls at Abby's finishing school in Philadelphia had come from the New Orleans area and had similar features. Magdalena's stunning appearance rivaled anyone Abby had ever met.

Nick cut a striking figure in his customary black slacks, embroidered vest, and white shirt with black ribbon tie. Instead of detracting, the patch over his left eye added to the rugged, yet debonair appearance, which caused women to openly admire him as he walked past.

Although Nick appeared significantly older, he and Magdelena were a remarkable looking couple for a frontier town in the middle of nowhere. More than once since Magdelena had arrived on the stage a few days before, Abby found herself wondering if something had driven them to establish a saloon this far west, in a town offering little in the way of cultural distractions. She'd let her imagination get the best of her several times, envisioning they were running from the law, settling someplace where no one could find and prosecute them for whatever crime they'd committed. Abby chuckled at the way her fantasies could run wild.

She came to a stop at the edge of the boardwalk and glanced around. To her left and across the street stood the boardinghouse. If she made a right turn, she'd end up in front of the blacksmith shop and livery. She hesitated for a brief moment before making the decision to check on Noah, just to make certain his injuries weren't more serious than Rachel let on.

Embers still glowed in the forge, the heat assaulting her as she stepped through the unlocked doors and into his empty work area. The sound of horses from the livery in back carried to the front. She skirted the forge and walked to the back door, wondering if Noah might be cleaning the stalls or tending the animals he boarded.

More than once Abby had left her old gelding, Willie, with Noah for various reasons. She smiled, remembering all the times she'd worked to come up with some reason to visit him. Willie had always been a good excuse. She suspected Noah figured out the ruse long ago, but he never said a word.

Abby walked through the back doors, looking around until her gaze landed on Noah, forking hay from a stack several feet away, then tossing it into each of the stalls. Although the night air felt chilled, he wore no shirt, the muscles of his back bunching with each movement. Abby could've watched him for hours, wishing she had the right to run her fingers down his shoulders and arms. Her fingers itched to trace a path over his hardened chest.

"Abby?"

She startled when she noticed him striding toward her.

"Do you need something?" He came to a stop a foot away.

"I...um...heard you'd hurt yourself. I wanted to see if you were all right." She glanced at his bandaged hand, now dirty from work. It seemed he'd ignored Rachel's advice to take it easy for a few days.

He shifted the pitchfork to his other hand and held up the bandaged one. "Not much of a wound. Burned myself a little, nothing more." He lowered his hand, not taking his gaze from Abby, letting himself enjoy the sight of her.

"Rachel told me you were to lay off a little, let the burn heal."

"Well, I suppose I don't listen too well." His sheepish grin had her laughing. "Something funny?"

"Do all men ignore advice from their nurse or doctor?"

"I can't speak for others, but I've never taken it too seriously. Only way to keep eating is to work." He leaned the fork against one of the stalls, searching for words that would keep her at the livery longer. "Have you seen your father again?"

Her gaze had followed each of his movements and now landed on his face, noting the bruising and cuts from the beating her father's men had given him were almost healed. "I'm to have supper with him on Sunday."

"You don't sound pleased."

She snorted at the thought of anything having to do with her father being pleasurable. "I am *not* looking forward to it."

"He's still your father, Abby."

Abby glanced at Noah, surprised he'd support her decision to see her father. "And that is the only reason I agreed to have supper with him. He's sending one of his men to town to escort me. The problem is I won't be able to leave at will." She cast Noah a mischievous grin. "Unless I steal Willie and ride out."

Noah broke out in laughter at the image of Abby trying to escape on old Willie. "When was the last time you had Willie out for a run?"

"You mean as fast as he can go?"

"No, I mean as fast as other horses. I'll bet Rachel's old horse, Pete, could outrun Willie, and Pete is about the oldest horse around these parts. Come on." He motioned her toward one of the stalls holding a ten-year-old gelding. "I took this horse in trade for some work. There's a saddle inside you can use. Take the horse and saddle on Sunday so you won't feel trapped."

The happiness on Abby's face felt like a punch in the stomach to him.

"Oh, Noah, are you certain? I can pay you something for riding him." She reached out to stroke the horse's nose, her eyes lighting up with pleasure.

He settled fisted hands on his hips and glared at her. "I don't want your money, Abby. Take the horse on Sunday. All I ask is that you put him in his stall if I'm not back when you arrive."

She flinched at the hardness in his voice, then swung her gaze at him. "Are you leaving town again?"

"I'm going to my cabin early tomorrow and don't plan to return until Sunday night, maybe even Monday morning."

"May I see it sometime?"

"What?"

"Your cabin."

"No." He regretted the rigid tone that made her jerk, but he didn't want Abby to see the small cabin he'd built. It suited him fine and he enjoyed his time there, but to a woman of Abby's background, it wouldn't even compare to the bunkhouse at her father's ranch. He had few niceties a lady of her stature would expect.

She clasped her hands, squeezing them tight and squelching the retort on her tongue.

"It's a small place, nothing special. One big room and a separate bedroom."

Her eyes blazed and her hands fisted at the implication. "You think I wouldn't appreciate it? Would think less of it and you because it isn't some grand home?"

He took a deep breath, not wanting to admit she was right. "It was built for me and no one else. No visitors, and no—"

"Women?"

"That's right. No women." The longer Abby stayed, the lower his mood fell. He couldn't be this close to her without wanting to reach out and draw her to him. He had plans for the two of them, and it didn't include accosting her in the hay of his livery. "Isn't Suzanne expecting you for supper?"

"Are you asking me to leave?" she snapped, then regretted her outburst.

Rather than answer, he stepped past her to grab his shirt and slip it on. "I have a few more chores to finish before I eat and go to bed. I need to get an early start in the morning."

"You're right. I should leave. Do I need to let Toby know I'm taking the horse on Sunday?" She hoped his offer to use the horse still stood, even with her petulant behavior.

"I'll let him know."

"Thank you." She kept her gaze on him a moment longer, then headed for the door before turning to look over her shoulder.

"What is the horse's name?"

"Hasty."

Chapter Eleven

"Are you boys going to ride to the Pelletier place tonight?" Gabe asked as Cash and Beau reined their horses toward the Wild Rose, the sun showing mid-afternoon. He knew Cash, Dax, and Luke went way back, growing up together in Savannah.

"I thought we'd stay in town tonight, ride out there tomorrow." Cash dismounted, tossing the reins over a post in front of the saloon.

"Isn't there a boardinghouse or hotel where we can bed down?" Beau asked.

"You'll want to see Suzanne Briar over there." He nodded across the street. "She may have space for you, and her meals are the best in town. We don't have a hotel yet, but one of the owners of the Dixie has talked about opening one. Why don't you check with Suzanne, then I'll meet you there for supper? I need to let Noah know I've gotten back."

Gabe slid off Blackheart and walked him toward the livery, expecting to see Noah working late, as was his custom. Instead, Abigail brushed past him on her way outside.

"Oh, good evening, Sheriff Evans. Did you just get back?"

"Good evening, Miss Tolbert. Yes, I did, along with a couple other men I met in Big Pine. Is Noah inside?"

"He is." She glanced behind her, still trying to make sense of the horse's name, wondering if it meant anything specific. "I'm going to Suzanne's for supper."

"I'll be heading over there myself after I've spoken with Noah."

"I'll let her know." Abby crossed the street and entered the boardinghouse. She slipped off her coat, hanging it over her arm as she looked toward the dining room, her eyes widening in recognition. She walked toward two men, a smile splitting her face.

"Mr. Coulter, Mr. Davis. It's good to see both of you again."

Both men stood at her greeting.

"Miss Tolbert, it's a pleasure to see you again." Beau made a slight bow.

"You two know each other?" Cash asked, his brows knitting together in confusion.

"We met in St. Louis a few weeks ago." Beau turned his attention back to Abby. "Will you join us for supper?"

She couldn't think of a reason to decline. Besides, she wanted to find out what the two men were doing in Splendor. "That would be lovely. Thank you."

"Tell me. Did you find work?" Beau asked after they'd taken their seats.

"Yes, I did. At the bank. Mr. Clausen hired me right away. Of course, it helped that his previous teller left the week before." The lines around her eyes crinkled in delight.

"That is wonderful news. And you're staying...?"

"Here at the boardinghouse. Have you spoken with Mrs. Briar, the woman who owns it?" She glanced toward the kitchen, expecting Suzanne to come out any moment to take their orders.

"Not yet. We've been told she might have space for us to stay while we're in town, although Cash may stay with the Pelletiers." Beau looked past Abby to see an older woman emerge from the back and head for their table.

"I wondered where you were," Suzanne said, spotting Abby with the two men. "Ah, Mr. Coulter. Welcome back to Splendor."

"It's nice to see you again, Mrs. Briar." Cash watched as Gabe and Noah entered the dining room. "There will be five of us for supper."

"Good evening, gentlemen." Suzanne's warm smile greeted Gabe and Noah. They pulled up chairs, joining the others. "Did you just get back into town, Gabe?"

"I rode in with these two." He nodded toward Cash and Beau. "You've probably heard about the rustling going on. They've been tracking a gang from Colorado and believe it's the same group who've been rustling over in Big Pine."

"And you think they're the same ones stealing cattle around Splendor?" Suzanne asked Cash.

"We do."

She nodded, then took their orders, noting the rigid way Abby sat in her chair. Noah had taken a place next to her, no doubt the cause of her slight discomfort. Sadness washed over her. How they felt about each other seemed plain to everyone—except the two of them.

Abby shifted in her chair, trying to get a few more inches between her and Noah.

When she saw Cash and Beau, she should've known Gabe might join them. She hadn't thought of Noah, though. He hadn't hesitated to select the chair next to her, letting his knee and thigh touch hers as he settled into it. Although she kept trying to gain space, his large form would fill the space, letting his leg rest, once again, along hers.

Without thinking, she touched the back of a hand to her forehead, feeling the dampness even in the cool room. She concentrated on her breathing in an attempt to quiet her heart rate, which had risen considerably since Noah entered the room. Twice she tried to talk. Each time her throat closed up and she found herself forcing down a lump that threatened to choke her. She didn't recall feeling anything similar when she visited him earlier at the livery, suspecting the heat she felt came from the way his thigh rubbed back and forth on hers. The sensations threatened to overwhelm her, clawing their way around her, stopping any normal response.

"Abby, did you hear Cash?"

Noah's voice broke through, bringing her thoughts back to the present.

"I'm sorry. What did you say?" Abby glanced at Noah, then Cash.

"I asked what your father thinks of you working."

She sighed. All except Beau knew her father well enough to guess what his thoughts would be about her taking a job.

"As you'd expect, he's not pleased. He didn't try to forbid me outright from working, but I'm certain the discussion is long from over. I'm to have supper with him on Sunday. Noah's been gracious enough to let me use one of his horses so I won't be trapped as I would be if one of his men delivers me from town."

"You won't be riding alone, correct?" Gabe asked.

"She won't be," Noah answered, surprising the others at the table. "I'll ride with her, then wait while she's with her father. We'll ride back to town together."

"Noah, you can't do that." Abby was unprepared for his surprise announcement.

His eyes crinkled in amusement. "Of course I can. I have no other plans for Sunday, so you can visit with your father as long as you want. I'll be waiting when you're ready to return to town."

She couldn't think of a single answer that would stop him from doing whatever he wanted. Even Gabe, his closest friend, didn't try to stop him when Noah made up his mind.

"If Noah finds he's unable to escort you, I'd be able to take his place." Beau's eyes sparkled at the prospect of spending more time with Abby.

"Nothing will interfere." Noah's eyes narrowed at Beau as his voice held a quiet emphasis not lost on the others.

Abby's head swung to Beau, then to Noah before she let out a sigh. "Thank you, Noah. I appreciate your offer, even though I doubt it's necessary."

Noah felt great satisfaction at Abby allowing him to accompany her. Even if she hadn't, he would have followed, making certain she returned safely to town. He also believed Tolbert wasn't above forcing Abby to stay at the ranch, at least long enough to assure Clausen would need to replace her at the bank. The man would do whatever he could to continue to assert his control over his only child.

"I suggest we ride to the Pelletier ranch tomorrow, talk with Dax and Luke about the rustlers." Gabe pushed his empty plate aside.

"Do you have any idea who is doing the rustling?" Abby asked, trying to conceal the way her gaze continued to shift toward Noah.

"We believe they're lead by Parnell Drake—" Gabe began.

"Drake? The man who worked for my father?" Abby interrupted, surprise in her voice.

"The same. Cash and Beau tracked him from Colorado to Big Pine. It appears they may have moved here."

"My God..." She glanced at Noah, then covered her mouth with a hand before closing her eyes tight.

"Drake *is* in Splendor. He made a deposit at the bank earlier this week," Noah said, looking at Abby. He hadn't thought of following them from town. If he'd had any idea they might be involved in the rustling, he would've tracked them to wherever they camped.

"Are they staying in town?" Cash leaned forward, resting his arms on the table.

"No. They rode south. I should've followed them."

"You had no reason to, Noah. We didn't put it together until a few days ago." Cash sat back and crossed his arms. "We're still not certain it's the same men who are rustling around Big Pine."

"Except nothing else makes sense." The fact Abby knew the man they suspected of leading the rustlers bothered Beau. "Is Miss Tolbert in any danger?"

"It's doubtful, although her father might be." Gabe knew Tolbert didn't like it when someone got the better of him. Drake had not only been his foreman, but had been behind numerous attacks against the Pelletiers, contrary to Tolbert's orders.

"I need to warn him." Abby began to stand before Noah wrapped a hand around her arm to stop her.

"I'll ride out in the morning," Gabe said, looking around the table. "He needs to know Drake is back in the area. Did you recognize anyone with him?"

"No. I thought perhaps one of the other two men who worked for my father might be with him, but they weren't." Abby gripped her hands in her lap, wishing she'd taken a better look at the men with Drake. She did recall one man had a scar which ran down the side of his face, but nothing more. "If they don't know we suspect them, they might return to the bank."

The others seemed to ponder her statement before Cash spoke up.

"It's possible they'll return. In the meantime, who knows how many more head of cattle will turn up missing."

"It may be they were scouting the bank before robbing it." Beau sat back as Suzanne walked in with a pot of coffee and cups, setting one in front of each of them.

"Are you able to join us, Suzanne?" In a silent plea, Abby reached up to touch Suzanne's arm.

"Let me lock up. I'd love to sit for a spell."

The table remained silent as Suzanne closed the door behind the last diners and joined them. Gabe explained what they'd been discussing, including Beau's thought about a possible bank robbery.

"It wouldn't surprise me. When they worked for Abby's father, Drake and his men came in here several times. I knew they were different from the rest of us." Suzanne's brows knitted together as she sipped her coffee. "I heard them joke about the wagon train of pioneers who'd been attacked by Indians—the group Ginny Pelletier was a part of before settling here. They laughed about the couple who died and the stupidity of the settlers."

"Did they come into the restaurant this week?" Noah asked.

"No, although I thought I saw Drake ride out of town with some other men a few days ago. Monday or Tuesday, I think. I didn't get a good enough look at the time, but now I know it must have been them. What can I do to help?"

"Nothing right now, except stay away from them if they come to town." Gabe didn't want Suzanne, Abby, or any of the townspeople coming to harm because of Drake. He glanced at the men sitting around the table. They needed to find him before he harmed anyone in Splendor.

"Are you certain you can't close the restaurant for one afternoon and ride to the Pelletier ranch with me and Doc Worthington?" Abby asked once more in hopes Suzanne would give her a different answer.

"I can't today. The place is full with boarders who'll expect supper. Perhaps another time when there are fewer people."

Abby noticed Suzanne didn't look too disappointed. The last year had been rough for her after the new restaurant opened at the other end of town. Now people had a choice. She imagined Suzanne appreciated the additional income the boarders provided.

"I'd better leave before Doc leaves without me. I'll see you tonight." Abby stepped outside, enjoying the feel of the midday sun on her face. The ride would be short if the weather held. She looked across the street to see the livery closed tight. She suspected Noah had gone to his cabin and felt a twinge of guilt he'd be riding back early to escort her to her father's ranch for supper. At least Sunday meals were early. She'd be finished in enough time to meet Noah and make it back to Splendor before dark.

"Well...hello, Miss Tolbert. I understand you'll be going with me to visit Rachel." Doc Worthington had pulled the wagon to the front and finished tossing a couple bags into the back as Abby stopped beside him.

"Thank you for taking me." She grabbed his outstretched hand and climbed onto the wagon seat.

"Believe me, it's my pleasure. I enjoy having company." He settled beside her, grabbing the reins, glancing behind him at the sound of approaching horses. "It appears we'll have others riding along with us."

Abby turned to see Gabe, Cash, Beau, and Noah rein up alongside the wagon.

"I hear you and Miss Tolbert are heading to the same place we are." Gabe nodded toward Abby.

"If you're going to the Pelletier ranch, that would be correct. You men ready?" Doc asked, then slapped the reins. "Seems Rachel invited half the town to supper." His voice sounded a little rough, even as a smile appeared. "She does like having a houseful."

Once they started out, Abby continued to cast quick looks behind her, watching Noah keep pace with the wagon. He'd smile at her each time he caught her looking his way, sending a wave of heat through her.

As if he'd found a way into her thoughts, he pulled alongside the wagon. "Good afternoon, Abby." He touched his finger to the brim of his hat.

"Hello, Noah. It seems you won't be making it to your cabin this weekend."

"No, ma'am. I'll have lots of time to spend up there."

"Is it far? Your cabin, I mean."

Noah grasped the saddle horn with one hand, keeping the reins in the other, and leaned back. "Depends on the weather. An hour's the longest, but even then, the ride is beautiful. Some nights in the middle of summer, I have light all the way. It's worth the trip to wake early in the morning to witness the stunning sunrise. Yellows, oranges, reds, and pinks—it's a sight."

She listened to him go on and on about the beauty of his home and wished he'd invite her to share it with him. And not just the sunrises. She wanted to see what he'd accomplished with the land the Pelletiers had given him for helping free Rachel, the doctor, and the Frey brothers from outlaws bent on killing them. She shuddered at how close they'd come to losing the four about a year ago. At first, Noah had turned down the gift of the land, but neither Dax nor Luke would give up. It was either the land or they'd deposit money into Noah's account at the bank. He finally took the land, building a cabin with a small amount of help from Gabe. She yearned to see it.

"Perhaps you'll take me there some day." Her low, wistful voice tore away at Noah's commitment to never let her see his home.

As proud as he was of it, Noah never intended it to be a place to bring a bride and raise a family. Until recently, he'd never believed he had any real chance with Abby. Even if he could change her mind and allow him to court her, the cabin wasn't fit for a lady. At least he'd been telling himself that for almost a year. Her leaving the ranch, living in the boardinghouse, and working at the bank opened his mind to the possibility they could have a life together.

"It's not a place for a lady, Abby."

It was all he could get out, yet Abby saw it as an opening. "How do you know if you've never had a lady visit?"

A low chuckle rumbled from Doc Worthington's chest. He'd stayed silent during the exchange, guiding the wagon toward the entrance to the Pelletier ranch.

"She's got you there, Noah." He cast an amused glance at Noah, believing the man daft for continuing to put off such a prize as Abigail Tolbert.

Gabe, riding on the driver's side of the wagon, watched Noah shift in the saddle. The situation with Abby seemed to be coming to a head and he sure hoped he'd to be around to see it.

"She has a point, Noah. No reason not to take her up the mountain, get her opinion of the cabin. Didn't you say you wanted some ideas on curtains or some such thing?" Gabe braced his face at the lie he spoke.

Noah glared at him, knowing full well he'd never mentioned a word about curtains, or tablecloths, or any of the niceties a woman would expect in a home. "Don't believe I recall such a discussion, Gabe," he ground out, wishing Gabe had kept his thoughts to himself.

Abby turned to Noah, her eyes wide in anticipation. "It would be an honor to give you suggestions on the cabin. Running a home was part of my course work at finishing school." Abby cringed at what she'd said, feeling heat creep up her cheeks. As soon as the words were out, she wished they could be dragged back. "I mean...well..." Her voice trailed off. Anything more and she'd find herself in a deeper hole.

"I'm sure Noah would appreciate any help he could get with fixing up the place. Right, Noah?" Gabe grinned, enjoying watching his friend squirm.

Noah's jawed worked as he tried to control the fire in his gut at Gabe's suggestion. Even though he'd known Gabe since they were kids in New York, he never remembered a time he wanted to land a fist to his friend's face more than right now. It was good the wagon, Doc Worthington, and Abby stood between the two of them.

"It's all right. I'm sure Noah will reconsider inviting me when he's ready."

"Hope we're not all six feet under by then," Gabe mumbled under his breath, nudging Blackheart into a gallop as the ranch house came into sight.

Chapter Twelve

"We gonna hole up here forever?" Lem Pruett, one of Drake's cronies from their war years, sat on his horse, eyeing the cattle milling around the open space they'd found within the walls of the nearby mountain range.

"The cattle are doing fine. There's plenty of grass and water, and we're far enough out that no one should find us." Drake knew there'd be plenty of grass available during the drive south, but he wanted to fatten them up as much as possible before they started out.

"Drake's right. Those cattle need to feed on the grass several more days or we'll lose too many on the drive." Archie Swaggert, another of Drake's cronies, swung back up on his horse and looked up at the towering valley walls.

"This is a good spot, south of the Murton ranch. There are no other ranches for miles. Wish it weren't so far from the Pelletier and Tolbert ranches, though. Once we raid them, we'll have enough to leave."

"'Course, we don't have to go after more cattle, Drake. We got plenty to move and make a nice profit." Lem had been pushing to move the herd ever since he'd spotted the men who'd been tracking them ride into Splendor with Sheriff Evans. He'd been headed for the saloon, but hid in an alley before they spotted him, then rode toward camp with the news. If the sheriff, Coulter, and Davis joined forces with the local ranchers, it would be difficult to hide the herd much longer. If they did what Drake wanted and rustled from Tolbert and the Pelletiers, it would double the risk.

"No more discussion on this. We're going after their cattle." Drake reined his horse around and headed toward their camp.

For Drake, this wasn't about stealing cattle as much as revenge against the ranchers whose actions forced him, Lem, and Archie to disappear a year ago, before their plans had been completed. The three had expected so much more than mere wages as ranch hands for Tolbert. They'd hoped to turn local sentiment against the rancher, setting him up as the lawbreaker for the crimes the three committed. As their boss, they believed it would be a simple matter to focus the blame on Tolbert.

With him out of the way, Drake convinced himself it would've been easy to force his daughter, Abigail, to go along with their plans. Seen as a soft female with little ranching experience, Drake envisioned marrying her, taking the ranch in the most basic and legal way possible.

It now appeared she'd had a falling out with her father. He'd been shocked to see her behind the teller counter, pretended he didn't recognize her, and hoped she didn't recognize him. Drake doubted she had the ability to utter a convincing lie.

He had pondered what to do since that day. The action he preferred included her father dying in a ranch accident, leaving his substantial holdings to a daughter with little skill or interest in running a ranch. He'd step in, take it off her hands or marry her—either worked for him. It wasn't as if he'd be stuck with her long before she met a similar fate as her father. Drake chuckled to himself. There were a hundred ways to die and disappear on a ranch the size of Tolbert's. He just needed one.

They arrived at the perfect time for Abby to help Rachel and Ginny with the final preparations for supper. It kept her busy and away from Noah. He'd avoided her after they'd returned to Splendor, spending time at his cabin and not coming to Suzanne's for meals. After two weeks, she'd grown desperate to get one glimpse of him. She'd seen him in town, and asked him to help when Drake appeared at the bank. Other than stopping at the livery the day before, she'd done her best to give him the space he seemed to need.

His actions at supper last night, on the ride out today, and volunteering to escort her to her father's tomorrow had her confused. She didn't know how to react. No matter how much she wanted it, being around him hurt more than she'd imagined. Cutting him from her thoughts hadn't worked, and now he appeared in agonizing regularity. The man didn't realize or care about the effect he had on her.

"Abby, would you mind carrying this to the table?" Rachel held out a platter brimming with sliced beef and boiled potatoes. Although she still appeared to have plenty of energy, the pregnancy had begun to affect her movement and length of time she could stand before feeling pain in her back.

"Of course."

"Oh, and let the men know supper is ready."

She wanted to protest, ask Ginny to call the men, but knew it would seem petty. Besides, she needed everyone to see her as the grown woman she'd become, making her own way on her own terms. It wouldn't happen if she looked to others to help her over the many hurdles in life, which was how she saw Noah.

Setting the platter on the table, she turned toward the front door in time to see Dax and the others walking in, laughing. With all the hardships they faced with men like Drake, it was good they could find reason to joke.

"Supper's ready." Her eyes met Noah's before she looked away and turned toward the kitchen, passing Ginny as she set a basket of warm bread on the table.

Ginny settled her hands on her hips as the men milled about, ignoring Abby's request. "Luke, come sit down before your supper gets cold."

"Coming, sweetheart," Luke called to his wife, winking and receiving a blush in return.

"If you'll help Rachel with the last of the food, I'll go get the orphans." Ginny didn't wait for a reply from Abby before dashing out the front door.

Dax, Luke, and a few other men had discovered the children—Lydia, Billy, Samuel, Selina, and Margaret—hiding in a cave up the mountain from Luke's place on Wildfire Creek. At nineteen, Lydia was the oldest. From what everyone could tell, she'd taken a shine to Bull Mason, one of their top hands, and the feeling appeared to be mutual.

Except Billy, all had chosen to live at the Pelletier ranch, Redemption's Edge, doing what they could to help. Billy had decided to live with Frank and Hiram Frey at their ranch located several miles southwest. Fifteen, proud, and stubborn, he'd originally wanted nothing to do with any white ranchers, but changed his mind when he got to know the Freys. His seven-year-old sister, Margaret, had been torn. She wanted to stay with her brother, but there were no other females living at the Frey ranch. Her close relationship with Lydia and Selina, and her friendship with Ginny's younger sister, Mary, made the decision to stay with the Pelletiers easier. Most Sundays, Billy made the long ride to have supper with everyone and spend the day with Margaret.

Ginny found them in the barn with Bull, hovering around a foal born a few days before.

"Rachel wants all of you to come inside for supper. You, too, Bull." Ginny looked into the stall, admiring the beautiful colt, now part of Luke's horse breeding program.

"Come with me," Ginny said to her sister, Mary.

"I want to go with Uncle Bull."

"Me, too," Margaret chimed in, each of the girls taking one of Bull's hands and pulling him toward the house, the others following behind.

Fourteen-year-old Samuel, Lydia and Selina's brother, dashed ahead, determined to find a chair with the men and not be relegated to the children's table. He worked with Luke and Travis, another ranch hand who had considerable experience breeding horse stock at his family farm before the war began. The war changed everything for Travis. Similar to many others, he'd come west, hoping to put the pain of the past behind him and start over. He'd found the opportunity with Luke and Dax.

Abby watched everyone crowd around the two tables, reminding her of what Noah had told her about Christmas supper. All the ranch hands attended that day. A lump formed in her throat, remembering she'd invited Noah to have supper with her and her father. She'd swallowed the extreme disappointment when he told her Rachel had already extended an invitation for him and Gabe, which they'd accepted. She so wished to spend Christmas with someone other than her father. It would never have occurred to him to invite their ranch hands. They'd shared a quiet meal alone before she retreated to her room, filling the emptiness with a book.

"May I sit next to you, Abby?"

Noah's warm voice flowed over her and she found herself smiling up at him. "Why, yes. That would be lovely."

He pulled out a chair for her, then seated himself, scowling when Beau sat on her other side. Twice in two days Davis had shown an interest in her, and in Noah's mind, that was twice too many. He needed to have a talk with the man, let him know to back off and find his own woman.

Dax said a blessing before plates were filled and the room fell silent, except for the continual chattering at the children's table. Today, only Mary, Margaret, and ten-year-old Selina sat around the small table Luke had brought in from the storage shed behind the bunkhouse. Lydia and Samuel squeezed into the adult table, making for a tight fit, although no one complained.

Abby experienced a combination of excitement and apprehension at being wedged between two imposing men—one she enjoyed as a friend, the other she wanted so much more from, even though she'd told him otherwise.

As he'd done at supper the previous night, he let his leg rest against hers, not allowing her to end the contact. Each time she moved, he'd shift enough to touch his leg to hers again. At one point he rested his hand on his thigh, letting his fingers stroke the side of her leg, sending rays of heat flashing through her body and making her heart race. She glanced up at him, trying to draw his attention away from a conversation with Bull. Although she could see his lips quirk upward as he listened to something Bull said, he didn't look at her. Instead, he increased the pressure of his fingers against her thigh, stroking her through the thin cotton of her dress. The sensations created by his movements overwhelmed and scared her, causing beads of moisture to form on her forehead.

"Excuse me," she mumbled, pushing back, trying not to run from the room as she sought refuge in the cool night air.

"Abby, are you all right?" Rachel asked as Abby covered the distance between the dining table and front door in seconds.

"I'll check on her." Noah followed her, shooting a warning look at Beau who had also started to rise, then sat back down.

Noah pushed open the door and stepped onto the porch, spotting Abby running toward the corral next to the barn. "Abby, wait." He didn't wait for her to respond, jogging to a stop next to her. "Are you all right?"

She rounded on him, arms crossed, angry eyes flashing up at him. "What do you think you were doing in there? Do you have so little respect for me you think you can touch me like that at the supper table with others all around us?" She drew in a deep breath, letting it out slowly as her heart continued to beat almost painfully in her chest.

Noah's concern turned to discomfort at the agony he saw on her face. "I'm sorry. I'd never do anything to cause you embarrassment or pain."

"Then what was that about?"

He looked toward the western mountains, noting the sun touching the tops of the highest peaks, and took a deep breath. Shoving his hands in his pockets so he wouldn't do what he wanted and reach out to touch her, Noah took a step backward.

"Do you remember when you told me you no longer had feelings for me?" His voice was rough as he worked to swallow the lump in the back of his throat.

She let her arms drop, clasping her hands in front of her, feeling regret at how he'd interpreted her words.

"Yes…"

Noah had fought his attraction to her for too long. He needed to be honest, let her know how he felt, and discover if she still had any feelings for him at all.

"I need to know the truth, Abby. Do you feel anything for me?"

She bit her lower lip as her brows drew together. Her chest squeezed into a throbbing ball, making it almost impossible to breathe. Abby struggled to form the words, knowing what she said now would have lasting implications. She looked up, searching his face.

"Yes, Noah. I do have feelings for you. I always have."

He hesitated a moment before taking a step forward. "As a friend...or more?"

She glanced at him, then looked away before finding the courage to lock her gaze with his. "More. Much more."

He drew a hand from his pocket and stroked one finger down her cheek. "That's good, Abby. Very good." He moved his hand to the back of her neck and drew her toward him, lowering his mouth to hers, capturing it in a kiss that caressed her lips, causing heat to flare through him.

Abby could feel her body shudder at the gentle touch of his lips to hers. She raised her hands, resting them on his arms, steadying herself as she leaned closer.

Slowly, so as not to frighten her, Noah moved his other hand to her back, gently aligning her body with his as he deepened the kiss.

She gripped his arms, feeling the taut muscles tighten beneath his shirt. As he pulled her closer, her hands moved to the back of his neck, her fingers spearing into his hair, drawing him down to her.

A husky moan escaped his lips at the passion he felt build within him. The feel of her in his arms triggered sensations he believed beyond his reach, the building pleasure almost more than he could bear.

Her lips parted on a sigh, allowing him access to the deep recesses of her mouth. She didn't pull away as he expected. Instead, she followed his lead, drawing him more firmly to her, exploring his mouth as he did hers. Time passed until she pulled away on a ragged breath, feathering kisses over his face and down his neck before lifting her gaze to his once more, letting him take her mouth again.

In the distance, Noah recognized the sound of a door slamming and knew they had to stop. He drew away, placing another soft kiss on her lips before stepping back, letting his arms drop to his sides.

"Uncle Noah, are you and Miss Abby all right?" Mary ran up to his side, catching her breath as Margaret came to a stop behind her.

Noah bent over, offering the girls a warm smile. "Miss Abby and I are fine." He glanced behind him, then back to the girls. "We're ready to go back inside. We didn't miss dessert, did we?" He straightened, reaching out a hand to Abby, a thrill jolting through him as she linked her fingers in his.

"No. That's why we came out. We're all waiting for you." Mary didn't even pause as she and Margaret ran back to the house and up the steps, disappearing inside.

Noah turned Abby to him. "We'll take our time, make sure this is what you want. I don't intend to make any mistakes with you, Abby."

She reached up and stroked his cheek, a smile lighting her face. "You're who I want, Noah. I've known it for a long time. Please believe my feelings won't change."

Noah already knew he loved her, yet he couldn't help feeling they should take it slow. She'd just found her independence from a father who still hoped to bring her back under his control. Noah never wanted her to feel dominated by a man again. He'd court her, take his time while doing his best to convince himself he was a man deserving of her love.

Chapter Thirteen

Noah opened the livery earlier than normal on Monday morning, contentment he'd never known before flowing through him. On Sunday, he'd accompanied Abby to within a half-mile of her father's ranch, fished in a nearby stream until she returned hours later, then rode by her side back to Splendor.

After they'd taken care of the horses, he walked her to Suzanne's, giving Abby a quick kiss before returning to the livery. He'd lain in bed Sunday night, thinking of how he wanted to court her in the way a woman such as her deserved. He'd also thought of his commitment to help Gabe, Cash, and Beau locate Drake and his gang.

Dax and Luke agreed to provide men to help with the search, and Gabe would be talking with Tolbert today, trying to convince him to supply more men. They needed every man available to track and arrest the rustlers.

"Is the coffee ready yet?" Gabe stood by the door, watching Noah throw more wood on the forge.

Noah nodded toward a cook stove in the back. "Help yourself." He might not be a great cook, but no one had ever complained about his coffee. "You still riding out to see Tolbert?"

"I am. How did Abby's visit go yesterday?"

"She didn't say much except he tried to convince her to quit the job and move back to the ranch. She refused."

Gabe nodded, taking a sip of coffee. "I can't see why she'd ever want to move back. Her life is here with you now."

Noah glanced over his shoulder. "We've made no plans."

Gabe couldn't help grinning. He'd seen the look on both their faces when they returned to the house Saturday evening and knew they'd reached some kind of understanding.

"You will, my friend. You may want to draw it out a little, but in the end, she'll be picking out curtains for your cabin."

Noah turned, crossing his arms and glaring at his friend. "Do you need help saddling Blackheart, or can you do it on your own?" he ground out.

"All right. I'll say no more." Gabe tossed out the last of his coffee before saddling his horse and swinging into the saddle. "No matter if Tolbert helps or not, we meet with the Pelletier men at sunup tomorrow and ride out."

Noah nodded, watching as Gabe turned Blackheart toward the Tolbert ranch. He had more faith in Tolbert than Gabe or the others had. Not because he thought Tolbert gave a damn about the people. He'd do it to protect his property and for no other reason. Providing a few men to help stop the rustling would be beneficial for him, and that's all the reason Tolbert required.

He finished an order for Stan Petermann, owner of the general store. Afterwards, in an attempt to keep his mind off tonight, he completed tool repairs, fixed a wagon axel, and shod a pair of horses. He'd asked Abby to supper, his first attempt to properly court her. The nerves he felt surprised him. Social conversations came hard to him. Gabe would dispute this, citing all the times Noah had been considered gregarious when they were growing up.

They'd been an odd pair—Gabe, the son of a wealthy New York businessman, and Noah, the son of a laborer who worked for Gabe's father. Over the years, Noah's father had risen up the ranks, becoming a valued and trusted employee, but Noah's family often struggled, even with the increased wages.

While Gabe worked a few hours each day for an uncle who owned a prestigious hotel, Noah took odd jobs which started after school and ran late into the night. As expected, Gabe enrolled at Columbia College, intending to either work for his father or rejoin his uncle in the hotel business after graduation. Unlike Gabe, Noah never planned to attend college, believing his future existed following in the footsteps of his father. An unanticipated scholarship from Gabe's father allowed him to follow his friend to Columbia. Neither graduated.

The war changed the lives of both young men. Each volunteered for service in the Union Army, and although they'd planned to return to college after the war, neither had, preferring to venture west. What Noah witnessed during the war, including the killings he'd been a part of as a Union sharpshooter, changed him from an outgoing, sociable young man to someone who cherished his solitude.

Until Gabe returned to Splendor several months before, Noah ate his meals alone and seldom visited the Wild Rose, preferring to drink from his private bottle of whiskey.

Two events worked to change his self-imposed private existence. First, Gabe returned, refusing to let Noah suffer the effects of the war alone. Within weeks Gabe had him sharing meals, playing cards, and enjoying the occasional whiskey at the Wild Rose.

Second, he'd met Abigail Tolbert. Her impact on him had been immediate and intense.

"Still working I see."

Noah swung around to see the woman who'd captured his thoughts all day standing in the doorway. Abby took a few steps forward, then stopped as if waiting for an invitation to come closer.

"I saw the light from the forge and decided to see if you were still working." She hesitated a moment before continuing. "And to see if you still wanted to have supper with me."

His eyes narrowed on Abby as he walked forward, noticing her uncertain expression and how she clasped her hands so tight, her knuckles lost their color. He wiped his hands down his trousers, then reached out to take her hands in his.

"Of course I want to have supper with you. Give me a few minutes to clean up." The tension seemed to seep from her at his words, a tentative smile curving the corners of her mouth. He brushed a quick kiss across her forehead. "I won't keep you long."

Abby had thought of little else all day besides supper with Noah. If she were being honest, he'd rarely been out of mind since visiting the Pelletiers. She'd never anticipated his actions, the way he held and kissed her, making her body pulse with desire. The thought of anyone catching them fled as his touch created a heat that destroyed all rational thought. She knew if he hadn't pulled away, she would've allowed him to do whatever he wanted, his touch shattering any shred of restraint she possessed. The understanding of what he could do to her, how he made her throb with need, frightened and thrilled her.

She startled as warm hands rested on her waist and drew her back to rest against his firm chest.

"Are you ready?" Noah lowered his head, placing kisses along the soft column of her neck. He chuckled at the shiver he felt go through her.

"Noah..."

"Hmmm...?"

"Someone might see us." Her voice trembled, although she made no move to pull away.

He moved his hands to splay across her stomach as his mouth continued to kiss the sensitive skin below her ear. She squirmed in his arms, pushing back toward him, rubbing her body against his.

"Noah..." she breathed out as his hands moved up to her ribs. "We should stop." Her thick voice held none of the conviction he expected.

He knew she was right, yet the feel of her skin and the rose scent of her hair made it hard to let go. If it hadn't been for the loud voices and noises from the street, he'd have been content to stay this way for as long as she allowed.

She turned in his arms and pressed a kiss to his mouth. "It wouldn't do for anyone to see us together like this."

He clamped down his body's reaction, turned her toward the street, and pulled her arm through his. They drew little attention walking across the street and into Suzanne's.

"Good evening, Noah. Abby mentioned you asked to escort her to supper."

"Yes, ma'am." He glanced down at Abby and couldn't help the joy he felt at being with her openly. It was long past time he claimed her as his.

"I have the perfect table for you."

They followed Suzanne toward a corner furthest away from the entrance to a table adorned with a white tablecloth, candles, and vase with one red rose. Abby stopped and stared, then shot a look at Suzanne.

"This is beautiful."

"I'm so glad you like it. I found the rose on a wild bush out by the stream. Saw it this morning and hoped I'd have a reason to use it. Tonight I have roast beef, venison, and chicken stew."

Abby ordered stew while Noah decided on the beef, then both settled back as Suzanne left for the kitchen.

"You didn't talk much about your visit with your father yesterday." Noah leaned forward, recalling Abby's somber mood when she'd joined him after her supper. They'd said little on the ride home, both comfortable with the silence. He'd helped her from the saddle, wrapping his arms around her, welcoming the way she laid her head against his chest.

Lowering his head, one soft kiss became two, then more, until she clung to him, placing kisses at the base of his neck, his chin, letting him capture her mouth. He'd let his hands rest on her waist, enjoying the feel of her soft curves. He'd been sorely tempted to move them back into the shadows of the livery, letting it go as far as she'd allow before sanity returned. A few minutes later, he'd walked her to the boardinghouse.

"He'll never change, Noah. Father is a man who wants control, and not just of me." She quieted as Suzanne brought their meals, then turned to help other customers. "Yesterday, he talked of his desire to take a more active role on the Splendor citizens committee, leading the town in the direction he believes it should go." She took a bite of stew, chewing slowly.

"Did he say what that direction is?"

"He mentioned trying to move the territorial capital here to draw more people. The railroad will be expanding, and he's afraid Splendor will be left out if we don't have a strong voice advocating for a rail line here."

"Those aren't bad notions, Abby. It's what most towns want—to grow, be able to take advantage of opportunities. What bothers you so much about these ideas?"

"It's not the ideas. It's *my* part in them. He wants me to quit my job, be by his side, play hostess for him the way mother did before she died." She glanced up at Noah, lines of worry etching her face. "I told him I was content in town, working at the bank. He responded by saying he could get Mr. Clausen to fire me at any time. He cares nothing of what I want, Noah. He never has."

He reached across the table, placing his hand on top of hers. "I doubt Clausen would've hired you if he had concerns about your father withdrawing his money. A lot of people trust him with their savings. Many more than when your family moved to Splendor." He looked up at the sound of men's voices, not recognizing either of the two who walked in and took a table near the front.

Abby saw him stare and turned in her seat, placing a hand over her mouth to stifle a gasp before shifting back toward Noah.

"Do you recognize them?"

"I'm certain at least one of those men accompanied Drake to the bank. Don't they look familiar to you?"

Although he'd noticed the others, Noah had been focused on Drake, watching as he gave his money to Abby, making sure the man did nothing to threaten her. He leaned forward, focusing on the one facing them. As the man turned toward his companion, Noah saw the scar. It triggered a recollection in the bank when the same man glanced over his shoulder, flashing a feral smile at him. The memory jolted Noah.

"The one with the scar…"

Abby leaned over the table, closer to Noah. "Yes. I'm certain he was there."

Noah looked at their half-finished meals, knowing he had to notify Gabe, regretting their evening had to end so soon.

"Abby…"

"It's all right. We need to let the sheriff know." She pushed her chair back before Noah's hard gaze stopped her. "What?"

"*We* are not doing anything. *You* are staying here, where it's safe. I'll go to the jail."

"But what if—"

"If Gabe has questions, he can speak with you tomorrow. Right now, he needs to know they're in town." Noah's senses went on alert as he escorted Abby through the dining room and into the kitchen, keeping her on his side away from the men, a hand on the small of her back.

"Is something wrong?" Suzanne set down her towel and stepped toward them.

"At least one of the men who was with Drake at the bank is sitting at the table closest to the door." Abby felt a shiver course through her body.

"I need to tell Gabe and I want Abby to stay here. It's doubtful they'll do anything more than eat their meal, but I'd suggest you spend as little time with them as possible." He turned Abby to him. "Stay upstairs. I'll be by to escort you to the bank in the morning." He ran his knuckles down her cheek, then turned to leave.

"Noah?" Abby whispered. He stopped, glancing over his shoulder. "Be careful."

"Cash, you and Beau stay hidden alongside the Wild Rose. Noah will be watching from the livery, and I'll be near the bank. We follow them to their camp, nothing more until we locate the stolen cattle." Gabe checked his guns, holstered them, then grabbed his rifle. "Once we know their location, we send word to the Pelletiers and Tolbert."

"He agreed to your request?" Noah asked, surprised.

"Reluctantly, but yes."

They took their places and waited. It didn't take long for the men to emerge from the restaurant, mount their horses, and ride south, but instead of turning west, toward the mountains, they rode east. Following at a safe distance, Gabe and the others reined to a halt several times, moving off the trail when the men stopped. Each time, the two men glanced behind them, then moved on.

An hour passed before the two made camp without making contact with Drake.

"What now?" Noah dismounted with the others, moving their horses well off the trail.

"We'll wait the night, see if they meet Drake in the morning. They're our best chance of finding him." Gabe didn't like the tension in his gut. On the battlefield, he'd always taken heed of his instincts, coming to respect the warnings his body sent out. Tonight, something felt amiss, but he didn't know what.

"And if they don't go to Drake?" Beau kept glancing ahead, spotting the light from a campfire.

"We'll have no choice but to head back and wait for another chance."

"I don't like it." Cash slid from the rock where he'd been since early morning, watching the men but seeing no movement.

Noah scrubbed a hand over his stubbled jaw, recounting each moment from the time the men walked into the restaurant to them making camp. He knew they'd spotted him at Suzanne's. A brief nod between the two let Noah know they'd recognized him or Abby, maybe both, yet their expressions signaled no concern.

"Are Drake and his men wanted for anything?" Noah asked.

"Only Drake, for cattle rustling in Colorado. He's suspected of murder, but there's never been enough evidence to secure wanted posters." Cash finished cinching his saddle, preparing to either follow the men or return to town.

"Then all except Drake would have no fear of showing up in Splendor, walking around as if no one would be looking for them. I'm surprised Drake showed his face at the bank." Noah's gut clenched at the idea forming in his mind.

"He may have found out I left town and figured you wouldn't know about him," Gabe said. "Hell, I didn't know Drake was wanted until I did a little more digging."

"But they know you two have been tracking them, right?" Noah asked Cash and Beau.

"That's our guess. We've made no secret of our interest in locating Drake and whoever rides with him. I've never seen a gang more elusive, riding in and out like ghosts, leaving little to track." Beau crossed his arms, shaking his head in disgust.

"Hell," Noah muttered, shooting a concerned look at Gabe, who nodded in understanding. "We've been setup. We need to get back to town. Now." Noah swung up on Tempest, taking off at a quick pace, the others following close behind. The closer they got, the more his internal alarm sounded. As the four rounded the corner onto the main street, the number of people milling around outside the bank and in front of Doc Worthington's clinic confirmed his fears.

Noah jumped off Tempest and ran to the clinic, pushing past others to slam into the crowded waiting area, as Gabe and the others stormed toward the bank.

"What happened?" Seeing the look on the faces of those standing about, Noah's heart raced.

"The bank was robbed. They shot Clausen in the arm. He's in with the doc now," Stan Petermann answered. "Abby's all right, Noah. I believe she's still at the bank."

Noah backtracked, heading to the bank, and dashing inside to see Abby leaning against Gabe. The moment she spotted him, Abby left Gabe's side and rushed into Noah's arms.

He closed his eyes, wrapping her tight in his embrace, resting his chin on her head.

"Are you all right? They didn't hurt you, did they?" Noah's questions came out in a rush, his heart pounding as he thought of what might have happened.

"No," she mumbled, shaking her head against his chest.

"Your lady pointed her gun at the robbers, threatened to shoot if they didn't leave. That was right after they shot Clausen." Gabe shook his head. "I'd better speak with Mrs. Phelps."

"That right, Abby?" Noah pulled away and looked at her, feeling her shiver and seeing a mix of emotions pass over her face.

"I didn't know what else they'd do once they shot Mr. Clausen. Suzanne gave me the gun this morning, knowing you and Gabe were following those men. I never thought I'd have to use it." Her voice broke, although he saw more anger on her face than fear.

He squeezed his eyes tight as his arms clamped around her again. They remained silent for a long moment before he spoke. "Did you recognize the men?"

"They wore bandannas over their faces, but I'm certain one was Drake. I recognized the hat he wears with the distinctive band. I already told Gabe about it."

"You did real good, Abby—may even have saved Mrs. Phelps and yourself from harm. Who knows what those men would've done after they shot Clausen." Noah's rough voice almost broke as the full impact of the danger slammed into him.

"What the hell happened?"

Everyone turned at the sound of Tolbert's booming voice. He pushed past everyone, rushing through the door and walking directly toward Abby and Noah.

"Abigail, are you hurt?" He scowled at Noah, seeing his arms wrapped around Abby. She glanced at him, but didn't step away.

"I'm fine, Father, but Mr. Clausen took a bullet in the arm."

"I heard. You're leaving with me. Now. You will quit this job and return to the ranch. Get your belongings and meet me at the wagon."

"*No*, Father. I'm *not* quitting my job and I'm *not* returning to the ranch. Not now, and maybe not ever." Abby dropped her arms from around Noah and crossed them in front of her, her eyes showing a spark of anger.

"You most certainly are. I will not have you placing yourself in danger. Now, get what you need, or I'll send a man back to fetch your belongings."

She let out a breath, not wanting to get into this with him.

"I no longer live at the ranch. You sending me away proved to be for the best as I'm now doing what I've wanted to do for some time. This job and living at Suzanne's is what I want and there's nothing you can do to change any of it."

"You're a child—"

"I'm twenty and a grown woman. You have to stop seeing me as a little girl. I haven't been that in a long, long time."

Tolbert's countenance, which had been hard and unyielding, changed as if all the wind had been sucked from his lungs. His shoulders slumped as he paced away, then turned to face her.

"This discussion is not over, Abigail." His voice sounded firm, although it lacked the conviction of moments before.

She took a few steps toward him, her face softening. "Yes, it is, Father."

Tolbert showed the look of man on the verge of defeat, yet still fighting in hopes of turning the course of events. He reached a hand out to her, then let his arm drop. Tolbert raised his eyes to Noah, searching the man's face.

"You watch out for her, Brandt. There'll be hell to pay if you don't."

Chapter Fourteen

"How much do you think we got?" Lem asked as they rode into camp and dismounted.

"Enough to get the town to focus on the bank robbery and not the rustling." Drake tossed the one bag of money on the ground. "Archie, count it out."

"Sure thing." Archie retrieved the bag and pulled out a knife.

The two men Gabe, Noah, and the others had tracked rode in a few minutes later, smiling when they saw Archie spreading out the money on a blanket and sorting it into piles.

"It worked. I knew that girl would recognize me from when you took money to the bank. Four men tracked us, but gave up and turned back—just the way you said they would." Hal Reid absently stroked the scar on his face as he walked up to Drake. "And now they think we're camped away from the mountains. Anyone get hurt?"

"The banker tried to pull a gun. Archie shot him in the arm." Drake grabbed hardtack from his pocket and bit down on the dry biscuit, waiting for Archie to finish the count.

After leaving Tolbert's ranch with Archie and Lem, Drake had expanded the number of men working for him. Most watched the herd, while others helped with rustling and whatever else their boss ordered. Of all the men, Drake counted four as close allies—Archie, Lem, Hal, and Biff. He'd served in the Confederate Army with all of them at one time or another, but lost track of Hal and Biff until spotting them in Denver over the winter.

He'd taken Archie, Lem, and a few others with him to rob the bank, using Hal and Biff as decoys. It had been almost too easy. Drake never expected Sheriff Evans to take Brandt, Coulter, or Davis with him, leaving the town unprotected. Other than those four, there were few men proficient at using a weapon, and most worked at the Pelletier ranch.

"A hundred fifty dollars is all we got. Not much." Archie handed Drake the money.

"The amount doesn't matter. This will force Evans to split up whatever men he has available, some protecting the town, others searching for us. We'll make sure we run them in circles while the rest of our men raid the ranches. It won't be long before we'll have the number of cattle we need to drive the herd out of Montana." Drake reached into his saddlebag, pulled out a bottle of whiskey, and took a swallow. "Now, let's talk about going after the Tolbert and Pelletier cattle."

The bank stayed closed the rest of the day, Mrs. Phelps nailing a notice to the door stating they'd reopen the following morning. Doc patched up Clausen's arm and sent him home, glad the injury had been a nick and nothing major. Still, Doc knew it must hurt like hell.

"Where's Abby?" Rachel burst into the treatment room, her eyes searching. Once they reached town, it hadn't taken Dax and her long to hear what had happened.

Her stomach grew a little each day, but Doc decided to keep that thought to himself.

"The last I saw, she was with Noah, heading toward Suzanne's. She's…" He never finished as Rachel hurried toward the boardinghouse.

From the front window of the boardinghouse, Noah spotted Rachel running out of the clinic. He stood from where he'd been sitting with Abby in the parlor, trying to convince her to go upstairs and lie down. Perhaps Rachel would have more luck.

Bursting through the front door, Rachel stopped when she saw him. "How's Abby?"

"She's—"

"As you can see, I'm fine." Abby stood, accepting the hug Rachel offered while casting a frustrated look at Noah. "He thinks I should go to my room and rest."

"He's right, Abby."

"You, too?" Abby sighed, slumping back into her chair.

"I'm not taking sides. I'm only thinking what might be best for you. I saw it many times during the war when I treated men in battle. The body craves rest after going through a traumatic experience." Rachel sat in the chair Noah offered.

"I wasn't wounded."

"No, but you witnessed Mr. Clausen being shot, feared for Mrs. Phelps and yourself, then held a gun on the robbers. Don't dismiss what you experienced." She held out her hands, which Abby accepted. "Uncle Charles says the bank won't reopen until tomorrow. At least rest for a while. You may be surprised how fast you fall to sleep."

Abby closed her eyes. She hadn't told Noah, but she'd vacillated between nausea and exhaustion for the last hour, believing much of it due to the encounter with her father.

"All right. I'll go upstairs for a while, but it's doubtful I'll fall asleep."

Noah and Rachel watched as she walked toward the kitchen, trying to stifle a yawn.

"She's exhausted." Noah picked up his cup of cold coffee and gulped it down. "How are you feeling?" He studied Rachel, noting the dark circles under her eyes.

She leaned back in the chair and rested her hands on her protruding stomach. "All right. Not sleeping too good, but that will pass."

"Who brought you to town?"

"Dax. He's meeting with Gabe, Cash, and Beau now. He told me a group of you plan to head out tomorrow, try to find the robbers."

"We'd thought it would be a search for rustlers. Now we might be searching for both." Noah glanced out the window, seeing Dax cross the street toward the boardinghouse.

"The same men?" Rachel asked.

"I'd bet on it." Noah stood as Dax walked in, holding out his hand.

"Is Abby all right?" Dax asked, taking a seat next to Rachel, grasping her hand.

"Holding up well. Tolbert came in before I could get her out of the bank. He's using the robbery as an excuse to push her to return to the ranch. She told him no." Noah's lips curved upward, remembering how she'd stood up to her father.

"I can understand Tolbert's concern, but she doesn't need to be back under his boot." Rachel absently rubbed a hand over her stomach.

Noah couldn't argue with Rachel's comment. "Tell me what's been decided about going after the robbers?" he asked Dax.

"Luke and I, along with several of our men, will be here at dawn. If Tolbert's men join us, fine. If not, we won't wait for them. We'll leave three men in town in case Drake decides to hit the bank again. Seems odd he went after the bank when Cash is certain he's the one behind the rustling."

"I've been thinking the same, unless he needs the cash to pay for supplies until they can drive the cattle out of the area. I can't help feeling that when we catch Drake, we'll recover the money and find the missing cattle." Noah stood, glancing over his shoulder at the sound of the entry door opening. "Afternoon, Miss Campanel. I don't believe you've met Dax Pelletier and his wife, Rachel."

Dax stood as greetings were exchanged. Rachel tried, in a subtle way, to let her gaze wander over the beautiful day dress and hat worn by Magdelena, noticing she'd also piqued Dax's curiosity.

"We wondered about Nick's business partner. Guess we all thought it would be a man." Dax's comment didn't surprise Magdelena.

"Most people make the same assumption, Mr. Pelletier. I'm quite used to it."

"Please, join us." Rachel nodded to an empty chair.

"Actually, I came to see how Miss Tolbert is doing. I saw Mr. Brandt walk her over from the bank. She's such a sweet young woman."

"Abby's resting, although it was a struggle to convince her she needed it."

"If you don't mind, I want to talk with Gabe about some other matters before we head back to the ranch. Welcome to Splendor, Miss Campanel." Dax bent to place a kiss on Rachel's cheek.

"I'll head over there with you. Ladies..." Noah nodded at the two women, then followed Dax outside.

"If you don't have to return to the saloon right away, please, join me," Rachel encouraged, anxious for a chance to get know Nick's partner.

Lena's eyes widened at the invitation. It wasn't often women such as Rachel extended an offer to talk. She'd grown accustomed to being ignored, even scorned by the good people in the towns where they owned saloons. She'd never worked on her back as the girls in the saloons did. Nick had been the one to include her in a life where she made decisions along with him.

"Thank you, Mrs. Pelletier. I'd love to join you for a while."

"Please, call me Rachel."

"And you'll call me Lena as my friends do."

Rachel nodded, touched by the extension of friendship. "You'll find there isn't as much formality here as there is back east. At least not like in Boston, where I'm from."

"I visited Boston once, during the winter months. Nick wanted me to see big city saloons."

"Have you known Nick long?"

"We grew up together, a result of our mothers working in saloons. He's older and always took on the role of protector, similar to a brother or uncle." She glanced at the wall behind Rachel, a wistful look crossing her face before she masked it. "He dragged me to school, even though it was obvious the other students' parents didn't want me there. Nick refused to let them force me away, believing education would be my way out as it had been his." She snorted at how their education had helped them.

"Yet both of you stayed in the same business." Rachel cocked her head. So much about Lena fascinated her.

She laughed. "Believe me, it wasn't what we planned. Nick won a saloon in a card game in New Orleans, deciding to improve the place, then sell it. Instead, he started making so much money, it didn't make sense to sell when he understood so much about the business. You see, he has a way with numbers, and I have a way with people. Together, we built and sold several saloons over the years. Of course, if it hadn't been for him, I don't know where I would've ended up."

"You must have been quite young when you started." Rachel guessed her to be in her mid-twenties with radiant olive skin and expressive eyes.

"Nineteen when Nick declared I was old enough to work for him. He was in his thirties by then. I'd come back from finishing school, where he sent me to become a lady." She rolled her eyes. "The one rule he had was that I never worked as the others girls. I hired them, made sure they were clean, didn't work when they were sick, and didn't fleece Nick out of his cut. By the time I turned twenty-two, he'd given me some ownership. Now we're fifty-fifty, although I never thought we'd be opening a place in a town like Splendor."

Rachel laughed, deciding she liked Magdelena Campanel. "My guess is there are few of us who thought we'd settle in a place such as Splendor. Dax and Luke grew up in Savannah, sons of a wealthy businessman. My family was quite unhappy when I decided to become a nurse, work in Union field hospitals during the war, then venture west to help my uncle with his clinic. You'll hear similar stories as you get to know the townsfolk. Somehow, fate, luck, good fortune—whatever you choose to call it—brought us all here."

"Well, it's supposed to be a stop before traveling to San Francisco. Nick's always wanted to see the Pacific Ocean."

"And you, Lena…what do you want?"

The question surprised her. Long ago, practically another lifetime, she'd believed all her dreams stood before her in the form of one man, an Englishman who'd escaped his aristocratic life to seek adventure in America.

He'd stormed into her life, and Nick's, working his way past their defenses to become a friend and confidant. Tall and lean with a broad, charming smile and quick wit, both men and women were drawn to him, wanted to call him friend. Lena had fallen hard. He didn't bother to hide his attraction to her, and over the months he frequented their saloon, he'd bestowed on her the type of flattery common when courting a woman. Other than Nick, no man had ever shown her such respect or attention.

He'd asked Nick's permission to escort her to supper and the theatre, rented a carriage for picnics in the country, and taken her on long walks. They talked of his travels across England and the rest of Europe, of the title and wealth he left behind when spurning his father's appeal to take his place and accept the duties he'd been born into. Her

214

feelings for him grew, as did his declarations of love for her, and they talked of marriage and a family.

After months, her willpower faltered and she'd allowed him into her bed. He'd been the only man to ever walk across the threshold of her door and heart. He'd taken what she offered, as well as tens of thousands of dollars, and disappeared. All in one night, she'd lost her heart, virginity, and the savings Nick and she had slaved to earn. Neither had ever seen him again.

It took months before the keen sense of betrayal and pain began to fade. Nick's report of the theft was met with amusement by the sheriff and his deputies, even though most were steady patrons of their saloon. Nick hunted the Englishman with a focus that frightened her, until Lena convinced him to stop, to spend his time and energy rebuilding what they'd lost. She'd vowed to never speak of him again.

Although her pain never turned to hatred or complete distrust in men, it did force her to take stock of her life and accept realistic expectations of her future.

She still had dreams, but knew a woman in her profession wasn't allowed to hope for long. Most everyone expected she'd worked as a prostitute at some point, and over the years, she'd grown weary of trying to change their perception.

She clasped her hands together and leaned forward. "This is my life, the one Nick and I have built together. I'll go where he wants, doing what is needed to survive. Beyond that, I have no dreams."

Noah swallowed the last bit of supper, noticing the large amount of food still left on Abby's plate. After meeting with the men who would make up the posse tomorrow, he'd worked for a few hours, trying to give Abby time to rest. He found her sitting in the front parlor, reading a book. She was so engrossed, she didn't look up when he entered.

He stayed silent, watching her face change expressions as the story unfolded. One moment, a smile would curve her lips— the next, she'd furrow her brows or let out a sigh. He no longer tried to convince himself he wasn't right for her. Her decision to forsake life on her father's ranch, living under her own terms, altered all the hesitation in Noah's mind.

They were a perfect match, even if his meager cabin wouldn't be an adequate home for her. His chest tightened. If all his hopes came true, he'd be watching her reading this way until they grew old.

"Noah! When did you arrive?" Abby jumped up to join him by the entry, smiling as she slipped an arm through his.

"A moment ago. I didn't want to interrupt your reading."

She held up the book. "I've read this a hundred times and could recite most passages by heart."

He smiled at the pleasure she took in something as simple as reading a book. "I thought we could take a ride up the hill behind town and watch the sunset while we eat. Suzanne packed supper for us."

"It sounds lovely. Let me get my wrap."

He could hear her dashing up the stairs, returning a few minutes later with a bonnet on her head and wearing a light coat.

"The horses are out front."

Hasty, the horse she'd ridden to her father's on Sunday, had proven to be a gentle ride, responding to Abby as if they'd been together for years. Noah had already tied blankets to the back of her saddle and loaded their supper into his saddlebags.

They meandered up a path behind the boardinghouse, traveling to the top of a hill above the town. Wildflowers bloomed everywhere as spring turned into early summer. Noah reined up at a spot he'd found the summer before, offering a perfect view of the spectacular sunsets he'd come to expect this time of year.

Noah helped her down, taking it slow, letting her body brush his until her feet touched the ground. He kept his hands on her waist longer than necessary, wanting to pull her into his arms and kiss her until they both gasped for air. Instead, he dropped his hands and stepped away.

"This is a wonderful place. Have you come here before?" Abby made a slow turn, taking in the view in all directions.

"A couple times. It's rare when I'm able to stop work to ride up. I made an offer on the land a year ago, but the owner turned me down." He laid a blanket out under a pine, facing the eastern range.

"Who owns it?"

"Your father."

"My father?" Abby's shocked expression didn't surprise Noah. "Would he even listen to your offer?"

"No. Turned me down flat without explanation."

She remained silent, not surprised her father wouldn't even consider an offer from Noah.

"I thought I'd try again in the fall. He doesn't use it and it's miles from the ranch." Noah believed it would be the perfect spot for the house he planned to build for Abby. He could already see it—two stories with a wraparound porch where she could watch the sunrise in the morning and sunset at night.

They settled on the blanket, Noah handing her the chicken, biscuits, and pie Suzanne prepared. Neither spoke as they enjoyed their meal, watching as the sun moved to hug the western mountains.

Abby couldn't believe she'd never been up there. She suspected there were many beautiful places around Splendor, and a fresh wave of resentment wrapped around her. Her father had allowed her to come home for Christmas and a few weeks during the summer, totaling perhaps six weeks a year. She'd been allowed to ride into town and back, with an escort, but never beyond Splendor's southern boundary. She could count on one hand the number of times he'd allowed her to ride unaccompanied, and her joy of being permitted this small bit of freedom precluded striking out on her own to explore. Now, with Noah, she could.

He set their empty plates aside and moved so his back rested against the tree trunk. "Come here, Abby." He motioned for her to sit in front of him, nestled against his chest. She didn't hesitate, settling between his legs as he wrapped his arms around her stomach and drew her back. "See the twin peaks to the right?"

His breath teased her skin, producing shivers as her heart thundered in her chest.

"Yes," she breathed out, unable to say more due to the sensations flooding her body.

"If you trace a line down from where the two peaks meet, and if it weren't hidden by the forest and hills, you'd be looking at my cabin."

She sat up, trying to see where his home might be, even though they were miles away. Glancing over her shoulder, she shot him a brilliant smile, causing his chest to seize and the air to rush from his lungs.

"Tell me about it?" she asked, leaning back again.

He pulled her against him, trying to get control of a body on fire, hoping she didn't feel the proof of it as she snuggled closer.

"It's nothing special. You already know Dax and Luke gave me the property for helping to save Rachel, Doc, and the Frey brothers. I built a cabin made of logs, a barn, and work shed. It's large enough to run a few head of cattle and horses, but it will never be a working ranch."

"And the cabin itself?"

"There's a kitchen with cook stove, and enough space for a table and chairs. I hauled up an old sofa Luke found in the loft of their barn and built a table to set next to it." He shrugged, believing he'd summed up his home.

"Where do you sleep?"

He grimaced as an image of his bleak quarters popped into his mind. "There is a sleeping room, but all it contains is a pallet with blankets."

He leaned forward, losing his fight to nuzzle her neck, inhaling her clean scent with a trace of rose. His lips traced a path from her ear, down the soft length of her neck to her shoulder, then back up, nibbling her earlobe, feeling her shudder.

"Noah..." she breathed out, letting her head fall back against his chest as his hands splayed across her stomach, inched upward, then stopped. She turned to face him, settling on her knees between his thighs as she wrapped her arms around his neck, eager for his kiss. He didn't disappoint.

He drew her close, capturing her mouth and taking control, delving inside and exploring her with languid strokes. Ripples of sensation spread through him as his hands smoothed down her sides, settling on the graceful swell of her hips.

Abby could feel her body tremble at the intensity of the sensations. Heat flamed through her, curling around to pool low in her belly. A moan spilled from her lips as his mouth moved across her cheek to nip her earlobe, tracing the line of her jaw, then searing a path to the hollow at the base of her neck. She squirmed, trying to get closer, shocked at her own eager response.

He moved back up to claim her mouth in a smoldering kiss. Passion radiated from her, scorching each place their bodies pressed together. Noah had never felt the wild desire for any woman as he did for her, wanting to take everything she offered, knowing he had to stop. Raising his mouth from hers, he gazed at her face, seeing her damp lips swollen from his kisses, feeling a deep sense of satisfaction.

He traced a fingertip across her lower lip before kissing her once more, trying to calm his ragged breathing.

She swayed at the loss of contact, reaching out to grip his arms, her breath coming in labored gasps. She opened her mouth to speak, but words failed her the moment her eyes locked on his.

"We should start back before it gets dark." Noah kept his voice low and gentle, feeling his heart continue to thunder. He reached for her hand, threading his fingers through hers as he helped her stand, then crossed to where the horses grazed several feet away.

Noah lifted her onto Hasty's saddle, secured the blankets, and swung up on Tempest. He glanced at her, worried he might have pushed too far. What he saw humbled him. Her eyes still glistened with passion, a warm smile breaking across her face as she let her gaze settle on his.

They took their time down the path toward town. Noah wondered how he'd been blessed with such a creature, vowing he'd never do anything to hurt her.

Chapter Fifteen

"What do you think?" Noah asked Gabe, watching the posse mill about under the eaves outside the jail as the rain continued to worsen, turning the street into a mud pit.

"I don't see going out in this. Any tracks would be washed away by the time we reached the spot where we tracked the two men. We could wait, see if the storm passes." Gabe pushed his hat further down in an attempt to keep the wind from whipping it off his head. He looked at Cash and Dax, who stood off to one side, talking. "What do you boys think?"

"Dax and Luke have their men here. Might as well see if the storm passes." Cash's disgusted expression mirrored those of the other men. They'd been watching the storm increase in intensity over the last hour, becoming more frustrated with each crack of thunder.

"You all agree?" Gabe asked the others, who all nodded. "Might as well head over to Suzanne's for coffee then."

"I'm going to check the livery. I'll meet you there." Noah pulled his coat collar up, and, holding his hat firm, walked to the end of the boardwalk, then across the muddy street toward the livery. No matter how he tried to avoid water-filled holes, he found his boots and pants covered in thick, sticky muck.

"Noah."

He turned to see Toby standing out front of the tack and miner supply store. Changing directions, he dashed toward him, stomping his boots.

"Sorry to bother you, but I got a large order for tack from Tolbert's foreman."

"How big?" Noah asked, stepping into the store behind Toby.

"Appears they want to replace everything. They're starting with two dozen new bridles and two dozen halters. I can make the halters, but you'll need to decide how much time it will take for the bridles. They'll need reins, also. Tolbert's man will be back later to find out when the order will be ready."

Noah stroked his chin. Tolbert made it a point of avoiding his tack shop, preferring to send men straight to Big Pine where a shop kept plenty of tack on hand.

"He'll have the bridles and reins in a week."

"I can have the halters by then. Strange, isn't it? Tolbert's never even been in the store."

In Noah's mind, strange didn't begin to describe it. He found himself wondering if the order had anything to do with Abby and her determination to stay in town, near him. Hostile would be the word he'd use to define the look Tolbert shot him as he left the bank after Abby rejected his demands to return to the ranch. Now this.

"I need to check one of the horses, then I'm going to Suzanne's for breakfast. Come fetch me if the foreman has questions."

Fifteen minutes later, he knocked mud from his boots before entering the restaurant, spotting Gabe and the others at a large table. His heart skipped a beat when he saw Abby having breakfast with Nick and Miss Campanel at a nearby table, an empty seat next to her. She looked up and smiled, pointing to the chair beside her. It wasn't a hard choice.

"Mind if I join you?" He looked at Miss Campanel and Nick.

"Not at all," Lena responded.

He turned to let Gabe know he'd be having breakfast with Abby and saw him nod in understanding, although his gaze was focused on Magdelena.

"Have you had a chance to settle in, Miss Campanel?"

"Please, call me Lena. I'm still learning about the town. So far, I'm enjoying it, although I hear the winters will be rough."

"Brutal might be a better word," Abby said, sipping her steaming coffee.

"You get used to them." Noah scanned the room, noticing Gabe kept glancing over at their table—specifically at Lena. He'd have to ask his friend about that later.

"Abby tells us you built a cabin a few miles from town. Do you stay there every night?" Lena asked.

"No. Mostly I stay in a room in back of the livery."

"Here you are, Noah—your usual." Suzanne set a plate of eggs, potatoes, and a slab of ham in front of him. "I'll get more coffee."

"I can help," Abby said, starting to rise.

"Abby..." Suzanne warned, narrowing her eyes.

"You're right. Sorry." Abby's cheeks flushed at the slight reprimand in Suzanne's tone, then turned to the others. "She made me agree I wouldn't help since I was paying full rent for my room and board. It's hard, though. I've known her my entire life and it's obvious she needs the help. I wish she'd hire someone. Most nights, she falls into bed, exhausted."

"I'll speak with her." Nick set down his cup and leaned back in his chair, not explaining further. "Gabe said you're still hoping to ride out today, start the search for the robbers."

The rain continued to pound, making it difficult to even ride through town. Noah glanced out the window. "No way to track in this rain. If it's not Drake, the robbers will be long gone by now. If it *is* Drake, I suspect he'll be staying around."

"Why would they stay?" Abby asked Noah, a shiver running through her, remembering the gun blast that injured Mr. Clausen.

"Arrogance. If Drake and his men are also doing the rustling, he'll have his sights on the Pelletier or Tolbert cattle."

"Father's cattle?"

"And the Pelletier's. Remember, he left before Gabe had a chance to arrest him for the attacks against Dax and Luke. He may be looking to finish what he started." Noah shifted toward Nick and Lena. "Dax served as a general in the Confederate Army. Drake reported to him. He deserted the night before a particularly bitter battle." Noah fell silent as he finished his breakfast, remembering the "accidents" that befell the Pelletier men while Drake worked for Tolbert.

"Shouldn't we warn Father?"

"Gabe already spoke with him." Noah pushed his empty plate away, looking toward Gabe and seeing his friend's gaze still riveted on Lena. He turned toward Abby. "I'll walk you to the bank when you're ready to leave."

"I'll get my coat. Thank you for letting me share your table," she said to Lena and Nick.

"You're always welcome, Abby. I should be going to the saloon, Nick. Make sure everyone is all right this morning."

"Did you have trouble?" Noah asked, watching Abby disappear into the hall.

"A minor brawl yesterday evening. One of the girls got shoved around, ended up with a black eye and bruises. Sheriff Evans and Nick broke it up." Lena glanced in Gabe's direction, smiling when she saw him notice her.

"Must not have taken Gabe long to get there."

"Oh, he was already sitting at one of the tables, talking with a group of men. He comes in every night for an hour or so. Good to see you again, Mr. Brandt." She stepped outside, opening her umbrella to walk the short distance to the Dixie Saloon. At least she didn't have to cross the muddy street like Abby did.

"Gabe's been coming in every night?" Noah asked Nick.

Nick flashed a quick look at Gabe, then turned to Noah and chuckled. "Ever since Lena arrived, he's been stopping in once or twice a day."

"Interesting," Noah mumbled.

"Yes, quite."

The storm raged that night and the next day. By noon on the third day, it had finally passed by, leaving the town drenched and soggy.

Noah stayed busy with the order from Tolbert and spending time with Abby. He'd gone to the Dixie with Gabe for a drink more than once. Nick used Noah whenever he needed a blacksmith and to board his horse. He'd also bought a horse for Lena and boarded it at the livery until he had time to build a stable behind the saloon. From what he told Noah, Lena had become an accomplished rider, preferring to ride sidesaddle as did many women from the South.

The Dixie drew a rowdier crowd than the Wild Rose. Most nights, cigar smoke hung thick in the air, and off-key piano music spilled into the streets. Gabe had stepped in several times to break up fights and haul drunks to jail. Most slept it off and rode home the next day.

Tonight, he and Gabe sat near the piano, watching the activity around them. Gabe seemed to be spending most of his time watching Lena help with drinks, serve food from their small menu, and keep the girls moving from table to table. She'd stopped by their table more than once, chatting for a few minutes before returning to the bar. He noticed she never stood by Gabe, as if she didn't want to get too close to him. The idea made Noah chuckle.

Gabe had never been one to take much notice of the women who fell at his feet. If he'd wanted to, he could have a woman in his bed every night. Instead, he preferred women he'd gotten to know and felt comfortable around, such as Dolly at the saloon in Big

Pine. She knew her place and he knew his. Rather than start something with a woman in Splendor, he'd travel there, knowing it would never amount to much. Something about the way he watched Lena caught Noah's attention. He'd never seen Gabe watch someone with such a brooding interest, as if he were a caged tiger, ready to spring loose.

He sipped his whiskey, knowing Abby busied herself with bookkeeping for Suzanne. Lena had also asked her to help Nick with the books for the saloon, which she'd eagerly accepted. He'd met her for supper, then she'd shooed him away.

"Another drink, gentlemen?"

Noah looked up to see Lena standing next to him, Gabe narrowing his gaze at her from across the table, absently rolling his empty glass between his fingers.

"Another for both of us, Lena."

"A double for me," Gabe added, letting his gaze wander to one of the women who worked for Lena. She followed the direction of his eyes, and for a moment, something passed across her face before she hid it.

"Would you like me to send Deborah over, Sheriff?"

He slowly drew his gaze away from Deborah to focus on Lena. "No, thank you."

"Let me know if you change your mind. I'll get your drinks."

Noah leaned forward, resting his arms on the table. "You want to tell me what you're doing?"

Gabe watched Lena cross the room to the bar, not looking away. "Don't know what you mean."

"That right? Well, I've known you for over twenty years and have never seen you watch a woman the way you do Lena."

Gabe broke his stare and turned toward Noah. "I find her intriguing, that's all."

"Intriguing?"

"That's right." He kept his face impassive in an attempt to deflect further questions.

"Here you are." Lena set Noah's drink in front of him, leaning over the table to hand Gabe his. "And a double for you."

"Why don't you sit with us a minute? Get off your feet," Noah said, smirking at the warning glance Gabe sent him.

She caught the look Gabe flashed Noah and wondered what it meant. "Another time. With the weather clear, everyone's coming out for drinks. Let me know if you need anything else." She turned to the table next to them, then walked to the bar, Gabe watching the sway of her hips.

"Rumor is she's never worked upstairs," Noah threw out.

"What the hell are you talking about?"

"She's a businesswoman, Gabe, not the same as one of her girls who work in the rooms." Noah tossed back the last of his whiskey. "Thought you should know."

Gabe crossed his arms, his gaze following Lena as she moved through the room, never touching anyone unless it was to remove a customer's hand reaching out to grasp her. Odd behavior for a woman who made her money in a saloon.

He'd also heard the rumors, but hadn't put any stock in them—until now.

"Why don't you ask her to have supper with you?" Noah asked as he pushed himself from his chair.

"If you're thinking I want to court her, you're out of your mind. She's a beautiful woman who fascinates me, nothing more. Looking and then acting on it, like you are with Abby, doesn't interest me. Doubt it ever will." He drained his glass, shaking his head at the crazy notion of him courting a woman. "Let's get out into the cool air so you can start thinking straight." He clasped Noah on the back, chuckling again at his friend's ridiculous suggestion.

"How many?" King Tolbert asked, staring at his foreman, a man who'd been with him less than two months.

"Best we can tell, about twenty head. They came swooping in, making all sorts of ruckus and scaring the cattle, who spooked and then stampeded toward the river. They drove a group across the water. We tried following after we got the herd back together, but by then, they'd disappeared into the hills. You ask me, they're plenty smart, taking a few head at a time. They're easier to hide that way." Dirk Masters pushed his hat back on his head and laced his thumbs through his belt loops.

"If they were smart, they wouldn't have robbed me. I'll keep searching until I find and hang them. Are the men bringing the herd in closer?"

"Yes, sir, and I've doubled the watch."

"Good. I want you to select five men to ride out with you and me tomorrow. We won't return until we've found the rustlers and brought them to justice. Understood?"

"Yes, sir." Masters let himself out, swinging onto his horse and taking off at a run toward the herd.

Tolbert knew Sheriff Evans expected him to report any rustling and let the law handle it. He scoffed at the notion Evans and his friends could handle the gang any better than Tolbert could with a few select men. And his method wouldn't cost the taxpayers any money. He'd find and lynch them, leaving their bodies for the animals to dispose of, saving the town the expense of a trial and burials.

He'd never been a man to wait for justice to happen. He sought his own, believing one man's determination could accomplish more than a group of men without purpose.

Tolbert opened a cabinet, removing his rifle and enough shells to last through any confrontation. Next, he took out a matching pair of revolvers and ammunition. He set both on the table as he grabbed his gun belt from a nearby hook. Most of the ammunition would be stored in his saddlebags, along with his other gear. Although he owned no land to the west or south, he knew the area well. Hidden canyons and valleys covered that section. You needed to know where to look, and he did.

Pacing to the window, he gazed toward the barn, noting it needed a fresh coat of paint after the long winter. He stroked his chin, making a decision he'd been pondering since Abby chose to stay in town, ignoring his appeals to return to the ranch.

He sat down at his desk and pulled out paper. Grabbing his fountain pen, he began to write. His last will and testament was in order and kept in his safe across the room. There was no need to make more than one change regarding his property. Every other item he owned—land, cattle, buildings, money—would go to Abigail. As angry as he felt about her decision to stay in town, he wouldn't exclude her from her rightful inheritance. However, he did feel a strong compulsion to clarify how he wanted the ranch to continue if anything happened to him. He wrote for an hour, noting all he'd been considering the last few weeks.

Finishing, he signed and dated the document, set the pen aside, and folded the paper, securing it in his safe.

Chapter Sixteen

Gabe walked down the boardwalk toward his office, already hearing the sounds of a possible fight starting at the Dixie. The sun still hung above the western mountains, not allowing day to give way to evening. The end of a week always brought out those who needed to cut loose. Figuring it would be a long night, he pushed open the door of the jail, seeing Cash and Beau inside.

"No more reports of missing cattle around Big Pine, and nothing here since the last raid at the Frey ranch. Maybe they've left the area." Gabe dropped the latest telegram from Sheriff Parker on his desk, then sat and tilted his chair back on two legs.

"Is that what you believe?" Cash leaned against the door, his arms crossed.

"No. My gut tells me they're waiting, believing we'll think they've taken off and won't be as vigilant."

"Do you still plan a search?" Beau leaned forward, more than ready to stop sitting around. He wanted to head out, track down Drake and his men, hold them accountable for their actions. It didn't matter to him if they found the cattle or not. He believed Cash's assertion Drake was responsible for the deaths of his relatives on their Louisiana farm, as well as the bank robbery in Splendor. It would be difficult to find a single redeeming quality in the outlaw or any of his men.

"I've sent word to the Pelletiers and Tolbert to meet us here at dawn tomorrow with as many men as they can spare. We'll start at the spot where we tracked the two men, then split into groups to cover as much ground as possible."

"And the town?" Cash turned a chair around, straddling it while resting his arms on the back.

"Same as before. Dax will bring men, leave a couple in town for protection. It's doubtful—"

The door slammed open, Lena Campanel rushing inside. "Sheriff, you have to come right away. Nick's got himself into a mess with a group of drunk cowhands from the Tolbert ranch. They were roughing up one of our girls—" She didn't finish before all three men took off at a run. Following, she watched each draw their guns before stopping outside the swinging doors, looking over the top to the scene inside.

Two men held Nick while two others alternated landing blows to his face and chest. It didn't appear he'd last much longer.

"Cash, you take the right. Beau, you're on the left. I'll go straight in. Ready?" Gabe crashed through the doors, followed by Cash and Beau, all firing warning shots into the ceiling. "That's enough." His voice bellowed through the saloon as the three trained their guns on the men surrounding Nick.

"Guess they didn't hear you," Beau said as one man drew back, ready to send another fist into Nick's face. Beau didn't wait, but aimed and fired. The man screamed and tumbled to the floor, grabbing his ruined knee. "You all heard the sheriff. Step away from Barnett before I get angry enough to shoot another of you."

The men dropped their arms, letting Nick slide to the floor as they scrambled to do as Beau asked. Lena dashed behind Nick and knelt down, using both hands to help him to a sitting position.

"How's Deborah?" Nick choked out, grasping his chest as blood trickled from a cut near his eye.

"The girls have her in the office. They'll take care of her while we sort this out." She used a hanky to absorb the blood dripping from his chin, then pressed it to the corner of his eye.

He tried to stand, but fell back, wincing in pain. "My ribs hurt like hell."

"Don't move until I can get help. No sense making it worse." She glanced behind her to see Noah push past Cash and Beau as they escorted the four men outside.

"Everyone all right?" Noah asked as Gabe collected their weapons, then nodded toward Lena and Nick.

"I've got to lock the men in cells, then I'll be back." Gabe cradled the weapons before disappearing outside.

Noah crouched down next to Nick. "Need some help?"

"Yes. I think he's got some cracked ribs."

"I can speak for myself, Lena." Nick grimaced, clutching his arms to his chest.

"Lena, get the doc while I help him up." Noah took Lena's place at Nick's back, threading his arms under his. "This is gonna hurt."

Nick was a tall man, but Noah had him by at least four inches and twenty pounds. In one smooth move, Noah lifted him onto his feet, bracing a hand to his back. Nick leaned forward, then rose until he stood almost erect.

"Damn," he muttered. "It's not often I let drunk cowhands get the best of me."

Gabe crossed the street as Doc Worthington and Lena rushed into the saloon. By the time he walked back inside, the doc already had Nick's shirt open, exposing abrasions already turning black-and-blue.

"They got you good, Nick." Doc pressed two fingers to several spots, asking Nick to cough each time. "I feel three cracked ribs." Doc studied his face, glad the flow of blood near his eye had stopped. "The cuts on your face aren't serious. Your ribs are the worst." He looked up at Noah and Gabe. "I'll need you two to help Nick to the clinic." Doc stood and watched as the men braced Nick on either side. "I've got to wrap your ribs with adhesive plaster. It'll help with the pain when you breathe. 'Course, nothing will help if you have a coughing fit."

They didn't have far to go, but Nick cursed under his breath with almost every step.

"Take him into the treatment room. Noah, stay with Nick. I'd rather you two wait in the front." He nodded toward Gabe and Lena.

"But—" Lena began.

"Are you his wife?" he asked, his brow lifting.

She placed her hands on her waist. "You know I'm not."

"Then Noah will do. I need someone strong who can help when I apply the adhesive." He didn't wait for Lena to respond as he closed the door behind him.

She rounded on Gabe, her face flushed. "He has no right to keep me out of there. Can't you do something?"

"Afraid not. The doctor's in charge here. Seems we'll both have to wait, as he asked." He lowered himself into a nearby chair, stretched out his legs, and crossed his arms.

"I should be in there with him." She dropped into a wooden chair, gripping her hands together in her lap.

"Since you're not his wife, the doc may be trying to spare you from seeing Nick with his shirt off."

Lena snorted as the corners of her mouth tilted upward. "It's not as if I've never seen him without a shirt."

"Oh?" His left eyebrow raised a fraction.

She glared at his implication. "We grew up together, shared swimming holes, and took care of each other when one of us got hurt. I've seen him shirtless any number of times."

"Guess you aren't going to see him shirtless this time." Gabe grinned before tilting his hat forward to shield his eyes.

"You're going to sleep?"

He pushed the hat back up a fraction to look at her. "Thought I would. Unless you're determined to talk."

Lena's eyes narrowed in irritation as she pursed her lips, then stood, crossing her arms as she walked to the window. A moment passed before she spun around. "Why don't you go to the jail, keep your prisoners company? I'm sure it would be more to your liking."

Gabe sat up, accepting a quick nap wasn't going to happen. "I need to speak with Nick, get his version of what happened."

"*His* version? It seemed clear when you caught the men holding and beating him. What more do you need?" She swiped an errant strand of hair from her face, pacing to within a foot of him. "Two of them were roughing up Deborah. He stepped in to break it up and the four attacked him."

"You saw all of it?"

"I did."

"Good. Then his story should match yours."

Before she could say more, the door to the treatment room opened and Noah poked his head out. "Gabe, the doc says for us to help Nick to the boardinghouse. Says he shouldn't go back to the saloon tonight."

"I'll go with you." Lena brushed past Noah to see Nick closing his shirt over the bandages wrapped around his chest. "How are you?"

"I've been better."

She moved to him, resting a hand on his shoulder. "It could've been so much worse."

"Guess so." He slid off the table to the floor, placing a steadying hand on Lena's arm. "I've got to get back in case more of the group from Tolbert's ranch start another brawl."

"Doc says you're to go to the boardinghouse."

"Like hell," he ground out.

"You're not much good the way you are. Why don't you do as the doctor says? I can manage."

"She's right, Nick." Gabe stepped into the room. "Noah and I will help you to Suzanne's. I'll ask Cash and Beau to keep watch at the saloon, make sure nothing else happens tonight."

"I can't ask others to do my job," he growled, shaking off their attempt to help him from the clinic.

"You're not. I am." Gabe motioned for Noah to stand back, figuring if Nick wanted help, they'd know it soon enough.

Nick stopped twice, leaning on the side of the building to rest, then would start again. Suzanne had already heard about the beating and made up the one downstairs sleeping room she had. Ginny Sorenson and her sister, Mary, used it before Ginny married Luke. She kept it vacant for emergencies such as this.

Noah waited until Nick settled in the vacant room before joining Abby in the kitchen, explaining what he knew about the brawl. The two had just finished supper at Suzanne's when they heard gunfire. He'd pushed from the table, warning her not to follow until he'd discovered the source of the noise.

"Some of your father's men were pushing one of the women around. Nick tried to stop them. Guess they didn't appreciate his interference. Lena fetched Gabe, and between him, Cash, and Beau, they broke it up, arrested the men."

"And they're all from my father's ranch?" Her brows furrowed as she considered this.

"Appears so."

"He wouldn't condone what they did. Has anyone sent for him?"

"Don't know. Word travels fast, though, and several more of his men were in the saloon when Gabe hauled the others to jail. I'm sure he'll hear about it soon enough and ride in to pay the fines. You know, he'll want to see you."

Abby shrugged. "As long as he doesn't try to talk me into leaving town." She'd grown tired of explaining her reasons for keeping her job and remaining at Suzanne's. He would never understand and accept her decision. She glanced up as Gabe walked in and tipped his hat to her.

"Would you care for coffee, Sheriff?"

"No, thanks. I'm heading back to the jail to send Cash and Beau to keep peace at the Dixie tonight. Nick told the same story as Lena. He wants to press charges, which is his right, but the circuit judge isn't expected for a few weeks."

"Lena still with Nick?" Noah asked.

"She'll probably stay a while longer. He didn't want to rely on Cash and Beau to do his job, but he seemed relieved knowing they'd be watching over Lena and the girls. I'll see you in the morning, Noah."

"What's happening in the morning?" Abby poured more coffee in Noah's cup, her forehead creased into a frown.

"We're riding out to search for Drake and the missing cattle. Dax, Luke, and your father agreed to send men to help." He looked up to see the worry etched across her face. "We'll be leaving men in town this time so Drake doesn't try to rob the bank again."

She nodded, although Noah sensed the tension radiating from her.

"C'mere." His chair grated on the old plank floor as he scooted back, reaching his hand toward her.

She grasped it, letting him settle her on his lap, wrapping an arm around her waist.

"It will all be fine, Abby. I doubt Drake is dumb enough to try the bank a second time." He leaned forward, brushing a kiss along her neck, inhaling her unique scent.

"It's not me I'm worried about."

A slow smile lifted the corners of Noah's mouth. "Nothing will happen to me."

"Promise?" She traced a finger down his stubbled jaw.

He closed his eyes at her touch, enjoying the feel of her caress. Promises were something he didn't make unless positive he could keep them. He didn't want to worry her further, but couldn't commit to something out of his control. He drew her hand to his mouth, pressing a warm kiss to her palm, feeling a slight shiver radiate through her.

"I'll be back. You and I aren't over, Abby. We'll never be over."

Noah finished the last of his chores before locking the door of the livery. Leading Tempest and Blackheart to the front of the jail, he noticed Cash and Beau already astride their horses, talking with Dax and Luke. He recognized Bull and Travis from the Pelletier ranch speaking with several other men who Noah assumed worked for the Pelletiers. Bull slid from his horse when he saw him.

"Morning, Noah."

"Bull." The two shook hands, Noah nodding to Travis. "Are all these your men?"

"They work for Dax and Luke. All good with a gun, one a tracker during the war. We're hoping to make it a quick search, find Drake and the cattle, and get back to the ranch." He looked toward the jail. "We're leaving a couple men here to watch Tolbert's men. Odd he hasn't sent anyone to town to get them." Bull had been injured during one of the attacks the year before—one of several attacks most believed were instigated by Parnell Drake and his men. He'd be glad to see them brought to justice.

Gabe took Blackheart's reins from Noah, swung into the saddle, then turned toward the others. "Tolbert's men won't be joining us." He spoke loud enough for his voice to carry over the crowd. "Seems he took some men and started his own search for the rustlers several days ago. None of his men in jail know which way they rode or when they're expected back. Most of you have met Cash Coulter. He and Beau Davis have been tracking Drake and his men since they ran across them in Colorado. They're riding with us today." He turned Blackheart south, then looked over his shoulder. "Let's go."

The posse stopped at the spot where Gabe and the others camped after tracking Drake's men out of Splendor days before. The storm erased all signs of that night, yet Cash, Beau, and the Pelletier man who'd been a tracker continued to walk the area in slow circles, coming up with nothing.

"What do you think?" Gabe asked Cash as both men searched the horizon to the east and mountains to the west, Noah and Beau joining them.

"They're not gone. I'd stake my life on it." He shifted in his saddle, focusing on the tall pines and low hills this side of the western mountain range. "I think Drake's men led us here to throw us off, the same way they did when we followed them from town, leaving the bank undefended. They aren't hiding the cattle out here where they can be spotted. The herd is closer to the mountains where they have good grass and can be driven into any of a hundred canyons and valleys."

"The Murton ranch is the last one south for miles. Drake knows it's doubtful anyone other than a posse would find them." Noah reached behind him for his canteen, taking a long swallow. "We can be at the Murton ranch by noon, rest the horses, then head into the mountains."

Gabe reined Blackheart around toward Dax and Luke, who still searched an area a hundred yards away. "Find anything?"

"Nothing to indicate a herd of cattle have been in this area. Luke and I believe they're hiding them closer to the mountains." Dax always believed Drake would return to Splendor. His hatred for the Pelletiers ran deep, and Dax suspected the man felt the same about Tolbert. He wouldn't leave the area until he'd exacted his form of vengeance on the two families.

Gabe nodded over his shoulder. "The others want to ride to the Murton ranch, continue the search from there."

"Then it's time we head out." Luke shifted toward the rest of the Pelletier men. "Let's go."

Chapter Seventeen

Dirk Masters lay flat on his stomach, peering over the ridge to get a better view of the herd below. The valley where they grazed couldn't be more than a hundred yards wide, but it spanned over a mile in depth. There was only one way in and one way out, the noise of the herd stifled by the high canyon walls.

He lifted his field glasses once more, counting the number of men guarding the herd. Five at most, which made sense as the cattle had no place to move except through the narrow opening at one end. He wondered how long the lush grass below would sustain them, guessing another few days, at most. Tolbert would need to make a decision soon if they were to go after the rustlers before they transferred the herd to another spot.

Dirk scooted back, not standing until ten feet separated him from the edge. He'd come here alone, telling Tolbert more men would increase the chances of being seen. The sun had risen midway toward its peak by the time he returned to their camp. He hadn't dismounted before Tolbert confronted him.

"Did you find them?" Tolbert demanded, eyes hard, hands fisted on his waist.

"The herd is in a canyon a few miles away. Didn't see the man you described as Drake, though." He slid to the ground, passing Tolbert on his way to the pot of coffee resting on the embers of a recent fire. He grabbed a nearby cup and filled it, wincing at the bitter taste. "About five men guard the herd, and there's only one way in." He lowered into a crouch, nursing the nasty brew. He doubted it tasted any better when hot.

Tolbert crossed his arms and stared down at Dirk. "Did you find where the rest of men are camped?"

"Nope. Thought you'd want to know where they've got the herd. I can head back out, but I go alone, same as before." He tossed out the remaining coffee and stood.

"I'll send one man with you."

"No. I can move better alone."

Tolbert stepped forward. He wasn't used to his hired men refusing an order. "I want a second man. If one of you is discovered, the other can ride back to warn us."

"You want this done right, let me do it my way. You want to send someone else, fine. I'll stay here in camp with the others and wait."

The two stared at each other, neither flinching. Dirk had worked for Tolbert long enough to know the man didn't know half of what he blustered about. Brute force and intimidation were his boss' primary weapons. As far as Dirk could tell, he had no real skills as a rancher. But he didn't need to as long as he had the money to hire those who did. The longer he worked for Tolbert, the more certain he became he'd be moving on at the end of summer to find work with men he respected.

Tolbert flinched first, not wanting to pass up an opportunity to find Drake. "Be back before sunset or I'll send men to find you."

"Wish I had more for you, Sheriff, but I haven't seen anyone around here." Ty Murton, the oldest of the Murton brothers, jumped from the back of the wagon where he'd been throwing hay into a nearby crib. "We've heard about the rustling at the Frey ranch, but so far, they haven't touched us."

The posse watched as two men rode toward them and reined to a stop.

"Sheriff, you know my brothers, Gil and Mark."

Noah nudged Tempest forward, focusing his attention on Gil Murton. He'd grown up with Abby, and, according to what Noah had heard, been sweet on her most of his life. As with Noah, Tolbert had discouraged Abby from associating with what her father considered a family well beneath her in wealth and social standing. Noah shook his head at the thought. In New York, Philadelphia, or Boston, social standing would matter. In Splendor, it meant little.

He liked Gil, knew him to be a hard worker with goals of building their small ranch into something to rival Tolbert. No doubt in an attempt to win Abby. Noah had little doubt Gil would be a success, but he sure as hell wasn't going to claim Abby.

Gabe finished explaining the reason for their visit, then dismounted, walking Blackheart to a nearby trough. Most of the others followed his lead as Ty, Gil, and Mark stood a few feet away, talking in quiet voices. When the three finished, Ty paced the few feet to stand by Gabe.

"We can't spare all of us, but if you need help, Gil or Mark can ride along."

Gabe knew the Murtons ran a thin operation. In fact, the only three ranch hands stood before them.

"Thanks, Ty, but we're good with the men we have. Any information you can give us on places where cattle could be hidden would be appreciated, though."

"Glad to. Bring everyone inside. Tilly's got plenty of stew and biscuits if you're hungry." Ty married Tilly the year before, pulling her from a life at the Wild Rose and giving her the family she'd never had.

As everyone filled their stomachs with hot food, Gil sketched out different areas where cattle could be held without detection. When he finished, adjusting the map after comments from Mark and Ty, he sat back, eyeing the others.

"You know, it might take weeks to find the herd. They could drive them over the mountains into Idaho, but they'd need to wait another month for the passes to clear of snow."

"What about Denver?" Noah asked, studying the map and noting the approximate distances Gil wrote down.

"It's possible. A little more risk of Indian raids and the drive will take longer. 'Course, they'll lose cattle no matter which route they take."

Mark leaned toward Ty, whispering in his ear.

"Might be best to start as far south as you can, then work north. They don't want to be found, and the chances of being seen are greater the further north they go." Ty nodded to Mark, who leaned back in his chair. Of the three, most knew little about Mark, other than he spoke little and was agonizingly shy to the point of being reclusive. "There's a natural break in the mountain range about here." He pointed to a spot on the map. "It's doubtful they'd keep them further south than this last canyon."

Abby closed her cash drawer. She'd finished with the last customer and had already counted the money, accounting for every penny. She felt more tired than normal today. She hadn't slept well, waking up several times, lying awake and thinking about the dangers Noah might be facing.

He'd been gone two days without word. They'd made no firm plans, he had yet to tell her he loved her, but she knew her world would crumble if anything happened to him.

"Are you ready, Abby?" Sally Phelps crossed behind her toward the safe where Abby stored her drawer each night. Mr. Clausen left early, still tiring easily because of the wound to his arm, leaving Sally in charge of closing up.

"I am." Abby stored the money, grabbed her wrap, and waited at the front door.

"Do you expect your man back tonight?"

A slow grin tugged at Abby's lips. "He's not *my man*, Mrs. Phelps."

"Well, darn close, if you ask me. And one fine man he is."

Abby could feel heat creep into her cheeks at the comment. "Yes, he is a fine man. Good evening, Mrs. Phelps."

"Don't worry. He'll come back in one piece." Sally closed and locked the door, leaving Abby to wonder how she could be so confident.

Taking a deep breath, she wrapped her shawl around her shoulders and walked across the street. As usual, the tinny sound of the piano in the Dixie drifted outside. Nick went back to work Saturday afternoon, just one day after the attack. She'd watched him struggle with his meals at the boardinghouse, finding it difficult to lift the fork to his mouth. Lena tried to help, but he'd brushed off her efforts each time. *So stubborn*, Abby thought. She glanced inside to see Nick and Lena near the bar, talking. He appeared to be doing his best to stand erect and ignore the pain.

She walked past the clinic toward Suzanne's. It seemed odd not to see images of firelight dancing through the door of the livery or hear the occasional clank of hammer to metal. She shifted toward the boardinghouse, placing a hand on her stomach. Abby had grown used to seeing Noah waiting for her, his large frame filling the doorway as he made a slight bow. He'd made a habit of greeting her after work, then returning to his work at the livery before escorting her to supper. Some nights, when he couldn't get away, she'd bring him supper, then sit until he finished eating.

Few tables were occupied in the dining room at this hour, even though travelers and locals tended to eat their evening meal early. She could smell a mix of aromas coming from the kitchen as she let her shawl slip from her shoulders. Folding and placing it over her arm, she stepped through the kitchen door, her brows creasing when she didn't see Suzanne.

Crossing the room, she pushed the back door open, peering toward the garden Suzanne kept next to the house. This time of year, all she could harvest were a sparse amount of herbs. By the heart of the summer, she'd have radishes, carrots, tomatoes, leeks, and onions.

"Suzanne." She waited a moment, then called again. Getting no response, she slung her shawl around her shoulders and descended the steps to the yard, walking toward the thin stream behind the buildings. She looked around and called once more before hearing laughter coming from the direction of the Dixie a few doors away.

She followed the sound to see Suzanne leaning against a tree trunk and laughing, her arms folded across her stomach. A man Abby had never seen stood near her, holding his hat in one hand, motioning with the other. She crept closer, not wanting to interrupt, but curious as to the man's identity. Looking down to avoid a branch spread across the ground, she startled at the sound of a man's voice next to her.

"Here. Let me help you."

She looked up to see the man who'd been talking with Suzanne next to her, holding out an arm and offering a warm smile.

"Thank you." She wrapped her arm through his. "I'm Abigail Tolbert."

"Yes, I know. Over the years, Suzanne has told me about you."

"Over the years?"

"My apologies. I'm Quentin Briar. Suzanne is my sister-in-law."

"You never mentioned you had other family," Abby said as they stopped next to Suzanne.

"Of course I did. You've just forgotten. Besides, you were back east at school when Quentin last came for a visit. He lives in San Francisco and traveled here to see Nick and Lena."

"And you," he added, looking at Suzanne, who laughed.

"Of course. Anyway, I've learned he's known Nick for years."

Abby cocked her head, a slight frown crossing her face. "Do you mind if I ask you a question, Mr. Briar."

"Not at all."

"Why would a sophisticated couple such as Nick and Lena move to a frontier town? Splendor is a wonderful place, but I'd think they'd want to live in a more vibrant city with more to offer."

"First, they aren't a couple, as most would believe. They're more like family—older brother and *much* younger sister. You'll understand when you've had more time to get to know them. They're devoted to each other, but that's it. As far as Splendor, I confess, I don't know the answer. They've done well for themselves. Nick is a genius with money, investing it in land, buildings, gold and silver mines, even a railroad. He's determined that Lena will want for nothing if something happens to him. He's quite protective of the women in his life. I had the opportunity to meet his mother before she died. Nick had set her up in a house outside of New Orleans. She must have been in her sixties, but still stunning. I believe he kept the place."

"Ah, there you are. Telling lies I wager." Nick came through the back door of the saloon, clasping Quentin on the shoulder.

"The ladies were curious about your businesses. I hope you don't mind I filled them in on some of it."

"No real secrets, I hope." Nick's gaze focused on Suzanne. They'd become friends since he moved to Splendor and took up residence in her boardinghouse.

"Don't believe I know any true secrets," Quentin joked.

"I came out to see if you'll join Lena and me for supper. Of course, you'll join us, Miss Tolbert." He shot a look at Suzanne, shaking his head. "You and I are going to sit down, go over the business. It's time you hired some help, Suzanne."

Her mouth opened, then closed. It had been a long time since a man tried to insert himself into her life. A part of her felt gratitude—another part felt offended. "I'm not certain I can afford help."

He offered her his arm. "Trust me. You can."

Dirk Masters left his horse several yards away, making his way through thick bushes and squeezing around boulders until he could get a clear view of the camp. He counted fifteen men, not knowing if five still watched the herd. He guessed they did. None looked similar to the description Tolbert gave him of Drake.

It appeared they'd been here for at least a week, maybe more. All were armed. Rifles leaned against bedrolls, rocks, and trees, and he noticed most of the men wore knife scabbards.

Rustling sounds to his right caused Dirk to shuffle backwards, hunkering down behind a large rock formation. A man emerged from a thick group of bushes, hiking up his pants as he strolled toward the fire. Drake.

"What's the decision?" A stocky man with a scar down his face stood as Drake approached.

"Tolbert first. He always keeps thirty or forty head near the ranch house. Rotates them every couple weeks and rarely leaves men to guard them. We'll take what's there and head out."

"When?"

Drake looked around, noting the men staring at him, waiting for a decision. He knew they were tired of sitting around, watching the herd and doing little else. These were men who craved action.

"I'll let you know as soon as Archie returns." He pulled a cheroot from a shirt pocket and lit it, letting the smoke out in a thin stream as the men returned to what they were doing.

Archie, Dirk thought. He'd heard the name, believed he was one of the two men who worked for Tolbert with Drake.

Dirk didn't wait to hear more. He needed to let Tolbert know his ranch would be next and where they planned to strike. Drake was right. Tolbert did keep a small herd close to the house and rotated them often, posting no more than two men to keep watch. Dirk had never asked him why, assuming it was another one of the peculiar quirks the man possessed.

Dirk shot one more look around the boulder, noting several men playing cards while others sat or stood around and watched. Drake and three others huddled several feet away, on the opposite side of the camp from Dirk. Time for him to leave.

He'd almost made it to his horse when it let out a whinny, loud enough he knew the others would hear and come looking. Dirk ran the rest of the way, mounted, and kicked the horse into a run as the sounds of shouting and men pushing through brush came from the direction of the camp. He leaned forward, flattening himself low across the saddle as a bullet whizzed past, followed by another. He hit open ground and gained speed, then reined his horse away from where Tolbert and the others were camped. In case some of Drake's men were able to get back to their horses and try to follow him, he didn't want to cut a straight path to the camp a few miles away.

Dirk changed directions again, riding up into the nearby mountain, losing himself, and his tracks, on the rocky path. Spotting a darkened cave, he guided his horse inside and slid off. He'd stay long enough to make certain no one followed, then he'd be back on the trail and head toward Tolbert's camp.

Sitting straight up from where he dozed near the horses, Noah scrubbed a hand over his face, certain he'd heard gunfire. It was still early, well before most turned in for the night. The others milled about, checked their guns, played cards, or sipped coffee. No one else seemed to have heard the sound, making him think he'd dreamed it. He tried to screen out the camp chatter and listened again. Nothing.

"Here, drink this." Gabe stood in front of him, offering a cup filled with coffee, then squatting down beside him.

"Did you hear anything a few minutes ago?"

"Like what?"

"Gunfire."

Gabe sharpened his gaze and stood, turning in a circle, listening. He could hear the low voices of the men as they filled their time.

"How many shots?"

"Just one. Probably a dream." Noah stood. "You plan on all of us staying together tomorrow or splitting into groups?"

"We've been talking about that. Cash and Beau want to split up into three groups, set up a base camp to meet tomorrow night."

"Makes sense."

"Maybe. With all the canyons, it'll be slow going in one large group. Problem is, three or four men aren't going to be able to do much if they run into Drake's gang. I don't want to ride back to Splendor with less men than we rode out with."

"For all we know, they've taken the cattle and left. It may be the money from the bank was what he needed until they sold the herd. They could be miles from here by now." Noah drank the last of the coffee and set the cup on a nearby rock.

"You believe that?"

"Nope." The corners of Noah's mouth tipped up in a grim smile. "I agree with what Dax and Luke think. Part of what Drake wants is revenge. If not, why come to Splendor at all? It'd be safer to bypass it altogether. The man's got a lot of greed and hatred built up inside, and from what I've heard, I believe he wants to take it out on the Pelletiers and Tolbert."

Gabe nodded, thinking the same and deciding the quicker they found the man, the safer they and the town would be.

"We'll plan to ride out in groups. You and I in one, Dax and Luke in the second, and Cash and Beau in the third. I'll tell the others we'll be heading out at sunrise."

Chapter Eighteen

Abby dashed across the street, dodging wagons and horses as she headed toward the telegraph office. Her father hadn't been seen in days, which meant his men still languished in the jail with two men from the Pelletier ranch watching them. Word traveled fast in a small community and she knew he would've ridden to town right away if he'd heard his men were behind bars.

"Good afternoon, Abigail."

"Hello, Mr. Griggs."

Bernie Griggs checked his pocket watch. "Bank must be closed for lunch. What can I do for you?"

"I wondered if you'd seen or heard from my father or his foreman since the posse rode out of town."

He scratched the stubble on his chin, shaking his head. "No, can't say that I have. Last time I saw him was the day of the bank robbery. Why?"

She bit her lower lip, knowing something was wrong. "It's odd he hasn't sent someone to get his men out of jail. It's been days and nobody from the ranch has come into town."

"I agree. It is unusual. Most weeks, someone from your ranch rides in for supplies, mail, or to send a telegram for your father. Can't remember the last time this amount of time went by without one of his men stopping in. Have you sent someone to the ranch to fetch him?"

"There's no one to send, and with my job, I'm not able to ride out until dark. I'm sure he's fine. It's just that..." Her voice faltered as she considered her words. She didn't believe all was well or someone from the ranch would've been spotted in town.

"Why don't you check with the Pelletier men who are watching the prisoners? They may have heard from your father."

"Thank you, Mr. Griggs. I believe I will."

A man leaned against a wall inside the jail, talking to the men behind bars. Abby heard a burst of laughter as she closed the door.

"Good day, Miss Tolbert." Travis Dixon said as she stepped closer.

"Oh, hello, Mr. Dixon. I didn't recognize you."

"Most people don't since I shaved off my mustache." He stroked the area above his upper lip. "If you came here to see Sheriff Evans, he's off with the posse."

"Yes, I know. Noah is with them." She could feel warmth creep up her face at the way she spoke of him with such familiarity. "I came to ask if anyone from my father's ranch has come to fetch the men." She nodded toward the cells.

"No one. Either Rude or I have been here the entire time," he said, referring to another of the Pelletier men. "You do know your father took a group of his men and rode after the rustlers before the posse took off, right?"

Her eyes snapped to his. "No, I did not." Worry gnawed at her, knotting her insides as she thought of the implications of her father going after Drake. Both men were arrogant, believing they were above the law. Except, as far as she knew, her father had never actually broken the law as they suspected of Drake.

Travis could see fear glittering in her eyes and tension lining her face.

"Your father has lived out here a long time and knows the dangers. I'm sure he'll be all right."

Abby twisted her hands in front of her, knowing anything could happen when men searched for rustlers and bandits. Worry surrounded her each day since Noah had left with the others. She'd pushed it aside as best she could, believing in his skills and his ability to stay calm under dangerous conditions. She had to trust he'd come back to her alive.

Her father, though, was a different type of man. Smart and arrogant, he often let his pride control his decisions. More than once, she'd seen him almost come to harm when he let his sense of superiority rule over good judgment.

"I'm certain you're right, Mr. Dixon. Thank you for letting me know."

"Good day, Miss Tolbert. I'll let you know if we hear from your father."

Her steps back to the bank were labored and slow as fear wrapped around her. As much as she didn't want to live with her father at the ranch, she didn't want harm to befall him.

"Did you find out anything, Abby?" Sally saw her shoulders slump as she slipped off her wrap.

"Travis Dixon said he took a group of men and rode after the rustlers a couple days before the posse left. That's why no one has seen him."

Sally stood, putting an arm around Abby's shoulders. "So now you have two men to welcome back when they return with that scoundrel who robbed us."

Abby couldn't help the amusement flickering in her eyes or the way her mouth tilted upward. "You're right, Mrs. Phelps. I should be planning a special welcome."

"That's the way. It's time to reopen the bank. You ready?"

"Yes, ma'am."

"You believe I'm wrong?" Tolbert glared at Dirk.

"Yes, sir, I do. Seems best to head back to your ranch and set up guards. They're after the cattle you keep in the small pasture. Why risk the men if we know Drake's plans and can stop him?"

"Doing it your way means bringing in the sheriff. I don't want Evans involved. This will happen my way. You can either go along with it or pack up and leave."

Dirk narrowed his eyes, frowning at Tolbert. He knew the man held little value for legalities when it came to his own brand of justice. In this instance, Tolbert had a choice which could mean little chance of losing men while capturing the cattle rustlers. Nothing about Tolbert's decision to confront Drake at his camp made sense. He couldn't stay and be a part of the man's madness.

"You're a damn fool, Tolbert, and I won't be a part of leading your men to possible slaughter." He spun away and grabbed his gear. Within minutes, he'd secured his belongings and took off in the direction of Splendor, hoping to find Gabe and obtain help before Tolbert made a terrible mistake—one that would cost lives.

Tolbert paced around camp. He'd never expected Masters to take off. Few men defied his orders, most deciding to do what he required and keep their mouths shut. Now he had one less man to confront Drake and return the stolen cattle.

He glanced at the men sitting around the fire, knowing he had nowhere near enough to do the job without some of them dying. Still, he would not change his plans. A few losses were nothing compared to letting a man like Drake roam freely, stealing and killing. Someone needed to take care of him.

"We've located Drake's camp and found where he's holding the cattle. Tomorrow, we go after him and his men. I want you ready to leave at dawn."

"What about Masters?"

"He won't be going with us."

"We'll camp here, then split up in the morning." Gabe nodded at Noah and the others for confirmation. He'd already explained how they'd continue their search, each group returning to this spot at nightfall. "If what Cash and Beau have learned is accurate, Drake has close to twenty men riding with him. Remember, we want to locate him, then plan how to confront and arrest them. No heroics, understood?"

"Understood, Gabe." Bull wanted to get the man who'd almost killed him months before, but not if it meant any of the men around him would be hurt...or worse.

"Good. Get some rest. Tomorrow will be a long day." Gabe unsaddled Blackheart, placing the gear under a nearby tree, leaning his rifle against the trunk, then turning at the sound of footsteps.

"Mind if I pack down here?"

"Not at all, Noah."

They lay out their bedrolls in silence, each grabbing jerky and hardtack before resting against their saddles. Noah took a long swallow from his canteen, glancing up at the bright stars and almost full moon, wondering about Abby and missing her.

"How's it going with you and Abby?" Gabe asked, as if reading Noah's thoughts.

"Good. Slow, which is as it should be." Noah tore off another piece of jerky, chewing slowly, wanting to get the search over with and return to Splendor. He'd decided to talk with Tolbert about the property above town now, rather than wait for fall. If Tolbert agreed to sell, Noah could start designing the house he planned to build for Abby...and him.

"Do you plan to add onto the cabin?"

Noah's gaze shifted to Gabe. "Nope."

Gabe's lips twitched. He knew Noah well enough to know he had plans, but wasn't quite willing to share. "That so?"

"Yep."

"Let me know if you change your mind. I might be able to arrange some time to help enlarge the place." Gabe tipped his hat low over his eyes and crossed his arms over his chest. Within minutes, Noah heard soft snoring. Gabe had always been able to sleep anywhere, while he'd be more apt to lay there for hours, his mind refusing to shut down.

He thought of Tolbert searching for the same man, believing if he found him, Drake's chances of ever making it back to Splendor for trial would be small. With a jury made up of his ranch hands, Tolbert's brand of justice would be swift.

Noah rested an arm over his eyes, sending a silent prayer they'd find Drake, no one would die, and he'd be in Splendor by sundown.

"I spotted close to fifteen men in camp. Not good odds, boss." Mal Jolly, one of the newer ranch hands, reported, believing Tolbert would call off the raid.

"Surprise is our chief weapon. We focus on Drake and capture him, then the others will surrender."

"And the cattle? We can't get the prisoners back to Splendor and herd the cattle at the same time."

"I said nothing of transporting prisoners to town." Tolbert spun around, facing the other men. "I want Drake. Nothing else matters as long as we get him." He pulled out his revolver, checked the cylinders, then snapped it shut. "Let's go."

Mal's stomach clenched. He'd fought as a Union soldier, never retreating. The word coward didn't figure into his vocabulary, and no one would ever describe him as one, yet his mind whirled at the insanity of Tolbert's order. Neither Drake nor his men would go down easy, which meant some of the men before him wouldn't make it home. He guessed Dirk came to the same conclusion. No matter, though. He'd signed on to do a job.

Mal and the rest of Tolbert's men positioned themselves as instructed and waited for their boss' command. Drake's men moved about, appearing restless, as if they'd stayed too long in one place. Not a good sign in Mal's opinion.

He'd chosen higher ground with a view of those milling around the camp. Settling between two boulders, he watched Tolbert, who took a spot across from him, his gun pointed toward Drake. He glanced away, noting the positions of the other men, and grimaced as another internal warning pierced his gut.

An instant later, gunshots blazed from all directions, bullets missing Mal by inches as they slammed against the rocks. Movement to his left caught his attention. He aimed and fired, hitting one of Drake's men in the chest. The cocking sound of a gun had him spinning to the right in time to get off another shot, this one planting itself in a shoulder, knocking the man to the ground. Mal grabbed the extra weapon and ducked behind the rocks, turning toward Tolbert's last position at the same time he realized the shooting had stopped.

He took small steps backward, leaving the protection of the rocks in an attempt to get a better view of the camp. What he saw turned his stomach.

Tolbert knelt before Drake, falling one way, then another, as the man hammered him over and over with the butt of his gun.

"Stand him up," Drake ordered. Lem and Archie grabbed Tolbert under each arm, steadying him. "You always thought you were better than the rest of us, old man. Guess it's not true. Before I'm finished, I'll own your ranch *and* your daughter. A shame you won't be around to see any of it."

With those words, Drake lifted his gun, centered it on Tolbert's head, and pulled the trigger.

"Did you see anything?"

Gabe held Tempest's reins, waiting for Noah to return from scouting the edge of the canyon. It had been slow going through thick shrubs and rocky terrain. If Noah didn't find any signs, they'd need to head back.

"Nothing. Thought I heard cattle. I must be losing my mind." Noah swung back up on Tempest.

"Sounds carry out here. You may have heard something, just not in that canyon. We'd better start back. Maybe the others have had better luck." Gabe turned toward the two men who rode with them. "We're going back, see if one of the other groups found something."

Fat drops of rain fell as they retraced their route to camp. Freak summer storms happened without warning, then disappeared. This one lasted not ten minutes before it gave out.

They entered camp, the last group to arrive, and could tell the others had no better luck. Noah knew they'd be going further north tomorrow, making gradual sweeps until they located the cattle or had to ride back to Splendor for more supplies. Giving up would never occur to any of them. The threat was too great.

Mal hadn't waited when Tolbert's lifeless body crumbled to the ground. While Drake's men focused on the carnage in their camp, he slipped around the rocks, past stands of tall pines, moving in silent steps toward his horse. Uninjured, he still felt the pangs of fatigue as he dragged his body into the saddle and grabbed the reins.

What he'd seen sickened him, but he let his mind go blank as he reined his horse around, riding through the trees before hitting open ground. He'd go south, then cut east and north toward Splendor, hoping to avoid any further contact with Drake. Finding the camp again wouldn't be hard. First, he had to convince Sheriff Evans to gather enough men to risk their lives by riding out to confront the rustlers. Mal shuddered at the vicious attack by Drake. Even during the war, he'd never seen a man destroy another without remorse.

By nightfall, he felt safe enough to rest. He'd been in the saddle for hours, traveling further south than intended in an effort to hide his tracks. Standing in an open circle surrounded by pines and low shrubs, he caught the aroma of burning wood and turned. Smoke wafted upward from beyond the trees on the north side of the opening.

From where Mal stood, he couldn't tell the distance. Worse, there'd be no way to identify who sat around the fire—friend or foe—until he rode closer. Bone tired, the thought of another skirmish held no appeal. He hadn't eaten since morning, and hadn't even thought about it until now. His stomach growled as he reached into his saddlebag, grabbed some jerky, and bit off a hunk.

The sun disappeared as he finished the last bite. He needed to make a decision. Ride toward the smoke, which continued to spiral upward, or stay put until morning.

"Hell," he mumbled to himself and stood. "No sense staying here alone when there could be hot food and help not far away, right boy?" He stroked a hand down his horse's neck, then mounted.

To his relief, the smoke led him to a campsite not far away. Better still, he recognized several of the men.

"Stop right there." The stern voice came from the other end of a rifle pointed at his chest. "Who are you?"

"Mal Jolly. I work for King Tolbert. Aren't you one of the Pelletiers?"

Luke lowered the gun and stepped forward. "You with the group Tolbert took out to find Drake?" Luke glanced behind him at the sound of footsteps to see Noah, Gabe, and Dax come to a stop beside him.

"All right if I get down? I've been in the saddle most of the day."

Luke nodded, letting his rifle drop to his side as Mal moved closer.

He walked up to Gabe and held out his hand. "Sheriff, I'm glad I found you." He glanced around at the others. "We located Drake's camp."

"And?"

Mal pulled off his hat, pushing his fingers through his hair. "It's not good."

Chapter Nineteen

Noah let out a string of curses as Mal finished his story. "Damn that man. Why couldn't he have waited, ridden out with the rest of us?" He didn't know how he'd break the news to Abby. Her disagreements with her father, although frequent and severe, never impacted the love she held for him. The ramifications of the man's death would be widespread, but to Abby, the loss of her father would be devastating.

Gabe watched Noah walk away, knowing he was thinking of Abby and how to tell her what happened. They couldn't dwell on it now. They had killers to hunt down.

"Anyone else get away besides you?"

"I don't believe so, Sheriff. It all happened fast." Mal scrubbed a hand over his face. "If I could've talked him out of it..."

"Don't dwell on it. Tolbert never listened to anyone's counsel but his own, and now he may drag good men down with him. I doubt Drake would leave any of Tolbert's men alive. Be thankful you got away."

Cash's jaw hardened at the amount of carnage the man had caused. He'd gunned down Cash's relatives in Louisiana, then continued west, killing at will without regard for consequences. "It's time we stopped that son of a bitch before he murders anyone else."

"We'll get him this time, Cash. Drake won't be leaving Montana." Beau clasped his friend on the shoulder.

"Can you lead us to the camp?" Luke leaned against a nearby tree, arms crossed. He never cared for Tolbert, didn't trust the man, but no one deserved the death sentence Drake imposed.

"I believe so." Mal stood and paced a few feet away as he looked up at the sky. He thought of the circuitous route he'd taken to get there, calculated the distance and how long he'd been riding. He faced Gabe with confidence. "Yes. I can take you to them."

"Good. We need as much information as you can give us."

Noah stoked the fire several times while Mal talked of the number of men, camp layout, and location of the cattle. He accepted a cup of coffee, sipping it, watching hot embers spark, then swirl into the air, trying to erase the image of Tolbert's death from his mind.

"Mal?" Noah asked when he didn't answer him.

"Sorry. I, uh..." He took a deep breath to clear his head.

"I asked if you know how many men guard the cattle."

"No. Dirk Masters scouted the herd and camp, but he took off before we went after Drake."

"Masters didn't go with you to the camp?" Noah had met Tolbert's foreman several times. Toby had taken the order for new tack from him. He'd impressed both of them.

"He and Tolbert had a falling out. Dirk took off..."

Gabe slapped his hands on his knees and stood. "He cannot get away from us this time. We leave before dawn. I want to be there when Drake wakes up."

"I think it's a damn fool idea. It won't take long before Tolbert and his men are reported missing. Then the sheriff will have the entire town looking for him." Archie lit a cheroot, inhaling a deep breath.

"We're changing nothing. With Tolbert out of the way, we have a straight path to his cattle. Hell, we can take more than the paltry thirty or forty we planned. We can take the whole herd and there'd be no one to stop us."

"I agree with Archie. We need to get out of here—drive the cattle over the mountains and into Idaho before anyone finds out about Tolbert." Although Lem held no love for Tolbert, he disagreed with Drake's cold-blooded killing. The man had changed since they'd served together for the Confederacy. He'd become obsessed to the point of being maniacal about taking over Tolbert's ranch. Now he talked of taking Abigail as his wife, securing his ownership of the ranch and other holdings.

Drake rounded on Lem, grabbing him by the collar and hauling him close. "You want out?" he hissed.

"No...of course not." Lem choked out the words, losing his balance and falling to the ground when Drake let go.

"Don't ever cross me, Lem. You either, Archie. Now, where's that bottle of whiskey? We should be celebrating our coming prosperity, not fighting each other."

Lem and Archie stared at Drake's retreating back.

"Whatever's going on with him is getting worse. He's talking crazy, Archie. It makes no sense to stay around any longer. We've got to get out of here before he gets us all killed."

Archie leaned toward him, glancing around. "Keep your voice down."

"But we've got to do something before he drags us down with him."

Archie nodded at Lem's comment, already working through a plan to take what he owed them and head for Idaho. They'd talked of it before, figuring the time would come when they'd leave their increasingly deranged partner behind. The two might be killers and thieves, but even *they* had their limits.

Mal led the posse up the steep terrain until it leveled out into a wide, flat expanse of open land. The moon provided enough light to get this far, but it wouldn't be long before the sun replaced it. They had to be inside the camp, guns ready, when that happened.

Another hundred yards and they'd disappear into the pines. Within those trees, they'd find Drake's camp and Tolbert's body.

Mal reined up and twisted in his saddle, motioning for Gabe.

"Not long now. The camp is about a hundred yards past the edge of those trees. Several rock formations ring their camp, providing cover. We should split up as soon as we're in the cover of the trees."

Gabe nodded, then signaled the others to come closer. They once again reviewed what each man would do, making sure there'd be no confusion once they reached Drake's camp.

"Be careful, and remember—it's Drake we want."

Gabe rode alongside Mal, the others following in single file until they disappeared within the trees. Several yards later, they slipped from their saddles to continue on foot.

Reaching the first of the rock formations, Gabe signaled for them to split up and surround the camp. They'd yet to hear a sound. So far, it had all gone as planned.

The closer Noah got, the more his gut squeezed. The plan had been to arrive before the men woke up, trapping them in their bedrolls, yet something seemed amiss. There should be sounds, even from a sleeping camp. Snoring, coughs, the sounds made when people changed positions, yet he heard nothing. He reached the point where he could lean around the rocks to see the camp a few yards away. His eyes narrowed as his brows knit together.

Noah moved a few feet closer, seeing Bull and Luke appear directly across the camp, Dax and Gabe to his right, and Mal with several others to his left. All froze at the sight before them

"Holy hell," Noah murmured as he continued to look around, confirming they didn't walk into a trap. He saw no one except the one person they most wanted.

Coming from all directions, the posse converged around the naked figure tied to a stake, his hands and legs bound, a bandanna in his mouth, eyes blazing as he recognized those circling him.

"I'll be damned." Luke stared at Drake, then glanced at the others. The thought of what he'd done to Tolbert was all that stopped him from bursting into laughter.

"Should we leave him here?" Dax asked, not taking his eyes off Drake.

"It sure would spare the town the cost of a trial and hanging." Beau lowered his gun, still glancing about to make sure no one else had positions around them.

"Bull, take some men and spread out, keep guard until we get Drake on one of the horses." Dax shifted back to Gabe. "Guess we better find the man some clothes."

"Yeah. Then get him to tell us what happened." Gabe walked to the one horse remaining at camp, figuring it must belong to Drake. He searched the saddlebags, pulling out pants and a shirt, but no boots.

"We should make him walk back to town," Noah muttered as he helped Gabe get Drake dressed, pulling the bandanna from his mouth. They kept him tied to the post until they'd secured the pants around his waist. The moment the ropes were released he tried to break free, twisting one way and then the other, kicking as he let loose with an ear-splitting roar.

Unable to take any more, Noah hauled back and landed an impressive blow to Drake's chin, dropping him to his knees, keening sounds coming from deep in his throat.

His dead weight slowed Noah and Mal as they dragged him to his horse, tossed him over the saddle, and used rope to tie him down.

Bull and the others returned as Noah led Drake's horse to the center of the camp. Their expressions signaled disappointment.

"Anything?" Dax asked.

"Tracks heading east. My guess is they've got the cattle hidden in one of the valleys nearby. Could take an hour or days to find them. What do you want to do?" Bull's gaze wandered to the man tied, stomach down, across the saddle. He'd rather see him swinging from a rope, but that day would come soon.

Dax glanced at Luke, who nodded. "We'll take our men and Mal, if he's agreeable, to see if we can find them. I'm not looking for a shootout, Gabe."

"I appreciate it, Dax, but I can't let you do that. There are still at least fifteen men out there, and none of them care if they put a bullet in any of you. We have who we came for. I'll notify the authorities east and south of here to keep watch for them. Maybe we'll get lucky."

"Who wants first watch on the prisoner?" Noah asked, holding up the reins to Drake's horse.

"I'll take him." No one seemed surprised when Cash stepped forward. Of all those present, he'd lost the most at the hands of Drake.

"What about the bodies of Tolbert and the others?" Bull asked, noting what appeared to be a mass grave in the trees a few yards away.

"I'll come back with a wagon," Noah said, knowing he had to be the one to return Abby's father to her. Several others offered to accompany him, including Bull and Mal. Now all he had to do was figure out a way to tell Abby.

"What's all the commotion, Mrs. Phelps?" Abby dashed from behind her counter to join Sally at the bank's front door.

"Appears the men are back."

Abby flashed a smile at her before rushing out the door, heading straight toward Noah. He and Gabe rode together at the front, and she thought her heart would burst at the sight of him alive and uninjured. The posse stopped at the jail and, as she got closer, she could see a man tied to a horse, face down, Cash holding the reins.

Her pace faltered when Noah slid off Tempest, spoke to Gabe, then turned to face her. She expected him to open his arms. Instead, he faced her with a somber expression, halting her steps several feet away, the smile slipping from her face.

"Who is it, Noah?"

"Drake."

"That's wonderful news, right?" Her heart pounded with worry the longer he stood apart from her.

"Yes, capturing Drake was what we wanted." Noah took a deep breath. He couldn't have the conversation out here where everyone could hear. He steeled himself and took a step closer. "We need to talk, Abby. Do you think Mr. Clausen will mind if you don't return for a bit?"

Tremors flowed through her. Whatever he had to say required privacy and time.

"He's at the land office, but I'll let Mrs. Phelps know." She started to ask why he wanted to talk, then changed her mind and retraced her steps to the bank, returning within minutes. "Where do you want to talk?"

He looked around, trying to come up with a place where no one would bother them, and where Abby's reaction wouldn't matter. He could think of only one spot.

"I know it isn't proper, but your room at the boardinghouse would be best." He moved to cup her elbow with a hand, guiding her across the street, spotting Suzanne standing outside.

"Appears you found Drake. Did anyone else get hurt?" she asked as the two joined her.

"None of the posse." He glanced at Abby, then back at Suzanne. "I need to speak with Abby in private. We're going to her room for a few minutes, if that's agreeable to you."

Suzanne's brows knit together as her lips formed a thin line. She didn't allow men in the rooms of her unmarried female boarders, but Noah's pained expression signaled the importance of his request.

"Of course. I'll be in the kitchen if you need me."

He escorted Abby inside and up the stairs, then stopped, scanning the hall.

"Here," she said, moving past him and opening the door to her room. She stepped inside, Noah a few paces behind.

"Sit down, Abby. I'll leave the door open."

She sat on the edge of the bed while Noah pulled the chair she used at the vanity toward her. He lowered himself into the small seat, dwarfing it with his size. At any other time, it would have made her laugh, but not today.

By now, her heart beat so hard, she found it difficult to breathe. She felt a shiver ripple through her and wrapped the shawl so tight, her knuckles lost their color. The silence continued, becoming oppressive.

"What is it, Noah?" she choked out, unable to control the tremor in her voice.

He stared at her, focusing his gaze on her beautiful blue eyes—wide, trusting, and confused. He saw all those as his mind struggled with how best to break the news.

Peeling her hands loose from their grip on the shawl, he wrapped them in his and leaned forward. "It's not good news."

He could see her swallow, then nodded for him to continue.

"It's your father, Abby. He's..." Noah took another breath. "He's dead."

She ripped her hands from his grasp and stood, stunned eyes looking down at him as she shook her head slowly. "No..." she breathed out in a strangled voice, still shaking her head.

He tried to reach for her again, but she backed away.

"Drake shot him. One of your father's men saw it happen. I'm sorry, sweetheart. So very sorry."

He watched as the color seemed to drain from her face. Again, he reached toward her, grasping her arms, not letting her step away. He guided her back to the edge of the bed, gently encouraging her to sit down as his warm hands moved up and down her trembling arms.

"Should I get Suzanne?"

She blinked several times before lifting her face to his. The emptiness he saw almost broke him. "What?"

"Suzanne...would you like me to get her?"

She continued to stare, unable to speak.

He started to turn, then crouched in front of her, taking her hands once more. "It will be all right, sweetheart. Please, trust me on this. You'll be all right."

Chapter Twenty

"The circuit judge will arrive in a few days." Gabe tossed the telegram on his desk, glancing at Noah sitting in a nearby chair. Two weeks had passed since they'd arrested Drake and each night Gabe had listened to the man rant about his innocence. He'd be glad to get the trial and punishment behind them. The town needed to get on with their lives and put the tragedy to rest. "How's Abby doing?"

Noah pinched the bridge of his nose, letting out a long breath. Soon after returning to Splendor with Drake, he and several others had retrieved the bodies of Tolbert and his men. Abby had screamed at him and Gabe when they'd restrained her from seeing her father's body. He'd never seen her so fierce and inconsolable. It had been a blessing when Reverend Paige and his wife came forward to comfort her, insisting she wouldn't want the last vision of her father to be in his current state. At least she'd listened to them even as she pushed Noah away.

"I don't know. She's been staying at the ranch since the funeral. I've ridden out a couple times, but, well…" He scrubbed a hand over his face. "It's more complicated now."

"Complicated?" Gabe asked, crossing his arms and leaning against the edge of his desk.

Noah stood, taking the few steps to the window and looking out on the midday bustle of their growing town. He found it odd how activities continued as if nothing major had happened. In his mind, the murder of a prominent citizen, such as King Tolbert, should impact the town in a more meaningful way. In truth, other than talk of the upcoming trial and sympathy for Abby, Noah had heard his name mentioned little, as if his passing would have scant effect on the town.

"The times I've gone to the ranch, she's been surrounded by people. Women from church, Rachel and Ginny Pelletier, Mr. Clausen and an attorney from Big Pine helping her understand the ranch and other property. Suzanne even closed the restaurant a couple days to stay with her, leaving the boarders to make meals on their own."

"I imagine it's a lot for anyone to handle, more so for a young woman who's never been involved in running the ranch. It'll take time to sort through all of it."

"The attorney's been staying at the ranch the last week. He's someone Tolbert introduced her to while he was doing his matchmaking."

"Ah..."

Noah spun away from the window, pinning Gabe with a stark look. "Meaning?"

Gabe looked up from the wanted poster he studied. "Meaning you'd best stake your claim if she's who you want. Abby's a wealthy woman now, and there'll be plenty of not-so-honorable men chasing after her. Settle this and marry her."

Gabe's words hit Noah like a punch to the gut. He loved her, wanted to spend his life with her as his wife, yet Tolbert's death changed everything. Her father's wealth was in the extreme. If he'd wanted, he could've bought all the ranches in the area and still had enough to live in grand style. Abby could no longer sever herself from the affluence, or choose to live in town and work at the bank. She held the keys to a ranching empire and all the responsibilities accompanying it. Noah could imagine no scenario where he still fit into her life.

"I need to get back to the livery."

"You riding out to see her tonight?" Gabe asked, not liking the troubled look on Noah's face.

"Thought I'd go to the Dixie, play some cards after supper. Care to join me?"

Gabe thought it a damn fool idea when Noah had a beautiful woman waiting for him at her ranch, but hell, it was Noah's life. "See you tonight."

"It's all so confusing. I don't know that I'll ever understand everything my father did." Abby rubbed her temples, trying to ease the headache she'd carried with her all day. "I had no idea he owned shares in a railroad, or a ranch in Colorado."

"*Part* of a ranch in Colorado. His partner is open to buying you out. It may be something you want to consider." Ernest Payson knew every detail of her father's substantial estate. Although a difficult man, he'd always found Tolbert to be fair in his business dealings. "I never did understand why he partnered on a ranch so far away, unless he speculated the railroad would be going through there. The one in Big Pine made sense and has a lot of potential."

"I suppose so, Mr. Payson."

"I wish you'd call me Ernie or Ernest. Mr. Payson makes me sound much too old."

Her mouth tilted in a vague smile. "All right, Ernest. But you must call be Abby or Abigail. Now, tell me your thoughts on Dirk Masters."

"I've spoken to him little since he returned after hearing of your father's death. Seems capable and has experience as a foreman. If your father hired him, I'm sure he has the skills you need."

"Remember, though, he also hired Parnell Drake." A quick, sharp pain shot through her before she concealed it with a shake of her head. "However, I do agree with you about Masters. If Father had listened to him, called off his plan to confront Drake with so few men, he might still be alive today."

"Supper is ready, Miss Abigail," Fanny said, poking her head into the office.

"Thank you, Fanny."

For years, Fanny Dobbins worked at the ranch as their cook and housekeeper. She'd stayed after Abby's mother died, making the decision to leave when Tolbert sent Abby away to school. Ruth Paige, the reverend's wife, sent Fanny a telegram notifying her of Tolbert's death. Within a few days, she returned to support Abby, planning to stay as long as needed.

Payson escorted Abby to the table, glad to put the business dealings behind them for a while. He'd seen how the sheer size of Tolbert's estate overwhelmed her. Unlike many men, Payson had worked with several women of wealth, most perfectly capable of taking over when their husbands died. They required his guidance with many decisions and paid him well for his sound direction. He'd thought it would be the same with Abigail. He'd been wrong.

He'd met her once at a party King Tolbert held at his home. The guest list included several bachelors, all considered a suitable match for Abigail. She'd spurned each one. Ernest had spent little time with her that day, preferring to watch, decide for himself if she might be worth pursuing. By nightfall, he'd determined she'd be more than worth the effort.

Living in Big Pine didn't afford the convenience of courting a woman a day's ride away. The untimely and tragic circumstances of Tolbert's death required Ernest to stay at the ranch for an extended period, providing the time and opportunity to get to know her, see if they might suit.

"Appears Mrs. Dobbins expected more to join us." Ernest's eyes scanned the table filled with plates of meat, chicken, potatoes, green beans, turnips, braised apples, and bread. His mouth watered at the aromas.

"She'll take whatever isn't eaten to the bunkhouse. Believe me, it will disappear within minutes." Abby shifted in her chair, adjusting her long skirt, trying to conjure up an appetite which had eluded her since learning of her father's death. The one person who seemed to understand and provide support came around little. She glanced at the chair where Noah sat on his few visits since the funeral.

He'd visited a few times, eaten supper twice, excusing himself soon after to make the journey back to town, leaving her to spend another strained evening with Ernest Payson. Each time Noah left, she wanted to run after him, hold up her arms so he could lift her into the saddle, and ride out with him. Her father's death had changed their relationship in a way she hadn't anticipated.

She didn't understand the distance he seemed to be building between them, especially after being so attentive for weeks. Most evenings before would end with her in his arms, Noah kissing her senseless, making her knees quake at the intensity of his desire. Each time, he'd pull away before going to a point from which neither could return, and each time, she wished he hadn't.

Abby loved Noah, wanted to share her life with him in good times and bad. Her wealth complicated matters, at least in his mind. She knew he struggled with her affluence, comparing it to his job as a blacksmith, believing his status too far beneath her. Abby didn't give a whit about social status or money. She wanted Noah.

Weeks before, she'd believed it wouldn't be long before he asked for her hand. Then Drake murdered her father. Days were filled with visits from neighbors and friends, expressing their condolences, cooking meals, and helping to make arrangements for the funeral.

Abby moved back to the ranch, at least for a while, to settle her father's affairs. Ernest Payson arrived within a few days, taking a room near her father's downstairs study. Quiet and efficient, he seemed to care only for helping her understand her father's estate and make the required decisions to keep Tolbert's businesses running.

Noah had taken one look at Ernest and come to an immediate and, as of yet, unspoken decision. Although cordial, she sensed a chasm grow between them—one not of her making.

Noah didn't know she had no intention of making the ranch her home, unless he stayed by her side, which seemed doubtful. He ignored her cautious hints about a future together, at times looking at her as if she were a wayward child, incapable of grasping the reality as he saw it. Those times angered her the most. She'd built a life in Splendor, worked at a job she enjoyed, and had every intention of continuing once the affairs of the ranch had been settled.

Ernest's suggestion to Noah that he become her foreman caused an intense reaction. He'd glanced between her and Payson, opened his mouth to say something before clamping it shut, then stormed off without explanation. He hadn't returned, leaving her angry, hurt, and confused.

"You've been cooped up here for weeks. Why don't I accompany you to town tomorrow? You can visit friends then, if you agree, I'll escort you to supper." Ernest delivered the invitation in a genial manner, not sounding as a man intent on courting her would, for which she felt grateful.

She had an almost desperate need to see Noah, spend time with him, ask why he'd stayed in town and didn't bother to visit. Perhaps they'd have lunch together, or maybe he'd join her and Ernest for supper.

"I *have* felt as if the walls are closing around me, Ernest. A visit to town would be wonderful. There are some questions I have for Mr. Clausen, and it would give me a chance to see Suzanne."

"The owner of the boardinghouse?"

"Yes. We are quite good friends." She chewed a bite of roast, eyeing Ernest from under her long lashes. "Would you mind if I invited Noah Brandt to share supper with us?"

Ernest picked up his napkin, dabbed at the corners of his mouth, then placed it back on his lap. "Not at all." Sipping from the wine Fanny had poured, he noticed Abby's glass sat empty. "Are you certain you don't care for wine? It is quite good."

"I'm certain it is or my father wouldn't have purchased it. It doesn't take much wine for my head to feel as if it's spinning off my body."

Ernest grinned at her description. "Some sherry then? It might help relieve your tension."

She blinked, not realizing he'd noticed her stress. "Perhaps I'll take a glass upstairs with me. It may help me sleep."

"Are you having trouble sleeping?"

"A little. I wake up, then lay there for what seems like hours, thinking of my father, the ranch, and of all I still must do. More times than I can count, I awaken with a headache." She pushed two fingers against a temple, as if to emphasize the point.

"This might help." Ernest pushed from the table and walked around to stand behind her chair. "Lean forward a little."

She glanced over her shoulder before bending forward and feeling his hands rest on her shoulders, massaging the tense muscles. At first, his touch startled her, but as he continued to apply pressure to the sore tissues, she relaxed, feeling some of the tension slip away. She closed her eyes, letting a sigh escape her lips. Although his hands felt good, they couldn't compare to the spark she felt whenever Noah touched her, wrapped his arms around her, drew a finger down her cheek.

Fantasizing Noah stood behind her, she swallowed the lump in the back of her throat. They'd come so far, become good friends, sharing so many dreams. Unless she did something soon, Abby feared she might lose him forever.

"Are you still awake?"

Her eyes popped open. She'd almost fallen asleep under his gentle ministrations and her musings of Noah.

"Yes, I'm awake. Thank you, Ernest. I feel much better." She pushed away from the table and stood, turning to face him. "I believe I'll retire now, unless you have more for me to review."

Seeing the weariness in her eyes, he shook his head. "We have plenty of time, Abigail. There's no reason to push further tonight."

"Goodnight then. I'll see you in the morning." She took the steps in slow fashion, as if floating up the stairs.

He watched her disappear near the top and picked up his wine glass, taking another sip. Ernest had never met her equal. The more time he spent around Abigail, the more he wanted to peel back each layer, as if she were a ripe piece of fruit, and learn all he could. He'd never seen himself as a romantic. Abigail Tolbert might prove his notion wrong.

Noah tossed his cards to the center of the table and grabbed his whiskey, holding it up, staring at the dark amber liquid as he swirled it in the glass.

"Damndest run of bad luck you've had in a while."

Noah shrugged at Gabe's comment. He didn't care about the game, the whiskey, or his friend's attempts to keep his mind off Abby.

"Good thing it isn't a big money game or you'd be betting your livery by now." Bull also tossed his cards aside, looking toward Travis, who continued the betting with Gabe.

The two had ridden to town for supplies, stayed for supper, then joined Noah and Gabe at the Dixie. Bull felt a stab of guilt at sitting here and not the Wild Rose. He'd been going there so long, it felt as comfortable as another home.

"You want my opinion?" Bull asked, looking at Noah.

"Probably not. But I'm not that lucky, am I?"

"Nope," Bull chuckled, picking up the cards Travis dealt him. "Abigail's going through a bad time. That girl doesn't need any lawyer from Big Pine telling her what to do. She needs a friend, someone who knows and cares about her."

"She's got friends. Plenty of them, including Suzanne, and Rachel and Ginny Pelletier." Noah tipped his chair back on two legs, rolling his glass between his palms.

"They're not who she needs." Bull's razor-like gaze fixed on Noah.

"She knows where I am if she needs help."

"You're a damn fool, Noah."

"I've been told that before."

"Good evening, Sheriff. Nick didn't tell me you came in tonight." Lena stood beside him, admiring his strong profile and the way his broad shoulders filled out his shirt. She'd thought him handsome the first time they'd met, finding herself more attracted to him with each encounter, but he'd never learn of it from her. "You boys getting everything you need?"

"We're good, Lena." Gabe let his gaze wander over her lush curves before locking on her bright blue eyes. Their gazes held a moment before he wrenched his away to focus on the cards in his hand. He didn't know what the hell was wrong with him when it came to her. Sure, her exotic beauty captivated him, urging him to discover what lay below the cool exterior, learn her secrets and share his, but damned if he knew why. There were plenty of other women, most respectable, he could fantasize about. Why did he obsess about a woman who owned a saloon, making her money by pleasing men?

"Let me know if there's something you want." She tapped Gabe's shoulder, her eyes glittering with amusement. "Deborah would still like to get to know you, if you're ever interested." Before he could respond, she turned and sashayed toward the bar, stopping to chat with other patrons.

Noah caught the way Gabe's eyes widened at Lena's comment, then followed her as she moved from table to table. He knew his friend would never take her up on the offer to visit Deborah. She wasn't the woman who caught his attention. If the need arose, Gabe would make the journey to Big Pine, visit with Dolly, then return to Splendor with his thoughts in order—at least for a time.

"I'm done." Noah pushed from the table, clasping Gabe on the shoulder before heading outside and into the cool night air. He took a deep breath, glancing up at the stars and wondering about Abby. Perhaps Bull had it right.

She hadn't asked him to stay away. *He'd* been the one to sense a need for distance. For Noah, the balance of their relationship shifted with Tolbert's death. While she lived in town, worked at the bank, and shunned her father's wealth, he felt on level ground with her—an equal. He'd let his insecurities slip away, began to believe himself good enough, one worthy of loving and marrying her. All that changed when he witnessed her work through the details and decisions of her father's estate with Payson. The reality of his position and hers slammed into him with an impact that shattered his previous beliefs.

He'd always took pride in his work, growing the livery and smithy business. The money he'd placed in Clausen's bank affirmed Noah's success. The miner's supply and tack shop he'd opened months before had made money within weeks of the first sale. Ideas for other businesses filled his mind as he hammered away at the forge every day. Thanks to his friendship with Gabe, he was well-read with a good education. Numbers came easily to him, as did an ability to grasp complex legal contracts. He had good friends, people he could count on. He'd built a good life and considered himself prosperous. But it wasn't enough—not for Abby.

Abby deserved the best. Ernest Payson, with his law degree and political contacts, could provide her a future well beyond Noah's means. He'd seen the way Payson looked at her, knew he had an interest beyond helping with the estate. Payson wanted her in the same way as Noah. The pain at the idea of another man winning her love pierced him as if a lance had been driven through his heart.

Yet, from what Noah had seen, Abby didn't return Payson's interest. In fact, she'd made numerous efforts to be alone with Noah when he visited, hinting at marriage and assuming they still had a future together.

Payson's suggestion of Noah working for Abby as her foreman hit a nerve. He still didn't know why he'd stormed out and hadn't returned, except because of the rightness of the suggestion, at least from Payson's perspective. He had no idea Noah and Abby had been seeing each other. For whatever reason, Abby had never seen fit to let Payson know the extent of their relationship.

He saw Noah as a man Abby could trust. A hard worker who understood how to deal with and lead men. The fact Abby hadn't jumped in and explained her feelings for Noah, squelching the idea, hurt more than a punch to his stomach. She hadn't slipped her arm through his or reached out in any way to let Payson know the folly of his suggestion. The fact she didn't do anything to proclaim her feelings sent him over the edge.

"Why don't you head out there tomorrow, see how she's doing, maybe take her on a ride in the hills? She must be feeling cooped up with no one to talk to except that slicked up lawyer." Gabe stood beside him, looking at the same stars that caught Noah's attention.

Noah dropped his gaze to the street, lifting a hand in greeting to a rancher with a full wagon who drove past. It amazed him how hard the people worked. Close to midnight and they didn't stop. Nothing seemed to phase or deter them. Was he giving up too easily?

"I'll think on it."

"Don't think too long. A woman has a way of conjuring up all kinds of bad thoughts when she doesn't hear from her man. Well, I'd best get back to the jail, make sure Drake hasn't escaped." Gabe had left the man alone in his cell, not worried at all that he'd get away. "The circuit judge is due soon. I'll be glad to get the trial over with and return to a normal life around here."

Noah didn't respond, his mind wrestling with the thought of riding out to see Abby tomorrow. Perhaps he would, if for nothing else than to confirm in his mind how well she could do without him.

Chapter Twenty-One

"Let me help you up." Ernest grasped Abby's elbow, providing support as she climbed into the buggy. He sat beside her, grabbed the reins, and slapped them with a light touch, starting their journey to town.

Abby tightened her bonnet before glancing at the clear sky. The weather had warmed up the last few days, dismissing the chill of spring for the heat of summer. No matter. There'd still be plenty of showers during the coming months to cool off the days.

She slid over a few inches, putting more distance between her and Ernest. The moment she awoke and remembered his idea to visit town, excitement had stirred in her belly. She'd taken special care with her hair, selecting a ribbon Noah had given her on one of their walks around town. Taking a dress from her wardrobe, she held it up, remembering how much Noah liked it, saying it brought out the cornflower blue of her eyes.

She glanced at Ernest, letting her hands smooth down her dress, smiling at the thought of seeing Noah. She hoped he'd take time away from his work for a walk. They needed to talk so she could understand why he stayed away. His actions confused and frightened her, made her feel vulnerable, none of which she felt around Noah before her father died.

"Will you be meeting with Mr. Clausen long?" Ernest asked, guiding the horse around a bend toward the north edges of Splendor.

"No, not long. I have a few questions to ask." The chief one being if he'd hold her job until she straightened out the affairs at the ranch and returned to her life in town. She had plans, and they didn't include being tied to a place so far away from Noah.

"There are some telegrams I must send. May I meet you at the bank when I'm finished?"

"Actually, I plan to visit Mr. Brandt for a bit before we eat. Why don't we meet at the restaurant?"

"Very well." He'd paid little attention to her friendship with Noah, assuming they'd formed a bond while she lived in town. For the first time, he began to think Brandt might mean more to her than just a friend.

Abby straightened her dress and sat up as they entered town, her heart pounding as they made the last turn. She didn't know why she felt so nervous, like a young girl about to stand before her class to recite a poem. Her chest squeezed as the schoolhouse came into view on her right, then the lumber mill on her left, followed by Noah's tack and saddle shop. She held her breath as the third building came into sight. She could see waves of heat escaping through the open door before the forge came into view. Trying not to be obvious, she craned her neck to glance around Ernest.

"I don't see him inside, Abigail."

She startled and straightened her spine, clasping her hands in her lap before clearing her throat. "Oh, well...thank you, Ernest. I'm certain he's around somewhere." At least she hoped he hadn't left to stay at his cabin. Then she thought of the forge. He'd never leave it burning if he planned to leave.

The wagon began to draw away from the smithy when the sound of a horse's whiny came from the livery in back. Abby shifted in time to see Noah ride out the gate on Tempest, then stop when he saw her. She waved, then set her hand on Ernest's shoulder.

"Stop, please." She didn't take her gaze off Noah as the wagon came to a halt and she stood.

"Wait, Abigail. Let me help you." Ernest secured the reins, jumped down, and dashed around the carriage.

She almost jumped off without waiting, her desire to see Noah overcoming appropriate behavior. Forcing herself not to be rash, she accepted the hand Ernest offered and gracefully stepped to the ground.

"I'll be at the telegraph office if you need me." He leaned close to her ear so she could hear over the noise of those riding past.

She barely heard, her attention so intent on Noah. Trying to calm her racing heart, she took a deep breath and walked toward him.

Noah didn't move from his perch on Tempest, his gaze staying locked on Abigail. He'd woken early, finished what needed to be done, then prepared to ride to the Tolbert ranch. Gabe knew him better than anyone, and he respected Bull more than most men in Splendor. If both believed his actions were that of a fool, well...perhaps they were right.

He'd spoken to Toby about keeping an eye on the livery, even posted a notice near the forge for anyone needing his services to go to the tack shop next door. Riding out the gate, he spotted the wagon, then recognized who drove it and the woman beside him. He'd reined Tempest to a stop as irritation raced through him. Instead of being glad to see her, anger built at the way she settled her hand on Payson's shoulder, then calmly waited for him to help her down, nodding when he leaned in to whisper in her ear.

"Noah?" Abby's soft voice cut through the rage he felt. He tore his gaze away from the retreating carriage to glance down at her standing next to Tempest, her brows creasing into a frown. "Are you all right?"

His hands tightened on the reins. Hell no, he wasn't all right. He was damn mad and confused at what he'd seen.

"Fine." He slid off Tempest, not reaching for Abby or indicating he felt glad to see her.

"Where are you going?" She stroked Tempest's neck as she spoke, loving the feel of the horse's strength below her fingers.

"To see Dax and Luke," he lied. He'd been headed for her ranch, planning to talk Abby into taking a ride with him.

"Oh, I see."

Her voice sounded strained and he saw disappointment cross her face. He should've told her the truth, but he'd started this lie and now had to see it through.

"Thought I might ride out to take a look at a broken down wagon Dax mentioned."

Abby nodded, but he could see her struggle with his explanation. She licked her lips as her gaze dropped to the ground, the disappointment crushing. A large part of her had hoped he'd been riding out to see her.

"What brought you to town?"

I came to see you, she thought. "I need to speak with Mr. Clausen before meeting Ernest for lunch." She braced herself and looked up at him, wanting to reach out and grab his hand, but keeping her arms at her side. "Would you care to join us? You haven't been out to the ranch in days."

Even with Abby at the table, Noah had no desire to spend a meal with Payson. His solicitous manner grated on Noah, yet she seemed to enjoy his fawning ways. He'd never be able to sit and watch without saying something he knew he'd regret later.

"Another time." He started to swing up on Tempest, then shifted back. "Dirk Masters ordered some tack from Toby a few weeks ago. The order is ready if you want to take it back to the ranch with you. If not, let Dirk know and he can get it the next time he's in town."

"So you heard about Dirk returning to the ranch."

"He stopped in town to speak with Gabe about your father and explain what happened between the two of them. Seems he got as far as Big Pine before turning back. He's a good man, Abby. The kind of foreman you'll need for a place as large as yours."

He stared at her a moment longer, wanting to take her in his arms and crush her to him. The belief he no longer offered her the life she deserved held him rooted in place. No matter what Gabe and Bull said, he couldn't shrug off his feelings of inadequacy when he looked into her eyes. Ernest Payson, for all his formal ways, would provide opportunities beyond Noah's limited means. Between her wealth and Payson's connections, she'd meet and become friends with the people who would build Montana.

She stepped up to him, resting her hand on his arm, his warmth seeping into her. "Payson was wrong to suggest you be my foreman. He never discussed his idea with me."

He shrugged. "You're right. I would've made a lousy foreman."

She gripped him tighter when he tried to turn. "That's not what I mean, Noah. What I mean is...well...you and I...we should run the ranch together. We should—"

"Ah, there you are." Ernest walked up behind her, holding out his hand to Noah. "It's a pleasure to see you again, Mr. Brandt." Noah accepted his hand on a nod. "Will you be joining us for lunch?"

Noah glanced at Abby, seeing her eyes widen, not missing the plea in her gaze.

"Another time. I'd best get back inside." He pulled away, seeing her shoulders slump as a look of despair spread across her face.

"Abby?" Payson held out his arm, waiting as she watched Noah's retreating back, then slipped her arm through his, a glazed expression covering her face.

Abby sat at the table, too stunned to speak or even order. Noah's cold, unfeeling reaction chilled her, as if ice were spreading through her body, taking root in her stomach. Noah had been her friend, her future. Now he wanted no part of her. The anguish at his rejection choked her, cutting off her ability to think, to breathe.

"Abby, is the chicken stew acceptable?" Payson watched with growing concern as she seemed to slip within herself. He didn't know what she and Brandt had spoken of but, whatever it was, she'd walked away a different woman than the one who'd ridden into town with him.

She nodded, seeing Suzanne standing by the table, the same distress Abby felt showing on her friend's face. "Abby, are you all right?"

The worry in Suzanne's voice almost caused the tears in Abby's eyes to fall. She took a deep breath, refusing to let anyone see how much Noah's dismissal hurt. No matter what, she wouldn't let his rejection damage her more than it already had. She'd fight her feelings for him, push her love for him to the back of her mind, and move on. If he didn't want her, fine. He could take his miserable blacksmith shop and cabin and let them burn for all she cared. No matter what, she was still her father's daughter—a Tolbert. She straightened her spine and lifted her head, jutting her chin toward Suzanne.

"I'm fine, and quite famished."

Suzanne's gaze narrowed at Abby. She didn't know what transpired, but guessed it involved Noah. She shook her head, turning toward the kitchen. Those two young people were either going to kill each other, or become one of the strongest couples this town had ever seen. She prayed it would be the latter.

"What's next, Ernest?" Abby sipped her tea as she read through yet another document he set before her, glancing up every few minutes to look through the window toward the barn. A few weeks after Abby's birth, her mother planted a tree near the corner closest to the house. It grew rapidly, and now supported a bird's nest filled with three chicks, as well as other birds who came and went, filling the air with their joyous chirps. She hadn't felt joy in a long time.

Weeks had passed since she'd seen Noah and experienced his rejection. The pain still felt as raw as it had the first day. She lay awake nights, trying to figure out what she'd said or done to make him turn his back on her.

She'd counted on him to be by her side and support her during the overwhelming loss of her father and Drake's trial. Although Noah had acknowledged her, he stayed near the back of the crowded courtroom, not joining her in the seat she saved. She'd sat between Ernest and Suzanne, other friends around her. Even though she glanced behind her more than once during the proceedings, he never made a move to come forward. The disillusionment in his refusal to be by her side still hadn't subsided.

"We have a tentative acceptance of your offer to sell the Colorado property to your father's partner. He's reviewing it with his lawyer, but I don't foresee any problems."

"The proceeds should be sent to Mr. Clausen. I don't want the money going to the bank in Big Pine."

"Any reason? Your father would've deposited the funds into the Montana Territory Bank."

"I trust Mr. Clausen. I've known him most of my life and worked for him." She emptied her cup and set it aside.

"It's important to keep accounts at more than one bank, Abby. You have too much cash to keep in one place. It's too risky."

She sighed, knowing Ernest was right.

"You might feel more comfortable if you met the bank president, let him answer all your questions and put your mind at ease."

"Perhaps."

She had no doubt it would help, but Big Pine meant a day's journey by wagon, a little less if she rode her horse. Except she didn't have a horse of her own. Noah had given her the use of Hasty whenever she needed. She'd bonded with him right away, loved the feel of him under the saddle, loved the way he responded to her slightest command. Of course, she had her pick of any horse on the ranch, but she wanted none of them.

"The horse I've been riding is at the livery. If I do decide to travel to Big Pine, he's the horse I want to ride."

Ernest waved a hand in the air. "Of course. I'll ask Dirk to send one of the men to town to retrieve him."

"There is a slight problem. Hasty belongs to Noah Brandt."

Ernest's expression showed his confusion before he shrugged and picked up the document she'd signed. "I don't see an issue. We'll have Dirk make Brandt a fair offer. More than fair, if needed."

They could try, but Abby felt certain Noah would shut them out as he had her.

"All right. It would be wonderful if he can strike a deal with Noah and bring Hasty back with him."

"Lena tells me you're feeling better." Suzanne filled Nick's cup, placing a hand on his shoulder. "I've never broken a bone and never want to."

Without thinking, Nick placed a hand over his ribs, sensing the pain even though it had been weeks since the beating in the saloon. "It didn't heal up near as fast as I expected. Guess it's my age."

She smacked his shoulder, laughing at his crooked smile. "I don't know what your age is, Nick, but if you're a day over thirty, I'd be surprised." She felt certain he was several years older, but he needed whatever boost she could provide.

A low rumble turned into a full belly laugh. "I can assure you, I'm a good deal older than that."

"Well, whatever your age, none of those men would've been crazy enough to go up against you alone. It took four, and from what I recall, they're all much younger." She turned toward another table, stopping when he reached out to grasp her hand.

"Thanks, Suzanne." He squeezed it before letting go and picking up his coffee, watching as she moved through the tables, talking to everyone. Nick believed she worked too hard, getting up before dawn and going to bed close to midnight. He didn't know how she'd kept up the pace over the years, taking no days off, asking no one for help.

She'd mentioned having a respite twice. Before Ginny Sorenson married Luke Pelletier, she and her sister, Mary, lived in the cramped downstairs bedroom. Several days a week, Ginny helped with cleaning and meals when she wasn't serving drinks at the Wild Rose. Abby also helped while she lived upstairs, although Suzanne refused it most of the time since she paid full room and board. She needed a regular helper, someone who could carry some of the load in exchange for room and board, and maybe a small wage.

Nick finished his coffee and prepared to stand when he saw Noah. He'd been wanting to speak with him, find out about Abby.

They'd spoken several times when she lived at the boardinghouse, and he'd visited her once on the ranch with Lena, but he hadn't seen her in town for weeks.

"Morning, Noah. Have a seat."

Noah nodded at Suzanne, then pulled out a chair. "How have you been? Ribs healed up?"

"Fine. You probably heard Abby paid for all the damage—Doc Worthington's fee and the fine Gabe imposed. She was quite generous. How is she doing?" He smiled up at Suzanne as she filled his cup and set one down for Noah.

"I wouldn't know." He didn't meet Nick's gaze before glancing up at Suzanne. "How about some eggs and bacon?"

"I'll bring it right out, Noah." She wanted to stay, hear his explanation as to why he hadn't seen Abby, but knew Nick might get him to talk easier if she didn't hover.

Nick held the cup between his palms, letting it rotate, feeling the warmth. Most of his life, he'd believed men would talk when they were ready and resented being prodded. As he grew older, he'd become less patient with friends who struggled, yet had too much pride to reach out for help. He'd already heard Noah had severed ties with Abby, but asked about her as a courtesy, and to see if their circumstances had changed. Secrets in a small town could never be kept hidden for long.

"I never intended to stay in Splendor. It was supposed to be a place where Lena and I could make some money before moving on to California." Nick continued to stare at the cup, not looking at Noah. "Now I'm not so sure."

"How's that?"

"You know Suzanne's brother-in-law, Quentin Briar?"

"I met him when he visited."

"Lena and I have known him for years, invested our money with him, and partnered with him in a couple saloons. He's always done right by us." Nick leaned back in his chair and sipped his coffee, then smiled. "Suzanne does make good coffee. Anyway, he traveled out here to talk about a saloon in San Francisco. It's a big place, makes lots of money, and is near Portsmouth Square, a prime location. The owner died. No heirs, but he left some kind of document appointing Quentin to handle the business—either close it down or find someone to take over and run the place. He wants us to partner with him. Since we'd already planned to head west at some point, I thought his proposition sounded good, and expected to feel excited about the opportunity." Nick shook his head. "Nothing. Lena couldn't believe I hesitated going along with Quentin's offer, and honestly, I didn't understand my reaction, either." He stopped as Suzanne appeared with Noah's breakfast, setting it before him.

Noah took a few bites before glancing at Nick. "Did you figure it out?"

"Took a while. Maybe because the answer was so simple." He leaned forward, resting his arms on the table. "It's the town, Noah. Splendor got to me like no other place I've ever lived. And what forms a town? The people, pure and simple. I declined a lucrative business in a place I always thought I wanted to live because I wasn't ready to leave the friendships behind. It's the first time this has ever happened to me."

Noah bit off another piece of bacon and chewed, thinking over Nick's words. He'd never thought much about it before now, figuring he'd move on at some point, maybe back to New York where his parents still lived. He'd grown comfortable here, built his businesses, and had plans to open others. But it was more than that.

Similar to Nick, he'd made deep friendships with people whose lives included helping their neighbors and sticking together during tough times. New York, with its huge population and divergent interests, couldn't compare to the bonds formed in a small town. He'd helped save lives, built his cabin, and fallen in love. Love...Noah stopped chewing, his mind closing down as he tried to push aside his feelings for Abby—something he'd been unsuccessful at doing for weeks.

Noah watched Nick's gaze follow Suzanne around the room as she moved between tables, picking up dirty dishes with one hand while pouring coffee with the other. If he didn't know better, he'd think—

"The more I thought about it, the more I knew this would be a place I could put down roots. Maybe even consider falling in love and marrying. Noah, it's a rare gift to meet the right woman and share your life with her. No one should throw away such an opportunity."

Chapter Twenty-Two

Noah continued to sit long after Nick had left for the saloon. He already knew Gabe and Bull disagreed with his actions toward Abby. Now Nick had, too, except he hadn't come right out and said it. Although they were his friends, none of them understood the pain he felt in making his decision.

He'd spent many sleepless nights wrestling with what to do, knowing she loved him and he loved her. In his mind, love wasn't the issue.

The wealth she'd spurned to live in town and work at the bank could no longer be ignored. She had no choice except to embrace the affluent society it offered. Noah wanted no part of it.

He'd envisioned building a life with what he earned through hard work, not living off Tolbert's money with Abby holding the strings. If he couldn't stand tall as the man of the house, he wouldn't become a part of it. He knew the money would always come between them, a wedge that couldn't be dislodged.

Noah had struggled to deal with the differences between Gabe and himself when they were young. The Evans family held wealth beyond anything Noah could imagine, yet Gabe hadn't seen it as an obstacle. In Noah's mind, it had never been about how Gabe treated him. It had always been about Noah's feelings of inadequacy when compared to his friend.

For years, he tried to compensate for their differences in living and social standing by working harder and excelling in school. They'd taken different paths during the war, although each gained a measure of success. Afterwards, they decided to ride west, start fresh. For the first time, Noah felt he and Gabe were on equal footing. He believed he'd left the barriers of his youth behind him—until now.

He loved Abby more than she'd ever know, and wanted her to find love and happiness. It just wouldn't be with him.

"Noah...Toby told me I could find you here." Noah's head snapped up at the sound of Dirk Masters' voice. "I came to pick up the additional tack, and I have another business matter to discuss."

"Let's head over to the livery." He tossed money on the table and led the way across the street, assuming he needed more tools or tack. Opening the door to let the heat from the forge escape, he turned toward Dirk. "We'll get your tack in a minute. What is it you need to talk about?"

"I've come to buy a horse. Miss Tolbert says his name is Hasty."

"He's not for sale. Anything else?" Noah's gut twisted at losing the horse Abby always rode. He'd planned to give him to her. Now he kept him to remember the times they'd ridden together, how she'd fit him perfectly, as if they were born as a pair.

Dirk shifted his stance toward Noah. He'd heard the rumors about him and Abigail, as well as talk their courtship had ended. Didn't matter. His job was to buy a horse and he didn't want to disappoint his new boss.

"Everything is for sale, Brandt. Name your price. I'm certain she'll pay it."

Noah crossed his arms, settling his feet shoulder-width apart. He had no intention of selling Hasty, now or ever...even to Abby. "As I said, the horse isn't for sale. I've got a couple others if you want to check them out."

Dirk pushed his hat further back on his head and planted his hands on his hips. "I'm afraid she won't settle for another horse. Hell, she doesn't even want us to cut one from the remuda for her."

Noah shook his head, the corners of his mouth lifting at the thought of her selecting one from the extra horses they broke for the cowhands. "Well, now, I don't know what to tell you. She rode Hasty a few times. Most likely, that's why she wants him."

"You certain we can't come to some arrangement? I hate disappointing her."

"Sorry, Dirk. He's not for sale, never will be. Guess we'd better move on to the tack shop and get your order."

As Noah watched Dirk drive the wagon, loaded with new tack, out of town, he thought again of how Abby looked atop Hasty. He remembered his nickname for her, one he'd never said aloud, but thought each time she rode. Princess. He'd begun to think of her as *his* princess and no one else's.

Disappearing behind the gate to the stables, he grabbed a bucketful of supplies. He pulled out two brushes, one for each hand, sweeping them in easy strokes along Hasty's neck, withers, and back, then along a strong thigh. He repeated the process on the other side before cleaning his hoofs. It didn't take much time. The horse hadn't been ridden in weeks, causing a pang of guilt to pass through Noah. He had four horses—Tempest and Hasty, who he never planned to sell, and a couple others he had every intention of trading or selling, whatever came along first. Too bad Dirk wouldn't take one of them.

"Anyone back there?"

Noah tossed the brushes aside and moved in the direction of the voice, recognizing Gil Murton.

"Good to see you, Gil. Thanks again for letting the posse camp out at your ranch."

"Heard the jury found Drake guilty. Did they recover the herd?"

"Gabe received a telegram from a sheriff in Idaho. He and his deputies cornered them not long after they crossed the mountains. Several of the outlaws got away, but they've got some in custody. Don't know what's going to happen now."

"At least they won't be coming back our way." Gil turned, nodding toward a woman a few feet away. "I rode into town to pick up my cousin who came in on the stage." He motioned for her to step up beside him. "Sarah, this is Mr. Noah Brandt. Noah, my cousin, Miss Sarah Murton. She's from Ohio. The town hired her as our new school teacher."

"Congratulations, Miss Murton. It's a pleasure to meet you."

"Likewise, Mr. Brandt." She looked around at the tools, pots, and gear hanging inside the smithy where they stood. "You have a quite a business here."

"Oh, it's not much, but it pays for my food."

Gil's rumble of laughter filled the air. "Don't let him fool you, Sarah. He owns this, the livery in back, and the tack shop next door. We'd better head over to the bank and meet with Mr. Clausen." Gil glanced at Noah. "He's the one who sent Sarah the offer and money to come here. I believe she'll be staying at Suzanne's until the town can build her a house."

"You know, there's an abandoned house that Ginny Pelletier thought of buying before she married Luke. I believe the bank owns it. You might ask Clausen about it. If he agrees, I'm sure I could round up a few men to get it fixed."

"Thanks, Noah. I'll mention it and let him know my brothers and I will help. Guess we'd better get going, Sarah."

Toby passed them as they walked out, letting his gaze follow her. "Who's that?"

"Our new school teacher. The last one moved to Big Pine and got married right after school let out for the summer. I'd say the town did a good job finding someone so fast."

"She have a name?"

"Sarah Murton. She's Ty, Gil, and Mark Murton's cousin. Something you wanted?"

"Dirk Masters picked up the tack and ordered more. He wants it next week." Toby shoved his hands in his pockets and shuffled his feet.

"You got something else on your mind?"

He let out a sigh. "He asked if I'd work on you a little to see if you'd reconsider selling Hasty. Seems Miss Tolbert won't take any other horse and is willing to pay whatever you ask for him."

"Dirk asked you to talk to me?" Noah found it hard to believe the foreman would try to finagle Toby into being a go-between.

"No, not exactly. He mentioned it, saying he hoped you'd change your mind. Seems he hates disappointing her after all she's gone through the last few weeks. Thought it best to mention it to you."

"Fine, you've mentioned it. Now you can head back to the shop and get started on the new order. I'll be over in a bit."

Noah stoked the forge, looked at the pile of broken tools that needed fixing, and grabbed one. As he turned the tool in his hand, he thought of Abby's desire to own Hasty. The thought of selling him didn't set well with Noah. Given more time to think it over, he might change his mind, but not today.

"What are your plans now?" Gabe didn't take his eyes from the telegram he'd received from Sheriff Sterling in Big Pine as he spoke to Cash and Beau. They'd stayed through the trial and hanging, then spent time at the ranch with Dax and Luke.

"We've been talking about where to go next. Any suggestions?" Cash's meaning was clear. As bounty hunters, he and Beau needed to identify their next outlaw. Gabe's stack of wanted posters would be their best source of information.

Gabe pulled the posters from a drawer and tossed them toward Cash. "You can look through these, but I may have another idea for you."

"Yeah? And what's that?" Beau took a seat, starting to flip through the images of suspected murderers and thieves, setting aside those who'd last been seen within the closest states and territories. They hoped to stay in this region. Although they traveled all over to hunt the men they sought, both talked of making Splendor their base, maybe buy some land and build homes.

"This telegram is from Parker Sterling. Appears there is more than one set of rustlers." He held it out to Cash who read it, then passed it to Beau.

He read it twice, shaking his head. "This makes no sense, unless it's a new gang. I swear we tracked just one set of rustlers. Not once did we get the impression more than one gang operated in the region."

"Maybe they're new to the area. Or they could be from around here, heard what Drake did, and saw an opportunity to take over where he left off," Cash said.

"Or they could be some of the men who escaped capture in Idaho—remnants of Drake's original gang." Beau handed the telegram back to Gabe. "What are you thinking?"

"It doesn't much matter who they are or how they started. Sterling needs help, and so will Splendor if they move this way. It's doubtful a bounty has been set as no one knows who's behind the thefts." He rubbed a hand at the back of his neck as he thought through the possibilities. "I suppose you could be sworn in as deputies."

"You mean work for you?" Cash smirked. He hadn't reported to anyone since before his service in the Confederate Army, where he'd met Beau.

"Or Sterling. Makes no difference to me as long as you're willing to help find and arrest the gang."

"Think about it, Cash. Regular pay. Plus, we get to wear a badge, right?" Beau flashed a broad smile at Gabe. "Might be worth considering until we decide what's next for us."

Cash paced to the window, looking out on the crowded street and so many unfamiliar faces. He thought he'd met a good many of the residents during his two visits to Splendor. It seemed to him the town grew more each day, chipping away at the services supporting it.

Gabe could use a regular deputy, maybe two. He worked seven days a week, and people sought him out twenty-four hours a day. Time off came when Noah kept watch on the town while Gabe rode to Big Pine for some rest...and play. Cash heard they hired a new teacher, but the school itself begged for more space. Students sat three abreast at desks meant for two. Suzanne's boardinghouse remained the one place travelers could stay so they wouldn't have to bed down on the ground. The thought of how this town would continue to grow and thrive excited Cash in a way he never expected. He felt the need to be a part of it, at least for a while.

"All right, but we work for you, not Sterling."

Gabe reached into a drawer and tossed a couple badges on the desk, followed by a bible. "Now, this book isn't required for you to take the oath, but it doesn't hurt. Hold up your right hands and repeat after me..."

"Sorry, Miss Tolbert. Brandt refused to sell the horse. He offered two others, if you're interested." Dirk held his hat in his hands, fingering the brim.

"Thank you for asking him. I know you did all you could to change his mind." Noah's refusal didn't surprise her. Somehow, Abby expected him to decline any offer coming from her, even though he knew how much she cared for Hasty. At least he'd been kind enough to let her ride him whenever she asked. Noah had provided her the freedom she'd never experienced living with her father.

"I can try again when I pick up the last order of tack. He may change his mind. Or maybe you could ride in with me. He might soften if the request comes from you."

Abby snorted, putting a hand over her mouth to stifle the unladylike sound. "I'm afraid my presence may make it worse. He might refuse to take any further orders for tack and saddles, then we'd have to ship in what we need from Big Pine." She let out a sigh and turned toward the stack of papers on her desk, knowing she needed to get back to reviewing them. Instead, she changed subjects. "How is our new bull doing?"

A bark of laughter escaped Dirk's lips. "Keeping busy."

"That animal was the last purchase my father made for the ranch. He had high hopes that bull would create the next generation of cattle."

"I can't argue with him. He's a fine animal and your father paid a high price for him."

Ernest walked in from the kitchen, holding what appeared to be a cookie in one hand and coffee in the other. He stopped when he spotted Dirk.

"Mr. Masters, I didn't know you'd returned from town. Were you successful in obtaining the horse?"

"Afraid not, Mr. Payson. I'll keep trying. I'd better get back to the men." He nodded before settling his hat on his head and leaving Abby alone with Ernest.

"Perhaps if I talked to Brandt—"

"No...thank you. I'll not badger him about selling Hasty. If he decides to sell, I'm certain he'll come to me first." She didn't believe it, though. Abby suspected he'd sell Hasty to about anyone so as not to see her ride into town on him. "I'll ask Dirk to cut out a suitable horse from the remuda. We should still be able to travel to Big Pine within the week."

"You're certain you want to ride and not take the wagon?"

"Of course. I'm looking forward to being away without having to read and reread documents from sunrise to sunset. I keep thinking we're through, then you bring me another stack." She lowered herself into a chair and stared at the stack of papers.

Ernest chuckled as he brushed crumbs from his hands. "Those on your desk are the last." He sat across from her, steepling his hands below his chin, as if in prayer, then lowered them to his lap. "You've done a remarkable job, Abigail. I know your father would be proud of what you've accomplished, how hard you've worked to understand the extent of his businesses. Many men wouldn't be able to grasp the complications of his holdings."

She knew he meant his words as a compliment, yet her responsibility to the ranch and other businesses had driven a wedge between her and Noah. Why couldn't he understand she couldn't walk away and leave it for others to handle?

"Thank you, Ernest. I do believe I've made considerable progress since we began. It will be good to get the trip to Big Pine behind us." She stood and grabbed her bonnet. "I believe I'll speak to Dirk, then have a look at the horses available. Perhaps I'll find one even better than Hasty." She knew the odds were against it.

"I'll come with you."

"I'd rather go alone, if you don't mind. I'm certain you'll find work to keep you busy while I'm gone." Abby dashed out, not expecting him to follow as she disappeared through the front door and into the sunshine. The warm rays beat down on her as she lifted her face, hearing the chicks in the nearby tree.

As a child, she'd roll a barrel under the tree and climb up to see the nests, moving fast so her father wouldn't see. He did walk out of the barn once as she hurried to draw both legs up onto a large limb and hunkered into a ball. Abby had held her breath and watched, wide-eyed, as he walked past, not once looking up. Her mouth quirked up at the corners at the memory. Each day brought a little less pain when she thought of her father. She wished the same were true of Noah.

"Are you looking for me, Miss Tolbert?"

"I am, Dirk. If you don't mind, I want to select a horse from the remuda."

"Of course. Come with me." He grabbed a halter, then waited for her to catch up before taking long strides around the barn, past the first corral and to the second one, where a herd of about twenty horses grazed. "Do you know much about these horses?"

"Nothing, except the ranch hands use them for their work."

"Unless they have their own horse, which is common with our men. We use these when we drive the cattle to market or if a horse comes up lame." He opened the gate, holding it as Abby followed him inside the corral. "These aren't green broke. Every one of them is an experienced cattle horse, so you shouldn't have much work to do." He pointed toward a buckskin with black mane and tail, grazing about twenty feet away. "That's Joker. As solid as any horse on the ranch and takes an easy rein. He'd be my first choice for you. Next to him is Clem. He's older, not as spunky, but dependable." Dirk took a step further into the corral before Abby reached out a hand to stop him.

She'd been watching Joker, his beautiful lines, the way he raised his head and shook it. "I'll give Joker a try."

"Good choice."

Twenty minutes later, he finished cinching a saddle on the horse and handed the reins to Abby. "Give me a minute and I'll saddle my horse."

"It's all right, Dirk. I'd prefer to go out alone, see how we do together."

"Pardon me, but I don't think that's wise, Miss Tolbert. I have total faith in him and you, but you're new to each other. At least let me ride a couple miles with you."

She saw his concern, heard it in his voice, and relented. "All right. A couple miles."

"Fair enough."

"Let me go once around the barn, then we can head out." Abby led Joker outside, then mounted, reining him around the barn at a walk before moving him into a jog. He felt good beneath her. Not like Hasty—no horse had ever felt as right as him, but still solid.

"Ready?" Dirk asked as she joined him near the house.

"Yes."

For the first time in weeks, Dirk witnessed the smile she'd been unable to share since her father's death. Radiant and unguarded, it caused an upward tug at his own lips.

"All right then. Let's go."

They took the long road out of the ranch entrance and turned toward town. She let Joker move from a walk, to a jog, to a lope before reining him back.

"He responds so well. How did we get him?"

"I don't rightly know. He was part of the remuda when I arrived. How about taking the trail to the left?"

Abby nodded, then spotted a lone rider coming toward them. Too far away to recognize, she leaned forward, squinting against the sun, then jerked upright when he lifted a hand in greeting.

"Dirk, I believe that's Noah Brandt riding toward us."

He rode ahead a few feet, then turned back and smiled. "It is. And he's leading another horse."

Chapter Twenty-Three

Noah hadn't expected to encounter Abby. He hoped to leave Hasty with one of the men, then return to town without ever seeing her. Now he had no choice. Straightening in the saddle, he continued forward, feeling his chest constrict further as Tempest moved ahead.

"Afternoon, Abby, Dirk." He touched the brim of his hat with a finger. The sight of her after all this time knocked the breath from his lungs, a pain he hadn't expected enveloped him, causing him to shift in the saddle to find relief.

"Hello, Noah. It's good to see you." Abby's world tilted. She could almost feel the heat radiating from his body, reaching out to her and drawing her in. Gripping the saddle horn with both hands, she leaned forward, trying to clear her head.

"Dirk tells me you have an interest in acquiring Hasty."

Abby saw something pass across his face as his eyes bored into her, but it disappeared as fast as it had appeared.

"You know I've always loved riding Hasty. I've never felt a connection with any animal the way I do with him."

He nodded, turning in the saddle to look at the horse, remembering how she looked astride him. Noah swallowed the growing lump at the back of his throat and twisted back toward her. Nudging Tempest with his heel, he moved alongside her and held out the lead rope.

"He's yours."

She stared at his large hand, her lips parting before her gaze caught his. "Are...are you sure?"

"Yes. You belong together." He held his hand further out, wishing she'd take the rope and be done with it.

Her hand shook as she reached toward his, feeling a jolt as she wrapped her fingers around the rope, her skin brushing his palm. Neither moved for a moment, then Noah let his arm drop away.

Beside them, Hasty danced and snickered, his reaction not surprising Noah.

"Thank you, Noah. If you have time to follow us back to the house, I'll get the money and pay you."

"I don't want money for him. As I told Dirk, I can't sell Hasty. He's a gift."

"Noah, I can't—"

"Take him, Abby. Ride him whenever you can and embrace the freedom. You deserve more, but that's all I can give you." His face clouded a moment before his gaze darted away from her. "I need to get back." He reined around and moved Tempest into a lope, trying to put as much distance between him and Abby as he could.

"Noah, wait!" She handed the rope to Dirk and took off, encouraging Joker to move faster. "Noah, please wait."

He let out a deep breath, realizing he could ride all the way to Splendor and she'd probably still be right behind him. Reining Tempest around, he watched her come to a stop, glaring at him, a mixture of irritation and confusion clear in her expression.

Anger and uncertainty knotted inside her. She could feel her hands tremble as icy fear twisted her heart. She edged forward, so close she could've reached out and placed her hand on his.

"You have to tell me what I did to ruin everything. Did I say something, do something to turn you away? I have to know why you no longer want me." She choked on the words as pain radiated through her. "Please, Noah. I have to understand…"

He never intended to have this conversation. He thought after this long, he could avoid declaring his reasons for walking away. She'd never understand, think him a fool and a coward, the same as Gabe, Bull, and Nick. He had his reasons, whether anybody else understood or not.

The silence lengthened between them as he came to terms with what needed to be said. He rested a hand on his thigh, trying to relax and figure out what to say so she'd accept his decision and move on.

"Abby, I've had a lot of time to think, come to terms with my feelings for you. What I learned is I care for you a great deal, more than any woman I've ever known. When I'm with you, life is right, good." He stopped, trying to calm the thundering in his chest, telling himself this was right. "I've always known it wouldn't last. We're much too different for a life together. I'm a simple man. I work, spend time at my cabin, hunt, fish a little, and enjoy a game of cards. It's no life for you or any lady. Your wealth will allow you opportunities beyond what a blacksmith could ever offer. You may not believe it now, but at some point, my lack of money would create a chasm we'd never be able to overcome. Once you think about it, look at my life and yours, you'll know I'm right."

"Lack of money and the inability to use mine? What does that mean?" Her voice shook as her gaze remained steady on his. "If we built a life together, I thought we'd share all we had. There'd be no yours or mine." She glanced behind her, seeing the ranch house and barn in the distance, wanting to share it all with this man. Abby turned back toward him. "I can't do this without you, Noah."

He reined Tempest a few inches closer. "Of course you can." He reached over and ran a finger down her cheek. "I could never live on your money, Abby." The look in her eyes, the pain flowing across her face, tore at his insides. It took all he had not to drag her off the saddle, settle her on his lap, and crush his mouth to hers. Instead, he reined Tempest away.

"You're a coward, Noah Brandt." She thought her words hadn't reached him until he stopped, his back going rigid. He sat for long moments before his shoulders slumped and he slowly turned toward her.

Abby's mind reeled in confusion and shock. Her body shook so hard, she thought she'd fall from the saddle. She'd always prided herself on her ability to remain calm in difficult situations. Staying in control had been required while her father was alive. Now her emotions, her entire body felt out of control, ready to explode into a thousand pieces. She wanted, *needed*, to hold on to her pride, but she felt it slipping away, like everything else.

Gripping the reins so tight her hands ached, she lifted her gaze to Noah, seeing regret on his face. She opened her mouth to speak, then realized she had nothing to say. He'd made his decision. Begging wouldn't change it, nor would she allow herself the humiliation of trying.

She spared Noah one last look, then straightened her spine, loosened her grip on the reins, and turned toward the ranch. Lifting her head and jutting her chin out, she saw that Dirk still waited, along with Hasty—a gift she no longer wanted.

"Let him loose to go back to Noah."

"But, Miss Tolbert—"

"Please, Dirk, do as I ask."

He shook his head, but let go of the lead rope, swatting Hasty a couple times on the rump to get him started toward Noah, who stared after Abby. Dirk didn't know when he'd ever seen a more miserable, disconsolate man, even though Noah tried to hide it behind a stone-faced resolve. Dirk glanced at Abby. He'd been close enough to hear voices, but not what was said. Whatever had happened between them shattered every ounce of joy she'd shown earlier.

He waited until Noah reached for Hasty's rope and pulled the horse toward him. His expression didn't change as he turned and took the road to Splendor, never looking back.

"It's time we head back, Miss Tolbert."

Abby nodded, retracing their path to the ranch and a life she never thought she'd be forced to live—one she didn't want. What she dreamed of, almost had in her grasp, had disappeared with the twist of a few words.

"This was a mistake, Archie. We should've gotten as far away from here as possible. Gone back to Colorado or Wyoming." Lem took a long draw from his cigarette, blowing out the smoke in a rushed exhale. "We don't have to stay. We owe these fellas nothing."

"Maybe not, but they've ridden with us for months." Archie glanced over his shoulder, making sure the others couldn't hear. "And don't forget they helped us avoid the posse in Idaho, even when they knew we wouldn't be able to keep the herd. They've gotten nothing for their efforts, except a small amount of money from the Splendor bank robbery."

"You getting soft now that Drake's not around?"

"Hell no, but I'm not anxious to do something that will get us killed, either. We ride out, what's to stop them from coming after us?"

"We'd leave them the herd," Lem protested.

"Thirty head isn't worth the time to drive them to market. I'm telling you, Hal and the others will ride after us. He won't ignore betrayal." Archie watched as Hal stood up from his seat near the fire, fingering the scar on his face as had become his habit when agitated. "They're restless. We need to finish this, split the money, and take off."

"Why Tolbert's place? We don't need that kind of risk." Lem tossed his smoke to the ground, snuffing it out with a twist of his heel.

"I'm with Hal on this one. With Drake dead, they'll figure the chance of us coming back is low. The daughter doesn't understand ranching. We'll grab her cattle before she knows what happened and can round up the men to follow us. This will be the easiest take we've ever had."

"One hit and out, right? Then we take what we have and hightail it out of Montana."

"We'll go after the cattle he keeps on his eastern border. It's big enough to make us some cash, and small enough to control them during a drive south. A herd that size will give us the grubstake we need to start over someplace else." Archie nodded as Hal approached.

"Problems?" Hal eyed both men, not trusting either one.

"Discussing which herd to go after and when." Archie crossed his arms, tossing a look to the men who followed Hal from the campfire and now stood behind him. "Lem and I are thinking we'll ride to Tolbert's, make sure the cattle are still in the same section of land."

"You and I will go, Archie. Lem can stay here with the others."

Lem stepped forward. Archie reached out a hand and stopped him. "Any reason you don't want Lem along?"

"Nope. Just being cautious." Hal kept his gaze locked on Archie, ignoring the anger he saw on Lem's face.

"All right. We should head out tomorrow. It'll take a day to get there and another to ride back. We'll need a count of the number of cowhands guarding the cattle. My guess is it'll be down from when Tolbert was alive. With Drake dead, the woman won't be watching for us. Should be easy."

"Nothing about any of this has been easy. I don't expect that will change." He shifted toward the men behind him. "Biff, you handle the men and herd until we return."

"Sure thing, Hal." Biff sent a menacing look at Lem, daring him to challenge Hal's order. All the men had been loyal to Drake, not to Archie or Lem. When word of Drake's hanging reached the gang, they'd looked to Hal as their leader. His orders were followed, the same as Drake's.

"We'll go forward with plans to raid the spread north of here tomorrow, then you and I will leave for the Tolbert ranch. Any objection?" Hal narrowed his gaze on Archie, knowing he'd go along with the raid.

"No argument from me." Archie stood rooted in place as Hal and his cronies walked back to the fire, then muttered a string of curses. He couldn't control the unease spreading through him. Hal held no love for either him or Lem. He'd have more reason than not to put both in the ground once he knew where to find the Tolbert cattle. Perhaps Lem was right. He'd have to think on it, make a decision soon. Right now, the odds were neither he nor Lem would be participating in any profit from the stolen cattle.

"Never thought I'd see the day you'd be wearing a deputy's badge, Cash." Dax's chuckle came from years of friendship. "Does this mean you're staying around Splendor for a while?" He poured whiskey and handed glasses to Cash, Beau, and Luke, then held his own glass in the air. "To the newest residents of Splendor."

"You want to tell us why you decided to work for Gabe? Seems bounty hunting is a lot more lucrative." Luke settled into a worn leather chair, stretching out his legs, crossing them at the ankles.

Cash gazed out the window toward the barn and the men working to break a horse in the nearby corral. He took a sip of the whiskey, letting it slip down his throat, creating a soothing warmth.

"More money, if you don't die trying to find your prey. You move from one squalid hole to another, chasing desperate men who have no conscience and don't care how they make their money. It's rare you go to bed without a gun resting real close, and you always fall to sleep with your pants still fastened. Looking over your shoulder becomes a way of life, and the ability to trust diminishes with each hunt." He turned toward the others, catching the look Beau shot him. "Since the war, I've put away enough to buy a small place. Now I can look for a new career, a job where I can stay in bed all night with a pretty woman and not worry about someone breaking down the door to kill me in my sleep."

Luke drew his legs up and rested his arms on his knees, rolling his glass between his palms. "You always have a place here, Cash. You, too, Beau."

Cash lowered himself into a chair next to Luke and tilted his glass toward him. "Thanks, and we might take you up on it. For now, we want to get the latest threat out of the way, then we'll decide."

"Is that the reason you rode out here? To tell us we have more problems heading our way?" Dax leaned a hip against the edge of his desk, crossing his arms.

"The biggest reason, yes. Gabe got a telegram from Sheriff Sterling. The rustling has started up again around Big Pine. It may be a couple isolated raids, but it's best to be prepared."

"Any connection to Drake's gang?" Luke asked.

"Don't know."

"What's your gut tell you?" Dax believed Cash had already formed an opinion.

Cash looked at the others. Every instinct he had told him the remnants of the gang had returned to finish what they started. "Yes. I think it's a good bet."

"How do you think Miss Tolbert will take the news?" Beau asked as the Tolbert ranch house came into view. Dax and Luke volunteered to send a man to the Frey ranch to warn the brothers, letting Cash and Beau ride on to speak with Abby.

"As well as anyone. She's had a lot to deal with, and we both know she never had any intention of going back to the ranch—at least not so soon. Rustling is one of the hardships ranchers face. Abby won't like it, but she has no choice."

Sliding off their horses, they took several steps toward the door when it flew open and Dirk Masters came out. He stopped short at the sight of them.

"Cash, Beau, what brings you out here?"

"We need to speak with Miss Tolbert—"

"I'm here. Please, come in." Abby stood in the doorway, motioning them inside.

"You'll need to hear this, too," Beau said to Dirk as he followed Cash past Abby.

"Sit down. Can I get you both coffee?"

"No, thank you. This shouldn't take long." Cash took a seat and explained what they knew of the rustling in Big Pine.

Abby listened without interrupting, as Dirk paced back and forth in front of the window.

"We thought you'd want to know, maybe have more men guard the herd."

Abby lifted her hands from her lap and folded them on top of the desk. "I thought, *hoped*, the rustling would stop with Drake's death."

"Rustling never stops. It's the way of it out here." Dirk glanced at Cash. "Any raids near Splendor?"

"None yet. Maybe there won't be."

Abby took a closer look at the reflection coming from inside Cash's jacket. "Is that a star on your shirt?"

Cash's hand went to his shirt and felt the metal. He'd already forgotten he wore it. "Yes, ma'am. Beau and I signed on to help Gabe for a while. One man can't keep up with how fast the town is growing. Mr. Clausen and the town leaders approved us right off."

"Gabe didn't mention to them he'd already sworn us in," Beau joked.

Abby offered a vague smile that didn't quite reach her eyes. "I'm sure they would. We've needed more help for a while and I'm relieved you're the ones helping the sheriff."

"You'll let us know if you get any further word from Sterling?" Dirk asked.

"We will. The Pelletiers know and they're sending a man out to warn the Freys. It may be they'll never make it this far west." Cash rested his hands on the arms of the chair and pushed up.

"Excuse me if I don't share your optimism." Abby stood and walked around the desk, clasping her hands in front of her.

"Thank you for riding out. We'll take your warning seriously and be prepared."

She waited until they left, then motioned for Dirk to follow her back inside.

"Double the men with the herd on the eastern border. If they hit us at all, that's where it'll be."

"Yes, ma'am. I'll send Mal with additional men." He turned, then looked back over his shoulder. "If they come here, we'll be ready for them. There won't be any more tragedies at this ranch as long as I'm alive to stop it."

Abby blinked several times as he disappeared outside, swiping at tears as frustration and anger flowed through her. She felt scared and cornered, and didn't want to deal with any of this. In her mind, she shouldn't have to.

What she did want was no longer in her grasp, and no matter how she wished it different, she truly was alone.

Chapter Twenty-Four

"She'll be all right. Dirk will keep watch on her and take care of any threats," Gabe said to Cash and Beau, glancing up as Noah stopped in the doorway. He nodded at the three men.

"What threats and to who?" He grabbed a chair, turning it around and straddling it, resting his arms on the back.

"Abby."

Noah jerked upright. "Why the hell didn't you tell me?" He stared at Gabe, his mouth set in a scowl.

"Settle down. She's fine." Gabe explained about the telegram from Sheriff Sterling and why Cash and Beau had ridden out to the Tolbert ranch. "Dirk knows about the raids. He'll make certain she's protected."

Noah stood, pacing around the small office, mumbling to himself.

"You care to share what's got you so upset?" Gabe asked.

Noah stopped, resting his fisted hands on his hips. "Dirk hasn't been on the ranch long and doesn't know all the places rustlers could hide, waiting for the right opportunity. Hell, half the men who work for Abby are new, hired on in the last few months. Tolbert never could keep help around for long." He scrubbed a hand over his stubbled face, a knot growing in his stomach. "Abby's smart, but she's not a rancher."

"You can ride out there anytime you want, talk with her, make sure she's all right." Gabe clasped his hands behind his head and leaned back in his chair.

"You know I can't do that," Noah ground out before muttering a curse.

"Sure you can. Saddle Tempest and ride." Gabe knew he baited Noah, but he didn't care. He'd grown tired of watching him sulk around, acting as if his decision to stop seeing Abby made sense. "For the love of God, Noah. Abby can't help the fact she inherited everything. What do you want her to do? Give it all away, bury it, burn it?"

"Damn it. You know that's not what I want." Noah's face reddened at the exchange. It had been years since he and Gabe engaged in such a heated discussion.

"Then what? You're miserable, and according to Dirk, so is Abby. And it's not as if the woman earned the money or knows how to make it grow. You ever think about that?"

Noah glared at him, shaking his head in confusion. "What are you talking about?"

"Do you think that lawyer from Big Pine is the best person to help her make business decisions, invest her money?" Gabe asked.

"You know I don't."

"Then who else will she turn to? Clausen is all right for holding what the ranch earns, but not for growing it."

"Yeah?"

"Lord, you're thick." Gabe pushed away from his desk and stood. "Noah, you're one of the smartest businessmen I know. You can take a dollar and make it ten by taking it in one door and sending it out another. That's what you bring to a marriage with Abby. You're not taking a dime from her. You're growing a future." He walked around the desk and slapped Noah on the back. "You better start thinking straight about what you have to offer Abby, my friend, because it's a hell of a lot more than you realize."

Cash and Beau stayed silent, listening to the exchange, their heads shifting back and forth between the two, their expressions changing as the conversation shifted.

"I didn't ask for your opinion." Noah began to say something more before he thought better of it and clamped his mouth shut.

"Since when did I ever wait for you to ask?"

"Hell," Noah mumbled, shaking his head. "I've got to get out of here, get some fresh air. I want to know the moment you hear anything new from Sterling." He didn't wait for Gabe to respond before jerking the door open and storming outside.

No one spoke for several moments after he left, although Cash and Beau exchanged confused glances. Gabe broke the silence when he stood and slammed his hat on his head.

"Stubborn fool," he grumbled, strapping his gun belt around his waist.

"I'm guessing he made the decision to stop courting Abby." Cash grabbed his own hat and stood as Beau did the same.

"He did."

"So, if I understand this, Abigail Tolbert is available to court, right?" Beau asked, his brows flickering up and down.

"Damn it, Beau. This isn't funny," Cash growled.

Beau held out his hands, palms out. "Not saying it is. Just asking a question."

"Make sure you don't ask that question of the wrong man." Gabe tipped his hat lower and stepped off the boardwalk into the crowded street, then called over his shoulder. "I don't want to handle a murder on top of everything else."

Noah's heart had slammed into his chest the moment Gabe mentioned Abby might be in danger, and it hadn't slowed down since. If anything, the clawing sensation and icy knob in his stomach worsened, as did the throbbing in his head.

He stoked the forge and picked up a tool from the repair box. Hammering heated metal, focusing on the job, always helped him think through difficult situations—or helped him push them from his mind. Right now, he didn't know what he preferred. He raised the hammer three times, letting it fall with a heavy thud. If he worked hard enough, he might be able to drive the worry from his mind.

Gabe told him they had to wait, see if the rustling in Big Pine continued, and if so, where. If they hit ranches to the east, they'd be moving away from Splendor. To the west would be a signal the gang moved closer. For now, Noah had to wait, the same as everyone else.

The more important question pumping through his system had to do with Gabe's remarks about Abby's wealth. Gabe had an uncanny ability of explaining troubles in such a way that even an idiot could see the logic. After listening to his words, Noah did consider himself a fool. How could he have been so blind as not to see what he had to offer Abby?

Sure, she had wealth, but no idea what to do with it without direction from Eugene Payson or Horace Clausen. Good intentions meant nothing when your advice didn't impact someone in a personal way. It hit him like a slap in the face. Abby had almost begged him not to turn his back on her. She needed him, said she couldn't do it herself. It took Gabe to help him understand what she meant. He threw the tool in his hand aside, cursing as he watched it skitter across the dirt.

"Hello, Mr. Brandt."

Noah spun around. He hadn't heard anyone approach, his mind too focused on Abby and how to fix the damage he'd created.

"Miss Murton. What may I do for you?" He worked to keep the frown from his face.

"I hope it's all right, but you said I should come to you if Mr. Clausen approved the use of the abandoned house as my residence." Her voice shook at first, calming the more she spoke.

"And did he?"

"Yes, he did." Her face lit in a bright smile, helping to pull Noah from his dark mood. "And the town is providing money to help fix it up."

"That's good news. Now I need to gather the men. Give me a couple days, find out who's available. With enough help, we may be able to get most of the work done over two, maybe three days."

"Papa taught me how to use a hammer and whitewash boards. I'll do whatever you tell me."

"Let's not worry about that today. I know the men will need plenty of food and lots of water. I'm certain you can work something out with Suzanne to help with the food."

"That's a wonderful idea. I'll speak with her right away." Sarah placed a hand on his arm and looked up at him "Thank you so much, Mr. Brandt." She dropped her hand and stepped back. "I'll be ready whenever you have the men."

He nodded, pleased with her delight in the small amount of help he and a few other men could contribute to her new home. For a few minutes, she'd taken his mind off his mistakes with Abby and the possible danger. Enough time for him to calm down and realize he had to make some decisions, fast.

"So this is the Tolbert ranch?" Hal sat forward in his saddle, looking down at the grassy valley below dotted with cattle and several riders.

"A small part. It's the largest ranch in the area. The Pelletiers to the west are the next largest." Archie had ridden every acre of Tolbert's land when he worked for the man. "Below us is where the largest herd is kept, the ones they'll plan to drive to market. The timing is good. They'll be moving them out within a few weeks."

"We'll need to get closer, get a count on the number of men guarding the cattle." Hal reined his horse around, intending to head down a narrow path leading into the valley.

"Not yet. We wait until evening." Archie sat steady, watching as cowhands circled around the herd, cutting out a few head and moving them into a smaller group. "It's easy to spot riders coming down the trails in daylight."

"Not while they're working the cattle. They'll never see us coming."

"Don't underestimate them. Tolbert hired men good with guns and cattle." Archie slid off his horse. "Might as well settle in. There's nothing more to do until the sun sets."

Waiting did nothing for Hal's sour mood. He'd thought they'd ride the perimeter of the pasture, count the men, and head back to their camp. The raid the day before got them thirty head. By the looks of it, they'd take at least five times as many from Tolbert's daughter. When this ended, they'd have enough to drive the herd south, sell them, then lose themselves in the mountains of Colorado. Pushing his hat over his eyes, he fell into a heavy sleep, waking when Archie jostled him a few hours later.

"Time to move out."

The moon provided enough light to see as they made their way down the twisting trail. The wind blew in their favor, reducing the risk of the cattle picking up their scent and alerting the ranch hands. They moved at a slow pace, searching for the best vantage point to get a good count of men and cattle. Archie slowed up as they reached the bottom of the hill, reining his horse into a small clearing surrounded by thick shrubs.

"You see those men?" He pointed to their left where several men sat around a fire, their bedrolls tossed on the ground. "Now over there." Archie indicated a group to their right, hidden in the shadows, across the pasture. No fire burned and their silhouettes were barely discernible within the cover of the trees. "Tolbert always insisted on at least one group of men posted away from the fire. These men are the ones we must locate."

"Don't see why we need to look further. You've already spotted them."

Archie shook his head at Hal's inability to grasp the meaning. "There may be a third group. If so, they'd be between the first two, somewhere over there." He lifted his arm straight in front of him, to a location across the pasture.

Hal leaned forward in the saddle, squinting in the direction Archie pointed. "I don't see anyone."

"It may be they don't feel the need to be as cautious with Drake dead. I'm not willing to take the chance. We'll wait here, make certain there aren't other men posted as lookouts."

"All right, but if we don't see anything in the next hour, we return to our camp. It's time we finish this and head out of the territory." Hal reined his horse back among the trees. He'd wait, as Archie suggested, but not for long.

"Get Dax. And be quick." Rachel gripped her hands tight around her protruding belly, the pain so intense, she thought she'd collapse.

"Not until I get you in a bed." Ginny wrapped an arm around her sister-in-law and moved toward the downstairs guest room. Kicking open the door, she helped Rachel lay down, putting pillows behind her back. "Do you want water or anything?"

"No...just get Dax," she ground out as another intense pain coursed through her.

"I'll be right back." Ginny dashed out to find him.

As Rachel's uncle predicted, the baby had decided to come early. She'd scoffed at his declaration a week ago and now felt foolish for doubting him. Over his years as a doctor, he'd delivered over a hundred babies, many under desperate situations and in less than sanitary conditions.

"Rachel?" Dax slammed the door open and rushed to the bed, stroking a hand over her damp forehead. "Is the baby—"

"Yes, the baby's coming. Have you sent for Uncle Charles?" Her breath came in gasps as she tried to control her reaction to the contractions.

"Bull's already on his way." He smoothed hair from her face as his worried gaze traveled to Luke, who stood beside Ginny near the door. Dax and Luke had discussed his fears of childbirth in such an isolated location many times, usually while sipping whiskey after supper. Each time, Luke assured him Rachel would be fine and they'd summon Doc Worthington at the first signs of labor.

"Dax, look at me." Rachel gripped his hand, pulling him down, her eyes searching his. "I'll be fine. Our baby will be fine." She tried to smile, only to be drawn into the depths of another contraction. Her hand tightened on his until she feared the pressure would break his fingers.

"Water's heating, Dax. I'll grab towels and be right back." Ginny took off toward the kitchen, Luke on her heels.

"Is she all right?" He knew his wife had been through this before, helping her mother when Ginny's sister, Mary, had been born.

"Yes. From what I've seen, this is normal. The contractions could go on for hours with the pain coming in intervals, then receding before starting again. She had a few small pains, then her water broke. I fetched you and Dax right away." She grabbed towels from a drawer and nodded toward a simmering pot. "Please bring the water."

Luke didn't hesitate, hefting the large pot and following Ginny to the bedroom. He took a breath, not wanting anyone, especially Dax, to know Rachel's birth pains scared him more than any of the outlaws he'd faced as a Pinkerton agent.

A scream jerked him to a stop, causing warm water to slop onto the floor and over his boots. He froze, watching Dax as he cradled Rachel, trying to comfort her until the contraction diminished. Luke knew his inability to make the pain stop would drive his brother crazy. Nothing hurt more than watching the suffering of those you loved.

"Luke, over here." Ginny pointed to the marble-topped chest of drawers. "Luke," she hissed once more when he failed to move.

"Yeah...I'm coming." He almost stumbled toward Ginny, his eyes riveted on Dax and Rachel, both drenched in sweat.

"How's she doing?"

All eyes turned toward the door as Rachel's uncle, Doc Worthington, rushed in with his bag. He shrugged out of his jacket, tossed it on a nearby chair, and walked to the edge of the bed, looking down at his niece.

"How are you, my dear?"

She glared at him as if he had two heads. "How can you ask me that?" Her voice came out as a growl, surprising everyone in the room.

"Everyone out, except Ginny."

"But Charles—"

"No argument, Dax. I need to focus on Rachel, not a squeamish husband."

"But—"

Doc let out a breath, glancing at Luke. "Please take your brother outside. He needs fresh air before we're wasting time picking him up off the ground."

Luke grabbed Dax's arm, getting shoved aside for his effort. Luke followed him, grabbing glasses and a bottle of whiskey as he passed the study.

Dax stood at the porch rail, his hands gripping the top, his head hanging down. Luke watched him for a moment before pouring them each a shot, handing Dax one before he set the bottle aside.

"Ginny told me Rachel is doing fine. Doc didn't seem concerned and he's delivered a lot of babies." He clasped Dax's shoulder. "All we can do is wait."

Dax nodded, then took a sip from the glass, letting the liquid roll around in his mouth before swallowing. He turned, settling his hip against the porch rail.

"I can't recall the number of battles I saw or bodies we buried during the war. Fear became a way of life, as did death. As an officer, I felt a sense of control, no matter how delusional that sounds." He nodded toward the house. "Nothing during the war compares to how I feel now." He downed the rest of his drink and grabbed the bottle, pouring another round.

"If it's any consolation, you're not the only one thinking of Rachel and hoping for the best." He looked toward the bunkhouse where Bull, Travis, and Rude milled about, glancing toward the house every couple minutes. The contractions had begun late. Dax had no idea why they'd stayed up, but none of them were tired. He looked at the moon, guessing it must be after midnight.

Dax raised a hand and waved them over. "You'd better grab more glasses and another bottle."

"Tell me exactly what you saw." Dirk sat at the campfire, cradling a hot cup of coffee between his hands to ward off the early morning chill.

"I did as you asked, posted men here and in three other spots." Mal scratched in the dirt with a stick, drawing where the men were placed. "Nothing happened until close to midnight, then one of our men spotted two riders about here." He pointed to a location to the southeast of where they sat. "He got close enough to recognize Archie Swaggert, one of Drake's men."

"One of the men who worked here, right?" Dirk took a sip of coffee, staring at the ground.

"Tolbert hired me after they left, but several of the men said he used to work at the ranch with Drake and Lem Pruett."

"The Idaho sheriff said none of the men arrested with the herd was Swaggert or Pruett." Dirk scrubbed a hand down his face as he thought of the possibilities. "Seems those two, and whoever else rides with them, have decided to take another try at the Tolbert cattle. Did the men see which way they went when they rode out?"

"Followed them up the hill and east. Our men swear the two never saw them."

"Good. We'll be ready for them when they arrive. First, we'll combine the two smaller herds on the western border near the Pelletier land. A few men will stay with that herd while the rest guard the cattle here. I'll leave men to guard Miss Tolbert."

"Do you think they'll go after her?" Mal didn't want anyone threatening her.

"No. I think they're after the cattle, but I don't want to take any chances."

"We can combine the herds today and be back here before sunset, boss. Who do you want with Miss Tolbert?"

"Pick two men who've been at the ranch the longest, known her a while, and will do what's needed to protect her. You and I should be here." Dirk glanced at the men riding out to the herd and those still finishing breakfast.

"How long do you think before they try for the cattle?" The same as everyone else, Mal wanted to stop the last of Drake's men.

"I don't know. Could be as soon as tomorrow, depending on where they're holed up and if they bring the rest of the stolen cattle with them."

"That'd be darn stupid if you ask me." Mal tossed the rest of his coffee on the ground and stood.

Dirk grinned. "No one ever said these rustlers were smart."

Chapter Twenty-Five

It took both Luke and Bull to hold Dax back during the screams. They'd come and gone throughout the early morning hours until he couldn't take any more and decided to storm into the house.

"Not until Doc says it's all right for you to be with her." Luke gripped his arm tighter while Bull blocked the doorway.

"Sit down, boss. She's still screaming, which means she and the baby are fine. Doc's got Ginny and Lydia in there with him. Relax. The baby will come when he's ready and not before." Bull didn't budge, waiting for Dax to give up and sit down.

Dax heaved a deep breath, clasped his hands behind his head, and turned toward the barn, walking until he came to a stop next to the porch railing. "Never again."

"What'd you say?" Luke asked.

"When this is over, I'm never going through this again." He dropped his arms to his sides, then crossed them over his chest right before a loud wail came from inside the house. He spun around, but didn't step forward, his face a mixture of elation and panic. A moment later, Doc Worthington walked out looking as beat as Dax felt.

"Is she...? Is Rachel...?"

"She and the baby are fine, Dax, and she's asking for you."

He didn't wait another moment before rushing inside and into the bedroom, stopping on the threshold, his breath catching in his throat. Rachel rested against a stack of pillows, a blanketed bundle in her arms, a smile on her face as radiant as he'd ever seen.

"Come over here and meet your son." Her voice sounded raw, yet Dax saw joy in her face.

He swallowed, taking a few hesitant steps forward before looking down at a small red face and squinty eyes. Rachel pulled the blanket away to reveal two tiny fisted hands.

"What do you think?"

"I think you're incredible," he whispered, his eyes riveted on her face.

"No, I mean about your son, Patrick," she laughed.

"Patrick..." he breathed out. They'd decided if they had a boy, he'd be named after the man who bequeathed them Redemption's Edge—Dax and Luke's fellow Texas Ranger, Pat Hanes.

"Here. You should hold him."

Dax lifted his arms, palms out, and took a step back. "Oh, no..."

"Oh, yes. He's a tiny baby and doesn't weigh much. You'll be fine." She held the bundle out to him, her eyes bright.

Dax steeled himself and bent forward, reaching out for Patrick and letting Rachel slip him into his arms. He cradled him to his chest, staring at his own flesh and blood, and something inside shifted. Raising his head, he looked at Rachel, his son's mother, and knew he had everything he ever wanted right in this room.

"I can't tell you how much this means to me, Mr. Brandt. All these men taking their time to fix up the house." Sarah handed him a plate of chicken and biscuits, glancing over her shoulder at the house.

"Thank you, Miss Murton. Each man said yes right away. They're here because they want to make you feel welcome."

"Well, I do feel welcome. My cousins told me I'd love it here. I already do."

Taking the last bite of his meal, Noah noticed a small cloud of dust rising from the north edge of town, preceded by three riders. "Looks as if you might meet a few more of your neighbors."

"Morning, Noah. Doc Worthington mentioned you might need help fixing up that abandoned house for the new teacher." Bull reined up next to him and dismounted, followed by Travis and Tat, another longtime Pelletier ranch hand. "We decided to see if that was right and share some news."

"He'd be right about needing the help." Noah made the introductions and told the three what still needed to be finished. "What's the other news?"

"Rachel had the baby. A boy. They named him Patrick after Pat Hanes." Bull's smile spread across his face.

Noah's smile matched Bull's. "How are they doing?"

"She and the baby are fine. Dax may need some time to recover, though." Bull laughed, then scanned the work on the house. "Seems you've made a lot of progress."

"It's moving along. With your help, we might be able to finish today." Noah nodded toward a wooden box a few feet away. "You can grab whatever tools you need from the box over there. I'm taking the wagon to pick up some more lumber."

"I'll go with you." Bull climbed onto the wagon next to Noah for the short trip to the other end of town. As the town grew, the original one room supply shop had tripled in size over the last year. Residents no longer had to make the journey to Big Pine and back for windows, stoves, and other materials. "I hear Miss Murton is cousins with Ty, Gil, and Mark."

"That's right. They contacted her about the opening for a teacher. Seems like a real nice lady. Tell me about the baby."

Bull's face lit up at the mention of the new Pelletier. "He's a tiny thing, that's for certain. Red, crinkly face and hands. Dax brought him out of the bedroom for a couple minutes."

"It's fitting they named him after Pat." Noah pulled the wagon to a stop and set the brake.

"I agree. I've met few men as good as him." Bull and a few others worked for Pat, then stayed on when Dax and Luke acquired the ranch. It had been a good decision for all of them.

They had just finished loading the wagon and prepared to climb aboard when Gabe strode up, holding a telegram.

"Got word from Sterling. There's been another raid at a ranch near Big Pine."

"When?" Noah asked.

"Three days ago. He's been out with a posse, trying to find the rustlers."

"Any luck?" Noah asked, already tensing at the knowledge the rustlers hadn't left the area.

"Not according to this." He held up the telegram. "I plan to ride out to the Tolbert place and let them know what I've learned. Bull, can you go get word to Dax and Luke? You folks need to be prepared."

Bull nodded, then looked at Noah. "I'll help Travis and Tat for a bit, then ride out." Bull climbed up on the wagon.

"I'm going with you to Tolbert's. I'll unload these supplies at Miss Murton's house, then get Tempest."

"No need, Noah. Cash is riding out with me and Beau's staying in town."

"I'm going—with you or on my own," Noah growled, jumping up next to Bull and slapping the reins.

"Heard you aren't courting Abigail any longer."

Noah tossed a disgusted look at Bull. "Well, you heard wrong."

Bull nodded. "That's good news."

Noah cursed under his breath, pulled the wagon to a stop, and turned toward Bull. "Now I need to convince Abby to give me another chance."

Bull slapped him on the back, snorting out a laugh. "Hell, Noah, the entire town knows how you feel about her, and her feelings for you. That woman wouldn't care how many mistakes you make. She'd still marry you." He glanced at Tat and Travis. "I'd better help the boys, then get back to the ranch. You tell Miss Abigail hello for me."

Noah watched him grab a hammer and some boards from the back of the wagon before joining Travis. He looked over his shoulder, spotting Gabe ride Blackheart out of the livery. He needed to join him.

"Wait for me." Noah dashed past him, saddling Tempest in record time.

Gabe, Cash, and Noah road at a brisk pace, cutting the normal travel time almost in half in their rush to alert Abigail and Dirk. Noah didn't slow much when they reached the ranch house, dismounting and running up the steps to pound on the front door.

"Abby? Abby, are you in there?" When he got no answer, he pounded again until the door flew open.

"What in the world are you doing, Noah Brandt?" Fanny Dobbins stood on the other side, her hands resting on her ample hips.

He ripped off his hat and bowed a little. "Sorry, Miss Fanny, but I need to speak with Abby or Dirk. It's urgent."

"Well, Miss Abigail rode out at dawn with one of the men. She told me she may not be back for a few days."

"And Dirk?"

"He's been gone a few days already. I think she may be riding out to meet him and the other men." She watched as his face become tense, his hands fisting around the brim of his hat.

"Do you have any idea where?"

She rubbed her forehead. "Well, let me think. Dirk mentioned the herd on the eastern border. They might be there, but I don't know for sure."

Noah slammed his hat back on his head and turned toward Gabe and Cash. "We need to ride to the pasture on the far eastern border."

"Do you know how to get there?" Cash asked.

"I do."

He took them on a straight path north, then east, his fear growing with each mile. It wouldn't be uncommon for Abby to join the men during the workday. After all, as the ranch owner, she had a lot to learn and needed to gain the respect of her cowhands—not as a woman, but as their boss.

The sun touched the tops of the mountains behind them as they rode around a large stand of pine and into a clearing devoid of cattle or ranch hands. Noah took off his hat and swiped a sleeve across his forehead.

"Where to now?" Gabe asked, pulling out his canteen, taking a drink, then passing it to Cash, then Noah.

"If Fanny is right, they'll be another mile or two ahead." Noah handed the canteen back to Gabe and settled his hat on his head. "If not, then we keep riding until we find the herd."

They didn't need to change direction. Riding through the other side of the clearing, they spotted cattle a mile away in a vast pasture, men circling on horseback. The sounds of bawling and bellowing increased the closer they rode. Two riders broke from the circle and rode toward them. Noah squinted, recognizing Dirk, but not the rider with him.

Wearing slacks, a hat pulled low on his head, the other man appeared more slender and without the height of most cowhands. As they got closer, Noah squinted, then cursed as he spotted hair flying behind the second rider. Abby. He should have known. She rode the same horse the day he'd taken Hasty to her ranch.

"What brings all of you out here?" Dirk asked as he and Abby stopped, her eyes catching Noah's for a brief moment before shifting away.

"I received a message from Sheriff Sterling in Big Pine about more rustling over there." Gabe tipped his hat to Abby, ignoring the fiery glare Noah shot him.

"Guess I should've sent word to you. We spotted Archie Swaggert and another man around the herd. Most of our men are here, circling the cattle and rotating watch at night. If the gang comes, we'll be ready."

Noah nodded toward Abby. "And her?"

She shifted in the saddle as her eyes came up to fix on Noah's, anger sparking. "I would think that would be obvious, Mr. Brandt. I'm here because I own the ranch."

He moved Tempest forward until he sat within a foot of her, his gaze boring into hers. "Go home, Abby. Let your men handle this."

"As long as the cattle are in danger from rustlers, I'm staying." Her intense gaze never broke from his.

"You aren't prepared to deal with rustlers. You don't even know how to shoot a gun." Noah's voice hardened at her resistance.

Abby glared back at him. "Of course I do. *You* taught me."

"One lesson isn't enough for what may await us. Go back to the house, Abby. You shouldn't be here." Noah's voice rose, as did his annoyance at her refusal to listen. He wanted to protect her and keep her safe. He wanted...

They both turned at the sound of muffled laughter behind them. Cash and Dirk shifted, looking anywhere except at Noah and Abby as Gabe cleared his throat.

"Why don't Cash and I follow Dirk to the herd? You two join us when you're ready."

"I'm ready now." Abby began to turn Joker around when Noah reached out and grabbed her reins.

"Hold up a minute, Abby. We need to talk."

"There's nothing more to say. I'm staying and nothing you can say will change my mind."

Noah's jaw tightened, but he dropped the reins. She wasted no time catching up with the others, leaving him to work out his frustration on his own.

Abby hadn't expected to see Noah when she and Dirk took off to check the southern border. Her first reaction felt as if all the air had been sucked from her lungs, followed by a tight pressure in her chest and an ache in the area of her heart. The emotions spread over her in quick succession as her mind accepted the inevitable—she'd have to find a way to be cordial and gracious to the man who'd broken her heart.

She hadn't expected him to practically order her back to the house. Ignoring him wouldn't have done any good, but arguing hadn't achieved a solution either. He'd told her he didn't want her or the life she'd been thrown into against her wishes. Somehow, he still felt he had a right to order her around, bend her to his will. She didn't understand why he even cared.

"Miss Tolbert, do you have a minute to talk?"

She looked up to see Dirk standing over her. When they returned to camp, she'd secured Joker and found a spot near the fire. A few minutes alone would clear her head and help her deal with Noah being so close.

"Of course. Sit down."

Dirk lowered to his haunches, resting his arms on his thighs. "Don't jump down my throat, but I agree with Noah." He held up his hand when she started to interrupt. "Hear me out. You don't need to be here. In fact, you *shouldn't* be here. If anything happens to you, all the men, the ones who depend on you for their food and a place to sleep, will be tossed out on their own. The ranch will flounder until the estate is reviewed, which could take months. I understand you want to support the men as the owner of the ranch, but this isn't the way."

Her shoulders slumped as he explained his reasons for not wanting her to stay. She hated that he made so much sense. Most of all, she hated admitting she'd made a mistake riding out to the camp. She remembered other times when her father left to confront suspected rustlers. Each time, she huddled in her bed, afraid he'd never return. He finally hadn't, leaving the responsibilities of the ranch to her. Dirk made sense. She had no one to take over if any harm came to her. There truly was no choice. She never considered herself stupid and had no intention of letting others believe it of her.

"You think I should leave?"

"Yes, but not tonight. Tomorrow morning, I'll send men back with you."

She nodded, her face showing none of the emotions she felt.

"All right. I'll let the men know." He stood, watching as Noah, Gabe, and Cash walked toward them. "I'll tell them your decision."

"I'd like to tell Noah." She shot a glance at him. "And thank you, Dirk." He nodded before joining Gabe and Cash.

Noah approached the fire at a slow pace, taking a seat near her. His eyes studied her, not liking the slump of her shoulders or sullen expression. He knew he'd been out of line. She owned the ranch and could make decisions regarding her own safety. Unfortunately, his concern for her wouldn't let him ignore the danger.

"Don't say it, Noah." She didn't look at him, keeping her eyes focused on the flames before her.

His brows drew together in confusion. "Don't say what?"

She let out a deep sigh. "Dirk agrees with you. No doubt Gabe and Cash feel the same. I've decided to go back to the house tomorrow and I don't want to hear another word from you about it."

He kept his expression neutral as relief washed over him. The thought of Abby getting hurt or killed during a raid caused a chill to knot his insides. He didn't know how he'd live if anything happened to her.

"I'll ride back with you."

"No, thank you, Noah. Dirk will send men with me."

"All right, if that's what you want." He didn't leave. There remained so much to say and explain, but now wasn't the time to talk it through. They had to focus on the rustlers and saving the cattle. Once they eliminated the danger, he'd get her alone and do whatever it took to earn back her love.

Chapter Twenty-Six

Hours passed and she still lay in her makeshift bed, listening to the occasional sounds of cattle. Dirk positioned men in a circle around the pasture. Most would be difficult to detect, which was what he planned. Gabe, Cash, and Noah stayed in the main camp, at least until the rustlers arrived, which they all believed would happen.

Noah made no further attempt to talk or come near her. He'd found a spot yards away to sit and watch, his Spencer repeating rifle by his side. He'd once told her he used a Sharps rifle while in the army, which now hung on a wall in his cabin, a reminder of what he'd done to help preserve the Union. She knew years as a sharpshooter had taught him patience, which he'd need tonight as the vigil continued into the early morning. She watched him as long as she could until her eyes drifted shut, pulling her into a fitful sleep.

Shouting, loud cracks of gunfire, and bellowing cattle jerked her awake. She sat up, trying to get her bearings, then threw off her covers and stood. Before she had a chance to think, her body slammed into the ground, crushed beneath another body.

"Stay down, Abby." Noah's stern command and hard form kept her immobile. He lifted his weight, looking around, then grabbed her arm. "Come on." He pulled her behind a group of low shrubs. At least she'd be hidden, even if they wouldn't protect her from flying bullets. "Do not leave this spot." He pulled a gun from its holster, handing it and extra bullets to her. "Use this like we practiced. Do not hesitate to shoot. Do you understand?"

She nodded, her dazed face searching his. The harsh determination in his eyes strengthened her as she took the gun from his hand.

"Promise me you won't move from this spot, no matter what you hear or see."

"All right. I promise," she breathed out as the sound of gunfire came closer.

He grasped her chin, lifting her face to his, and lowered his mouth. The kiss lasted mere seconds before he dropped his hand and was gone. Moments later, she saw him ride out toward the scattering cattle.

Abby huddled, motionless, gripping the gun in both hands, her eyes searching the dark. No one remained in the main camp.

Noah hadn't mentioned the rustlers, but she knew they'd arrived as Dirk predicted. There could be no other explanation for the gunfire and stampeding cattle. She leaned back, resting the pistol in her lap, and took a deep breath, praying Noah and the others would return unharmed.

The sounds receded the longer she sat. Abby glanced around, deciding whether to stay put, as she promised Noah, or dash toward her horse. Hearing nothing except the distant shouts of men and gunfire, she picked up the gun, shoved it in the front of her pants, and slipped the extra bullets into a pocket, pulling her lightweight jacket around her. Taking a calming breath, she slid forward onto her knees, preparing to stand, when someone gripped her hair, hauling her to a standing position and turning her around. She gasped, recognizing Archie Swaggert.

"Well, guess we hit the jackpot, Lem."

She struggled and tried to pull away, the pain increasing as Archie's grip tightened.

"You're not going anywhere, girlie," he smirked, holding his gun slack at his side.

"Let me go," she snarled, kicking his legs and writhing in his grasp.

He yelped as her boot connected with a knee, then threw her to the ground, pointing

his gun at her head. "You best shut up."
Archie bent forward, rubbing his injured
knee and turning to Lem. "Get some rope."

"What do you plan to do with her?"

"She's our insurance for getting out of the
territory. As long as she's with us, no one will
try anything for fear we'll shoot her."

Lem's jaw hardened, knowing they had
little choice.

Tolbert's men had been waiting when
they came for the cattle. They'd been
surrounded within moments of reaching the
herd, warned to drop their guns and
dismount. Hal and the others ignored the
warning, drawing their guns and firing into
the dark. Most hadn't made it, taking bullets
when they refused to surrender.

Lem and Archie took advantage of the
chaos to ride out, keeping to the perimeter of
the pasture until they saw the faint glow of
the fire where they'd thought Tolbert's men
had camped. Now they knew it was a ruse to
draw them out.

Lem grabbed a rope, taking little time to
tie her hands and stuff a grimy handkerchief
in her mouth.

"Get her on a horse and tie her hands to
the saddle horn. We need to get as far away
as possible before they know she's gone."

Archie dragged her up, shoving her forward. Within minutes, they were on horseback, riding at a fast pace away from the ranch.

"Four dead and the rest are tied up. Swaggert and Pruett aren't among them." Dirk reined to a stop next to Noah.

"Do we know if they rode in with them?" Noah slid his rifle in its scabbard and shifted in the saddle, searching the nearby hills.

"They did. Must have taken off when they realized they were surrounded."

Noah scanned the pasture, his eyes drawn to the dim glow of the fire from their camp. He needed to get back, make certain Abby remained where he'd left her.

"I'm going to check on Abby."

"You left her in the camp alone?" Dirk hadn't had time to think of her during the mayhem.

Noah's mind shifted to Archie and Lem.

"Shit." Noah didn't wait for Dirk or the others, turning Tempest around and racing toward the camp. "Abby!" He slid to the ground, checking the area where he'd left her. "Abby!" He turned in a circle, searching the camp, seeing nothing until his eyes lit on the empty spot where Joker had been kept with Tempest and Blackheart.

Looking at the ground where she'd hidden, he noticed boot tracks and what appeared to be someone being dragged. He followed the tracks until they disappeared at the spot where Joker had stood. By the time he returned to his horse, Gabe, Cash, Dirk, and Mal were waiting.

"She's gone." He swung up on Tempest. "Tracks indicate someone took her by force. We have to find her."

"Swaggert and Pruett," Gabe spat out as Cash followed the tracks.

He moved from side to side, studying the tracks, kneeling to get a closer look, then standing and looking at the trail ahead. Pacing forward, he came to a stop and turned around.

"They took her this way."

"You lead, Cash." Noah rode up beside him, narrowing his gaze, a plea in his voice. "Find her."

Abby worked the ropes securing her hands to the saddle horn as Archie led Joker. Lem rode behind, glancing over his shoulder every few minutes and listening for the sounds of horses coming from their rear. It didn't take long for Abby to loosen the poorly tied knots and slide her hands free.

She could feel the hard metal of the gun secured within her pants, still surprised neither Archie nor Lem had discovered it. Her hands shook as she tried to reach inside her trousers, knowing any extra movement of her arm or elbow might alert Lem, who rode a few feet away.

They'd slowed their pace over the last hour, riding in a zigzag pattern, even backtracking on occasion to cover their tracks. Still, Abby knew where they were.

"Where are you taking us, Archie?" Lem asked, riding up next to his partner.

"To an old path Drake discovered a year ago. It bypasses Splendor, taking us through the hills several miles to the east of town. It will be almost impossible for them to follow us on the deer trails."

"If they're following at all."

Archie glared at Lem, growing impatient. "They *will* follow. Once they realize Miss

Tolbert is missing, they'll track us, and they won't give up."

"Why don't we leave her? By the time they find her, we'll be over the border and into Wyoming."

"We will, but not until we're away from Splendor, deep in the eastern hills."

Abby listened to the two men. If they left her, there were no guarantees she'd be found. If Noah didn't locate her by nightfall, the odds were great she'd fall victim to one of the predators common in the area. No. Being left behind wasn't an option. She needed to get away before they dumped her in some remote spot, tied and possibly gagged.

The sun peeked above the hills, casting a stream of light on the trail, making their travel easier. Lem continued to ride next to Archie, giving Abby the time she needed to reach into her trousers and pull out the gun. She knew Noah had left it loaded and ready to fire. As long as neither turned around to check on her, she'd be able to conceal it.

Archie and Lem stopped at the top, looking out on the dense forest which spanned for miles in front of them. He pulled Joker forward, allowing Abby a glimpse of what lay ahead.

"In the middle. There," Lem smirked, pointing to the center of the forest. "Then we ride hard and don't look back."

A shiver ran through her at the thought of being abandoned in such isolation. She needed to act soon.

"These tracks are fresh. We can't be more than a few miles behind them." Cash swung into his saddle, looking toward the trail below which led into a forest a couple miles across and a few miles long. He knew it ended near the main road between Splendor and Big Pine. Once the outlaws got there, they could ride in almost any direction.

"Why are they keeping her? If they didn't take her for ransom, then why?" Noah asked, scrubbing a hand down his face.

"Insurance. They believe we'll be less apt to shoot as long as they have her. The problem is that once they reach a certain point, they're as likely to leave Abby as to take her along." Cash reached into a saddlebag, pulling out a pair of field glasses, searching the trail ahead.

"Then we have to catch them before that happens." Noah urged Tempest forward, passing Cash and riding downhill at a brisk pace, unmindful of the loose rocks and dirt.

"Fool's going to get himself killed before he finds her," Cash muttered.

"Not if I can help it." Gabe gave Blackheart his head, letting him go at his own speed down the grade, not letting the distance between him and Noah get too great.

They rounded a bend in the trail to see a straight path ahead. Lem still rode with Archie, paying no attention to Abby, for which she felt a great deal of relief. All she had to do was raise the gun and point it straight ahead.

She lifted the weapon, letting the ropes fall away from her wrists. *You can do this,* she told herself. Taking a deep breath, she pointed the gun at Archie.

"It's time to stop, gentlemen." Sarcasm, unusual for Abby, dripped from her voice. Her hands shook and she prayed neither men noticed the slight movement of the barrel.

Archie and Lem swung their horses around, disbelief crossing their faces before dissolving into anger.

"You didn't check her for a gun?" Lem ground out, a hand moving toward his holster.

"Don't, Mr. Pruett, or I'll shoot."

"You won't shoot anyone, girlie. You don't have the guts." Archie began to move away from Lem.

Abby kept the gun trained on him, ignoring his comment while keeping Lem in her sights. She knew they could continue to divide her attention until she had to shoot one of them. If it came to that, she knew Archie would be her target.

"I believe you misjudge me, Mr. Swaggert. It would give me great relief to put you in the ground, although I'd prefer to see you hang."

Abby could see the beads of sweat form on Archie's forehead, feeling the same on her own. She shifted her gaze to Lem, then back to Archie in time to see him nod at his partner. An instant later, Lem let out a rebel yell and rode forward, pulling his gun from its holster.

She didn't take time to think, pulling the trigger at Archie, then swinging the gun toward Lem.

"Did you hear that?" Noah stopped, a panicked expression on his face as he looked at Gabe. Noah said nothing more, urging Tempest toward the sound of gunfire, the others right behind as one more shot rang out.

Rounding a curve, Noah spotted Abby, sitting rigid atop Joker, the gun he'd given her held straight ahead, her arms not moving. On either side of her lay two men, neither moving. He pulled out his gun, slowing his pace until he stopped behind her.

"Abby?" He kept his voice low and calm, seeing her shoulders and arms begin to shake. When she didn't respond, he moved Tempest a few paces forward, trying not to spook her. He'd seen this in battle when soldiers made their first kill. They were as apt to turn the gun on their fellow soldiers as anyone else until they accepted what they'd done.

"Abby, honey, give me the gun."

Her face turned toward him, a blank stare greeting him, the gun following her movement.

"Give me the gun, Abby. You did real good, but it's over. They can't hurt you anymore." He held out his hand.

"Noah?" she choked out as the gun slid from her grasp.

He grabbed it, then reached for her, hauling her onto his lap. "It's over, sweetheart. I've got you."

She didn't resist, snuggling into the protection of his chest and wrapping her arms around his neck as sobs burst from her throat. He held her tight, stroking her back and whispering into her ear. He could feel her body tremble and closed his eyes, wishing he could do more to help ease her pain. She lifted her face to his, tears staining her face.

"Are they...?"

He glanced at Gabe and Cash kneeling beside the men. Each nodded.

"Yes, they're dead. We don't have to worry about them anymore."

Chapter Twenty-Seven

A week had passed since the shootings. Noah visited several times to check on her, talk about what happened, but never broaching the subject she most wanted to confront.

Twice, he acted as if had had something important to say. Each time, he took her in his arms, kissing her until they were breathless and achy with need. On both occasions, an interruption had Noah pushing her away. Then he'd tip his hat and ride back to town, leaving her confused and wanting.

"I'm heading into town, Miss Tolbert. Anything you need?" Dirk stood in the study doorway, holding out a scrap of paper. "This is what I have on the supply list. Let me know if something is missing."

She read it over, then handed it back. "Not unless Fanny has anything to add."

"I already checked with her. If there's nothing else, I'll be off."

She made a snap decision. "If you'll wait, I'll go with you."

Dirk stood aside, letting her walk past him to grab the cowboy hat she'd taken to wearing since the shooting. Today, she wore a dress, although trousers had become her outfit of choice, saying they made more sense when riding.

"Do you want me to saddle Joker?"

"No, I'll ride in the wagon with you." She picked up her reticule. "I'm ready."

They rode in silence most of the way. Since the shootings, she'd had more time to consider what she wanted and now felt firm in her decision. Today, she planned to have the discussion with Mr. Clausen she'd put off after her father's death. Depending on his answers, she'd be meeting with others, finalizing her plans and securing her future—at least the parts she could control.

The shootings had done more than put two killers in the ground. After her initial reaction to ending the lives of Swaggert and Pruett, she experienced other, more puzzling feelings. A strange sense of strength and freedom greeted her each day. What she'd done had given her an unexpected confidence in her ability to protect herself and make the tough choices required to run a ranching empire. She smiled at the thought.

If time allowed after talking with Mr. Clausen, she hoped to stop by the livery, say hello to Noah and visit Hasty. She'd become quite fond of Joker, although, if she had another chance and Noah agreed, she'd purchase Hasty. She had plans for both horses.

"Where to first, Miss Tolbert?"

Abby glanced at the livery as they passed by, seeing Noah working inside, her heart rate tripling at the sight.

"The bank, Dirk."

"You're sure about this, Abigail? It's a big step, although I believe your father just might approve." Horace Clausen read her instructions once more, surprised at the detail she provided.

"I've had a lot of time to consider my future and I'm comfortable with the decision. Will you be able to help me work out the details?"

"Of course. Have you spoken to anyone else about this?"

"No. I decided to discuss it with you first. Oh, and I haven't mentioned my plans to Ernest Payson, either. This may sound odd, but I didn't want him to try to talk me out of any of it."

Clausen chuckled. "He's a good man, and your father trusted him with all his legal work. I'd still recommend him for the documents you'll need to complete your plans."

"It's a shame we don't have lawyers in Splendor. Perhaps that will change someday." She started to rise, then sat back down. "Oh, and the other?"

"If it's what you want, all you have to do is give me a date."

She nodded. "Thank you, Mr. Clausen."

Abby spoke to Mrs. Phelps before walking out into the bright sunlight. It had rained the night before, settling the dirt and clearing the air of the normal dust that usually circled the streets.

Summoning her courage, she walked toward the livery. As she stepped off the boardwalk, she noticed a woman she didn't recognize walk into the smithy carrying something in her hands. Abby's heart stopped at the implication and she slowed her pace, knowing it was wrong, but hoping to catch something of what was said inside.

"Miss Murton, you didn't have to do this." The sound of Noah's warm, masculine voice wrapped around Abby.

"After all you've done for me, Mr. Brandt, being such a good friend and all, I wanted to do something for you. My mother taught me to bake. I hope you like wild berry pie."

"It's my favorite."

"I wondered if you might be comfortable calling me Sarah."

Abby peeked into the smithy, watching Noah's eyes as he looked at the woman. "All right, if you call me Noah. Perhaps you have time to share the pie with me."

She'd heard enough. No other woman was going to come between her and Noah. She took a breath and swept through the doors, a broad smile on her face.

"Hello, Noah. Dirk brought me into town. How are you?" Abby's voice sounded strong and certain as she stepped toward him, glancing at the pie he held with both hands.

He took a noticeable step away from Sarah. "Uh...hello, Abby. I'm fine. Have you met Sarah Murton, the new school teacher? She's Gil's cousin."

"No, I haven't had the pleasure." She smiled at Sarah. "I'm Abigail Tolbert. It's wonderful to meet you. I've known Gil and his family for years."

Sarah glanced between the two. She'd heard rumors about them, but suspected it to be small town gossip as she'd never seen them together. However, the way they looked at each other changed her thoughts.

"I've heard so much about you, Miss Tolbert. It's a pleasure. Mr. Brandt made certain the house the town is letting me use received much needed repairs. Without him, I'd still be at the boardinghouse with my books and other belongings stored in trunks." She smiled at Noah.

"Oh, so the reason for the pie?"

"Yes. I couldn't think of a better way to thank him."

"It looks wonderful."

"You'll have to tell me what you think of it." She nodded at Noah. "Well, I must be going. Thank you again. What you did meant a lot to me."

"It was no trouble. Let me know if you need anything else." He winced as the words came out, knowing how they must sound to Abby.

He'd spent the last week visiting her as often has he could, trying to figure out the best way to explain his change of mind. Gabe suggested telling her the truth. That he'd been a fool and wanted her back. Noah had tried more than once, but they'd been interrupted each time. He needed to get her alone, away from the ranch and his livery. Someplace they could talk in private.

Abby watched Sarah leave, then turned toward Noah, her eyes sparking. "Let me know if you need anything else," she mimicked, her hands on her hips.

"Now, Abby. You're making too much of this. It's a pie, nothing more." He set it down, taking a step toward her.

She inhaled deeply, letting the air out in a slow stream. "Is she what you want, Noah? Is that what all this has been about the last week? You've met someone else and haven't been able to tell me?" Her heart broke at the thought.

"Of course not. She's a nice lady, nothing more." The only woman he wanted stood in front of him. He reached a hand toward her. "Abby—"

"Never mind. I shouldn't have asked. It's none of my business." She spun away, dashing outside before he could stop her.

"Damn it, Abby. Wait." He followed her to the door, watching as she ran across the street and disappeared into the boardinghouse. He muttered a string of curses, knowing he had to fix this with her soon before he lost her for good.

"Here. I've always found a piece of pie fixes almost anything." Suzanne set the plate in front of Abby, along with a glass of milk. "Now, tell me what's got you so upset."

She would've laughed if her heart didn't feel smashed to pieces. A pie had been what started this a few minutes before. "I think Noah's met someone else."

Suzanne crossed her arms and leaned forward. "And why do you think that?"

She explained the pie, meeting Sarah Murton, and Noah's invitation to help Sarah with whatever she needed.

"What else?"

"What do you mean, what else? I think he may be sweet on her." She took a sip of milk, pushing away the pie.

Suzanne's burst of laughter stunned Abby. "The only woman that man is sweet on is you. He helped Sarah because that's the kind of man he is. Did she mention he rounded up about fifteen other men to help with the work? I think she baked the pie for the exact reason she mentioned. To say thank you."

Abby could feel her face heat. "So you believe I'm wrong?"

"Yes, Abby, I do. Noah's having trouble accepting your wealth, but he'll work through it. When he figures out his pride isn't worth losing you over, he'll be out at the ranch, apologizing. You need to be patient."

"You believe he loves me?"

"Of course I do."

Abby took another sip of milk, thinking over Suzanne's words. Patience had never been her best characteristic. When she figured out what she wanted, she went after it. She saw no reason to change now. She pushed from the table.

"Thank you, Suzanne. I know just what I need to do."

The next two days passed in a whirlwind of activity. After leaving Suzanne's, she sent a telegram to Ernest Payson, then had Dirk drive her to the Pelletier ranch. The discussion with Dax and Luke didn't take long. That night, she finished the last of the paperwork and put it in a drawer, ready for her meeting the following morning.

Dax, Luke, Rachel, and Ginny arrived early, along with baby Patrick, who'd grown considerably since Abby had seen him right after his birth. She handed the men the ledgers, showed them her files, and took the women on a tour. Although they'd been to the ranch before, neither had ventured upstairs. Hers and the Pelletier house compared in size, with the same number of rooms.

After a while, they joined Dax and Luke in the study, discussed details, and agreed on terms. Less than two hours after their arrival, the Pelletiers rode away as the new owners of the Tolbert ranch.

Before they left, Luke mentioned seeing Noah the night before when he took Ginny to supper in town. He told them he planned to go to his cabin Friday night, staying until Sunday, making some long overdue repairs.

It took some strong persuasion, and encouragement from Ginny and Rachel, but Luke finally broke down, giving Abby directions to Noah's cabin. She now had everything she needed.

Noah grabbed another board, nailed it into place, then set the hammer aside. He glanced around. The cabin had never looked better, although it had a ways to go before he invited Abby to see it. It needed curtains, a few more pieces of furniture, and a couple more pans in the kitchen, but overall, he felt pleased with his progress. He knew she'd never want to live here, not with her large home at the ranch. At least he wouldn't be embarrassed to bring her up for a day or two when they wanted complete privacy.

He stood, raised his hands above his head and stretched. Pouring a cup of coffee, he walked outside, thinking of Abby and how much she'd love the glorious sunrises. The cabin sat on a spot the locals called Sunrise Ridge, and the name fit.

He leaned against the rail and sipped from the steaming cup. It wouldn't be long before he'd be able to bring her here, sit with her in the mornings and watch the brilliant yellows, oranges, and pinks light the sky. Then he'd make love to her, keeping her in his bed for hours. He swallowed a lump of fear in his throat, hoping his dreams became reality.

Noah put his tools away, cleaned up, and stoked the fire in the kitchen stove. Suzanne had packed stew, biscuits, and preserves for supper. He placed the stew on top of the stove, then took a seat in the rocking chair he'd hauled up for Abby and sat back, closing his eyes.

Even with Luke's directions, it took Abby longer than anticipated to ride up the trail. The beauty of the hills on this side of town took her breath away, stopping her several times to take in the magnificent view.

She rode into a clearing, watching the sun descend toward the peaks of the western hills. Luke said the clearing meant she had another quarter mile to travel. She nudged Joker forward, her hands beginning to feel moist on the reins, her heart rate increasing the closer she got. Joker took her around one more bend and there it sat—Noah's cabin.

Abby reined to a stop and slid to the ground. She took off the coat she'd worn to protect her dress, then smoothed her hands over her hips and down her skirt. Taking measured steps, she made her way to the cabin. A few feet from the porch steps, a light went on inside, then another. She clutched her hands together. She was almost there.

Noah lit the kerosene lamps, then dished up a bowl of stew and took a seat at the table. Taking a bite, he sat back, chewing as he thought of Abby. He wished she were with him now, sharing this meal. Taking another bite, he rested his arms on the table. He'd become accustomed to being alone at his cabin. For the first time since he'd built it, he felt lonely.

Finishing the stew, he pushed away from the table at the same time a knock sounded on the door. He stared at it a moment, believing he'd imagined the sound. Shaking his head, he grabbed the bowl and heard the knocking sound again. He set the bowl down and walked to the door, grabbing the gun he'd placed on a table. In one quick move, he grabbed the knob and opened the door, pointing the gun straight ahead...and froze.

Abby gasped, her eyes crossing at the sight of a gun pointed at her face.

"Abby?"

"I...I thought I'd surprise you. It appears I did." She took a step backward, a heel catching on a wooden plank.

Noah muttered a curse as he lowered the gun, reaching out with his other hand and pulling her into the cabin, crushing her to his chest. "God, Abby, I could've shot you," he whispered into her hair as he set the gun down and kicked the door shut.

Backing her up against the door, he cupped her face in his hands and lowered his mouth. The kiss started as a brush of his lips against hers, his tongue tracing her lower lip, coaxing her to open. Her lips parted and he delved inside, tasting what he'd been dreaming about for days. Heat flared through him as she sighed into his mouth, wrapped her arms around his neck, and drew him down to her, holding him in place.

Abby couldn't control the fire burning inside. His hands moved up and down her back, then rested on her hips, pulling her tight. Noah's body aligned with hers, his hands roaming over her. She squirmed against him, trying to get closer, wanting more.

He left her mouth, trailing kisses along the curve of her jaw, tracing a path down her neck, sucking the hollow at the base, soft moans escaping her lips. He continued down to the swell of her breasts, then moved back up, crushing his mouth to hers again.

Stroking her face with his knuckles, he pulled back on a ragged breath, resting his forehead against hers. "I've missed you, Abby."

"I've missed you, too. More importantly, I love you, Noah."

"Ah, sweetheart, I love you, too." He captured her mouth again, this time letting the intensity grow until they were both crazed with need. Slipping his hands under her knees, he lifted her to his chest, taking long strides to the bedroom and laying her on the mattress. Joining her, he stroked a finger down the curve of her jaw, along the soft column of her neck, stopping above her chest. He could feel a shiver run through her body.

"Make love to me, Noah."

The passion in her voice and eyes drove his need to a fever pitch. He wanted nothing more, but she had to be sure.

"Abby, it's important you're certain about this. If this isn't what you want—"

"I've wanted this, you, forever. I want you to love me, Noah."

"Abby, darlin', I will always love you."

He stretched, seeing the early sign of morning streaming into the cabin as he took her in his arms. "I need to hold you. After a while, maybe I'll believe you're actually here with me." He kissed the top of her head, drawing in her scent, feeling her softness surround him.

She snuggled closer, resting her hand on his chest, and closed her eyes.

"I've been a fool, Abby."

"I know," she said against his chest, hearing his chuckle.

"I should've asked you to marry me months ago."

"Yes, you should have."

He flipped her onto her back, staring into her eyes, seeing the love he'd been missing out on all this time. "Marry me, Abby. I don't have much, but what I have is yours."

She couldn't stop the tears, even as a smile spread across her face. She trailed fingers down his stubbled jaw, reached up and placed a kiss on his lips. "I'd marry you if you had nothing."

He pulled her tight, then pushed away. "We can live at your ranch. I'm fine with that."

"Um...that may be hard."

She watched his brows knit together, confusion in his eyes.

"I sold it to the Pelletiers. Luke and Ginny will be making it their home." She laughed at his shocked looked. "*This* will be our home as long as you want. I love you, Noah. Your home is my home. Always."

Epilogue

"Is this the spot?" Gabe asked, clasping Noah's shoulder and appreciating the view from the hill behind town—the same land where Noah always planned to build a home for him and Abby to share.

Abby discovered the handwritten addition to her father's will hidden under several documents in his safe. He'd left no explanation other than stating his wish to leave the property to Noah in the event of his death. Nothing more. A few sentences and the land Noah dreamed of living on with Abby was his.

"The porch will wrap all the way around. She'll be able to watch the morning sunrise and evening sunset from right here."

"And keep watch on your whereabouts in town," Bull laughed, handing him a glass of punch and nodding toward the livery below.

"She won't have to. Abby wants to work at the bank a little longer, at least until we have a child. It's what she always wanted to do and is her way of meeting new people."

Abby and Noah had married in a quiet ceremony a week before. At night, they either stayed in the small room off the livery or rode to the cabin. Today, the entire town had been invited to celebrate on Abby's Mountain, as Noah referred to it.

"You've got plenty of friends ready to help. Just give the word." Cash popped a cookie into his mouth, chewing as he turned in a slow circle. "This sure is a beautiful place, Noah."

"I figure there's enough flat land for the house, barn, a corral, and pasture. We don't intend to run cattle, but she wants a few chickens and a garden."

"Chickens?" Luke asked.

"That's what she wants." Noah smiled at the thought of his wife chasing after a chicken, then preparing it to eat. He wasn't even sure she could cook. They'd eaten most of their meals at the boardinghouse.

"Noah." Abby walked up, holding baby Patrick. "Suzanne says it's time to join the rest of us." She cut a look at Cash. "The food is ready...real food, not the dessert you've already discovered."

Cash grinned, showing no remorse as he slid the last cookie he'd pilfered into his mouth.

Noah slipped an arm around Abby's waist, nuzzling her neck as they returned to the main gathering. As with each day since they married, he couldn't wait to get her alone and in his bed.

Long tables held platters loaded with beef, venison, ham, potatoes, vegetables, and bread. Suzanne and several women from church had prepared the food. Nick and Lena provided the music, hauling up the piano and the gentleman who played it from the Dixie. Dax and Luke brought the punch and a large barrel of water, while Ginny and Rachel made pies and cookies. From the looks of it, Noah guessed most everyone for miles around had ridden in for the shindig.

Noah glanced around, spotting Gabe standing next to Lena, Nick, and Suzanne. From what he'd heard and seen, Nick appeared to have more than a cursory interest in his landlord. He guessed the same could be said of Gabe and Lena, although neither would ever admit it, and Noah suspected nothing would ever come of it. He leaned into Abby, kissing her cheek.

"I'll be back in a moment," he said, walking toward the small group. "Thank you again for bringing up the piano." Noah extended his hand to Nick, who gave it a vigorous shake.

Nick glanced around. "You can't have a party without music. Fact is, in New Orleans, we'd sometimes have two or three pianos going at once."

"And a fiddler or two," Lena added with a laugh.

Gabe shifted toward Lena, grinning at her spontaneous laughter. "Do you miss it?"

Lena's brows knit together, her head tilting. "New Orleans? Sometimes, but not enough to move back and start over. Besides, it's nice to be around regular people and not be surrounded by professional scoundrels."

Gabe grinned at the disdain in her voice. "You met a lot of them, did you?"

"More than you'd think, and at least one more than I wanted." She sipped her punch, a hand moving to her stomach at the memory of the man who'd deceived her so completely.

Everyone turned at the sound of approaching horses to see Gil and Ty Murton ride up and dismount, broad grins on their faces, waving to their brother Mark and Ty's wife, Tilly, who sat at one of the tables.

"Sorry we're late, but we got held up." Gil removed his hat, nodding at Suzanne and Lena. "A rider came by with some big news. Seems there's been a gold strike at the site some Englishman's been working up in the mountains. A big one, according to the rider who came through."

Gabe stood next to Lena, sensing her body tense at the announcement, deciding to ask her about her reaction later.

"That so?" Gabe asked as the circle closed around Gil and Ty.

"We knew some foreigner had been prospecting the area, but never met the man."

"You remember an Englishman buying supplies from you?" Gabe asked Noah.

"Can't say as I do. Toby might remember."

"You have a name for the man, Gil?"

Everyone crowded around, waiting.

"Sure do, Sheriff. The rider said the miner's name is William Randolph Carlyle."

Lena gasped, a hand going to her throat as she glanced at Gabe. Her eyes rolled to the back of her head just before she fainted into his arms.

Thank you for taking the time to read Sunrise Ridge. If you enjoyed it, please consider telling your friends or posting a short review. Word of mouth is an author's best friend and much appreciated.

Please join my reader's group to be notified of my New Releases at:
http://www.shirleendavies.com/contact-me.html

I care about quality, so if you find something in error, please contact me via email at:
shirleen@shirleendavies.com

About the Author

Shirleen Davies writes romance—historical, contemporary, and romantic suspense. She grew up in Southern California, attended Oregon State University, and has degrees from San Diego State University and the University of Maryland. During the day she provides consulting services to small and mid-sized businesses. But her real passion is writing emotionally charged stories of flawed people who find redemption through love and acceptance. She now lives with her husband in a beautiful town in northern Arizona.

Shirleen loves to hear from her readers.

Write to her at:
shirleen@shirleendavies.com
Visit her website:
http://www.shirleendavies.com
Sign up to be notified of New Releases:
http://www.shirleendavies.com/contact-me.html

Comment on her blog:
http://www.shirleendavies.com/blog.html

Facebook Fan Page:
https://www.facebook.com/ShirleenDaviesAuthor

Twitter: http://twitter.com/shirleendavies

Google+:
http://www.gplusid.com/shirleendavies

LinkedIn:
http://www.linkedin.com/in/shirleendaviesauthor

Pinterest:
http://www.pinterest.com/shirleendavies

Tsu: http://www.tsu.co/shirleendavies

Other Books by Shirleen Davies

Tougher than the Rest – Book One
MacLarens of Fire Mountain
Historical Western Romance Series

"A passionate, fast-paced story set in the untamed western frontier by an exciting new voice in historical romance."

Niall MacLaren is the oldest of four brothers, and the undisputed leader of the family. A widower, and single father, his focus is on building the MacLaren ranch into the largest and most successful in northern Arizona. He is serious about two things—his responsibility to the family and his future marriage to the wealthy, well-connected widow who will secure his place in the territory's destiny.

Katherine is determined to live the life she's dreamed about. With a job waiting for her in the growing town of Los Angeles,

California, the young teacher from Philadelphia begins a journey across the United States with only a couple of trunks and her spinster companion. Life is perfect for this adventurous, beautiful young woman, until an accident throws her into the arms of the one man who can destroy it all.

Fighting his growing attraction and strong desire for the beautiful stranger, Niall is more determined than ever to push emotions aside to focus on his goals of wealth and political gain. But looking into the clear, blue eyes of the woman who could ruin everything, Niall discovers he will have to harden his heart and be tougher than he's ever been in his life…Tougher than the Rest.

Faster than the Rest – Book Two
MacLarens of Fire Mountain
Historical Western Romance Series

"Headstrong, brash, confident, and complex, the MacLarens of Fire Mountain will captivate you with strong characters set in the wild and rugged western frontier."
Handsome, ruthless, young U.S. Marshal Jamie MacLaren had lost everything—his

parents, his family connections, and his childhood sweetheart—but now he's back in Fire Mountain and ready for another chance. Just as he successfully reconnects with his family and starts to rebuild his life, he gets the unexpected and unwanted assignment of rescuing the woman who broke his heart.

Beautiful, wealthy Victoria Wicklin chose money and power over love, but is now fighting for her life—or is she? Who has she become in the seven years since she left Fire Mountain to take up her life in San Francisco? Is she really as innocent as she says?

Marshal MacLaren struggles to learn the truth and do his job, but the past and present lead him in different directions as his heart and brain wage battle. Is Victoria a victim or a villain? Is life offering him another chance, or just another heartbreak?

As Jamie and Victoria struggle to uncover past secrets and come to grips with their shared passion, another danger arises. A life-altering danger that is out of their control and threatens to destroy any chance for a shared future.

Harder than the Rest – Book Three

MacLarens of Fire Mountain
Historical Western Romance Series

"They are men you want on your side. Hard, confident, and loyal, the MacLarens of Fire Mountain will seize your attention from the first page."

Will MacLaren is a hardened, plain-speaking bounty hunter. His life centers on finding men guilty of horrendous crimes and making sure justice is done. There is no place in his world for the carefree attitude he carried years before when a tragic event destroyed his dreams.

Amanda is the daughter of a successful Colorado rancher. Determined and proud, she works hard to prove she is as capable as any man and worthy to be her father's heir. When a stranger arrives, her independent nature collides with the strong pull toward the handsome ranch hand. But is he what he seems and could his secrets endanger her as well as her family?

The last thing Will needs is to feel passion for another woman. But Amanda elicits feelings he thought were long buried. Can Will's desire for her change him? Or will the vengeance he seeks against the one man he wants to destroy—a dangerous opponent without a conscious—continue to control his life?

Stronger than the Rest – Book Four
MacLarens of Fire Mountain Historical Western Romance Series

"Smart, tough, and capable, the MacLarens protect their own no matter the odds. Set against America's rugged frontier, the stories of the men from Fire Mountain are complex, fast-paced, and a must read for anyone who enjoys non-stop action and romance."

Drew MacLaren is focused and strong. He has achieved all of his goals except one—to return to the MacLaren ranch and build the best horse breeding program in the west. His successful career as an attorney is about to give way to his ranching roots when a bullet changes everything.

Tess Taylor is the quiet, serious daughter of a Colorado ranch family with dreams of her own. Her shy nature keeps her from developing friendships outside of her close-knit family until Drew enters her life. Their relationship grows. Then a bullet, meant for another, leaves him paralyzed and determined to distance himself from the one woman he's come to love.

Convinced he is no longer the man Tess needs, Drew focuses on regaining the use of his legs and recapturing a life he thought lost. But danger of another kind threatens those he cares about—including Tess—forcing him to rethink his future.

Can Drew overcome the barriers that stand between him, the safety of his friends and family, and a life with the woman he loves? To do it all, he has to be strong. Stronger than the Rest.

Deadlier than the Rest – Book Five

**MacLarens of Fire Mountain
Historical Western Romance Series**

*"A passionate, heartwarming story
of the iconic MacLarens of Fire
Mountain. This captivating
historical western romance grabs
your attention from the start with an
engrossing story encompassing two
romances set against the rugged
backdrop of the burgeoning western
frontier."*

Connor MacLaren's search has already stolen
eight years of his life. Now he is close to
finding what he seeks—Meggie, his missing
sister. His quest leads him to the growing city
of Salt Lake and an encounter with the most
captivating woman he has ever met.

Grace is the third wife of a Mormon
farmer, forced into a life far different from
what she'd have chosen. Her independent
spirit longs for choices governed only by her
own heart and mind. To achieve her dreams,
she must hide behind secrets and half-truths,
even as her heart pulls her towards the
ruggedly handsome Connor.

Known as cool and uncompromising, Connor MacLaren lives by a few, firm rules that have served him well and kept him alive. However, danger stalks Connor, even to the front range of the beautiful Wasatch Mountains, threatening those he cares about and impacting his ability to find his sister.

Can Connor protect himself from those who seek his death? Will his eight-year search lead him to his sister while unlocking the secrets he knows are held tight within Grace, the woman who has captured his heart?

Read this heartening story of duty, honor, passion, and love in book five of the MacLarens of Fire Mountain series.

Second Summer – Book One
MacLarens of Fire Mountain
Contemporary Romance Series

"In this passionate Contemporary Romance, author Shirleen Davies introduces her readers to the modern day MacLarens starting with Heath MacLaren, the head of the family."

The Chairman of both the MacLaren Cattle
Co. and MacLaren Land Development, Heath
MacLaren is a success professionally—his
personal life is another matter.

*Following a divorce after a long,
loveless marriage, Heath spends his time
with women who are beautiful and
passionate, yet unable to provide what he
longs for . . .*

Heath has never experienced love even
though he witnesses it every day between his
younger brother, Jace, and wife, Caroline. He
wants what they have, yet spends his time
with women too young to understand what
drives him and too focused on themselves to
be true companions.

*It's been two years since Annie's
husband died, leaving her to build a new
life. He was her soul mate and confidante.
She has no desire to find a replacement, yet
longs for male friendship.*

Annie's closest friend in Fire Mountain,
Caroline MacLaren, is determined to see
Annie come out of her shell after almost two
years of mourning. A chance meeting with
Heath turns into an offer to be a part of the

MacLaren Foundation Board and an opportunity for a life outside her home sanctuary which has also become her prison. The platonic friendship that builds between Annie and Heath points to a future where each may rely on the other without the bonds a romance would entail.

However, without consciously seeking it, each yearns for more . . .

The MacLaren Development Company is booming with Heath at the helm. His meetings at a partner company with the young, beautiful marketing director, who makes no secret of her desire for him, are a temptation. But is she the type of woman he truly wants?

Annie's acceptance of the deep, yet passionless, friendship with Heath sustains her, lulling her to believe it is all she needs. At least until Heath drops a bombshell, forcing Annie to realize that what she took for friendship is actually a deep, lasting love. One she doesn't want to lose.

Each must decide to settle—or fight for it all.

Hard Landing – Book Two
MacLarens of Fire Mountain
Contemporary Romance Series

Trey MacLaren is a confident, poised Navy pilot. He's focused, loyal, ethical, and a natural leader. He is also on his way to what he hopes will be a lasting relationship and marriage with fellow pilot, Jesse Evans.

Jesse has always been driven. Her graduation from the Naval Academy and acceptance into the pilot training program are all she thought she wanted—until she discovered love with Trey MacLaren

Trey and Jesse's lives are filled with fast flying, friends, and the demands of their military careers. Lives each has settled into with a passion. At least until the day Trey receives a letter that could change his and Jesse's lives forever.

It's been over two years since Trey has seen the woman in Pensacola. Her unexpected letter stuns him and pushes Jesse into a tailspin from which she might not pull back.

Each must make a choice. Will the choice Trey makes cause him to lose Jesse forever? Will she follow her heart or her head as she fights for a chance to save the love she's found? Will their independent decisions collide, forcing them to give up on a life together?

One More Day – Book Three
MacLarens of Fire Mountain Contemporary Romance Series

Cameron "Cam" Sinclair is smart, driven, and dedicated, with an easygoing temperament that belies his strong will and the personal ambitions he holds close. Besides his family, his job as head of IT at the MacLaren Cattle Company and his position as a Search and Rescue volunteer are all he needs to make him happy. At least that's what he thinks until he meets, and is instantly drawn to, fellow SAR volunteer, Lainey Devlin.

Lainey is compassionate, independent, and ready to break away from her manipulative and controlling fiancé. Just as her decision is made, she's called into a major search and rescue effort, where once again, her path crosses with the intriguing,

*and much too handsome, Cam Sinclair. But
Lainey's plans are set. An opportunity to
buy a flourishing preschool in northern
Arizona is her chance to make a fresh start,
and nothing, not even her fierce attraction
to Cam Sinclair, will impede her plans.*

As Lainey begins to settle into her new
life, an unexpected danger arises —threats
from an unknown assailant—someone who
doesn't believe she belongs in Fire Mountain.
The more Lainey begins to love her new
home, the greater the danger becomes. Can
she accept the help and protection Cam offers
while ignoring her consuming desire for him?

*Even if Lainey accepts her attraction to
Cam, will he ever be able to come to terms
with his own driving ambition and allow
himself to consider a different life than the
one he's always pictured? A life with the
one woman who offers more than he'd ever
hoped to find?*

All Your Nights – Book Four
MacLarens of Fire Mountain
Contemporary Romance Series

**"*Romance, adventure, cowboys,
suspense—everything you want in a***

***contemporary western romance novel.**"*

Kade Taylor likes living on the edge. As an undercover agent for the DEA and a former Special Ops team member, his current assignment seems tame—keep tabs on a bookish Ph.D. candidate the agency believes is connected to a ruthless drug cartel.

Brooke Sinclair is weeks away from obtaining her goal of a doctoral degree. She spends time finalizing her presentation and relaxing with another student who seems to want nothing more than her friendship. That's fine with Brooke. Her last serious relationship ended in a broken engagement.

Her future is set, safe and peaceful, just as she's always planned—until Agent Taylor informs her she's under suspicion for illegal drug activities.

Kade and his DEA team obtain evidence which exonerates Brooke while placing her in danger from those who sought to use her. As Kade races to take down the drug cartel while protecting Brooke, he must also find common ground with the former suspect—a woman he desires with increasing intensity.

At odds with her better judgment, Brooke finds the more time she spends with Kade, the more she's attracted to the complex, multi-faceted agent. But Kade holds secrets he knows Brooke will never understand or accept.

Can Kade keep Brooke safe while coming to terms with his past, or will he stay silent, ruining any future with the woman his heart can't let go?

Always Love You– Book Five
MacLarens of Fire Mountain
Contemporary Romance Series

"Romance, adventure, motorcycles, cowboys, suspense—everything you want in a contemporary western romance novel."
Eric Sinclair loves his bachelor status. His work at MacLaren Enterprises leaves him with plenty of time to ride his horse as well as his Harley...and date beautiful women without a thought to commitment.

Amber Anderson is the new person at MacLaren Enterprises. Her passion for marketing landed her what she believes to be the perfect job—until she steps into her first meeting to find the man she left, but still loves, sitting at the management table—his disdain for her clear.

Eric won't allow the past to taint his professional behavior, nor will he repeat his mistakes with Amber, even though love for her pulses through him as strong as ever.

As they strive to mold a working relationship, unexpected danger confronts those close to them, pitting the MacLarens and Sinclairs against an evil who stalks one member but threatens them all.

Eric can't get the memories of their passionate past out of his mind, while Amber wrestles with feelings she thought long buried. Will they be able to put the past behind them to reclaim the love lost years before?

Redemption's Edge – Book One
Redemption Mountain – Historical Western Romance Series

"A heartwarming, passionate story of loss, forgiveness, and redemption set in the untamed frontier during

the tumultuous years following the Civil War. Ms. Davies' engaging and complex characters draw you in from the start, creating an exciting introduction to this new historical western romance series."

"Redemption's Edge is a strong and engaging introduction to her new historical western romance series."

Dax Pelletier is ready for a new life, far away from the one he left behind in Savannah following the South's devastating defeat in the Civil War. The ex-Confederate general wants nothing more to do with commanding men and confronting the tough truths of leadership.

Rachel Davenport possesses skills unlike those of her Boston socialite peers—skills honed as a nurse in field hospitals during the Civil War. Eschewing her northeastern suitors and changed by the carnage she's seen, Rachel decides to accept her uncle's invitation to assist him at his clinic in the dangerous and wild frontier of Montana.

Now a Texas Ranger, a promise to a friend takes Dax and his brother, Luke, to the untamed territory of Montana. He'll fulfill his oath and return to Austin, at least that's what he believes.

The small town of Splendor is what Rachel needs after life in a large city. In a few short months, she's grown to love the people as well as the majestic beauty of the untamed frontier. She's settled into a life unlike any she has ever thought possible.

Thinking his battle days are over, he now faces dangers of a different kind—one by those from his past who seek vengeance, and another from Rachel, the woman who's captured his heart.

Wildfire Creek – Book Two
Redemption Mountain – Historical Western Romance Series

"A passionate story of rebuilding lives, working to find a place in the wild frontier, and building new lives in the years following the American Civil War. A rugged, heartwarming story of choices and love in the continuing saga of Redemption Mountain."

Luke Pelletier is settling into his new life as a rancher and occasional Pinkerton Agent, leaving his past as an ex-Confederate major and Texas Ranger far behind. He wants nothing more than to work the ranch, charm the ladies, and live a life of carefree bachelorhood.

Ginny Sorensen has accepted her responsibility as the sole provider for herself and her younger sister. The desire to continue their journey to Oregon is crushed when the need for food and shelter keeps them in the growing frontier town of Splendor, Montana, forcing Ginny to accept work as a server in the local saloon.

Luke has never met a woman as lovely and unspoiled as Ginny. He longs to know her, yet fears his wild ways and unsettled nature aren't what she deserves. She's a girl you marry, but that is nowhere in Luke's plans.

Complicating their tenuous friendship, a twist in circumstances forces Ginny closer to the man she most wants to avoid—the man who can destroy her dreams, and who's captured her heart.

Believing his bachelor status firm, Luke moves from danger to adventure, never dreaming each step he takes brings him closer to his true destiny and a life much different from what he imagines.

Sunrise Ridge – Book Three
Redemption Mountain – Historical Western Romance Series

"The author has a talent for bringing the historical west to life, realistically and vividly, and doesn't shy away from some of the harder aspects of frontier life, even though it's fiction. Recommended to readers who like sweeping western historical romances that are grounded with memorable, likeable characters and a strong sense of place."

Noah Brandt is a successful blacksmith and businessman in Splendor, Montana, with few ties to his past as an ex-Union Army major and sharpshooter. Quiet and hardworking, his biggest challenge is controlling his strong desire for a woman he believes is beyond his reach.

Abigail Tolbert is tired of being under her father's thumb while at the same time, being pushed away by the one man she desires. Determined to build a new life outside the control of her wealthy father, she finds work and sets out to shape a life on her own terms.

Noah has made too many mistakes with Abby to have any hope of getting her back. Even with the changes in her life, including the distance she's built with her father, he can't keep himself from believing he'll never be good enough to claim her.

Unexpected dangers, including a twist of fate for Abby, change both their lives, making the tentative steps they've taken to build a relationship a distant hope. As Noah battles his past as well as the threats to Abby, she fights for a future with the only man she will ever love.

Dixie Moon – Book Four
Redemption Mountain – Historical Western Romance Series

Gabe and Lena's story. Releasing 2015

Reclaiming Love – Book One, A Novella

Kerrigans of Peregrine Bay – Contemporary Romance Series

Adam Monroe has seen his share of setbacks. Now he's back in Peregrine Bay, looking for a new life and second chance.

Julia Kerrigan's life rebounded after the sudden betrayal of the one man she ever loved. As president of a success real estate company, she's built a new life and future, pushing the painful past behind her.

Adam's reason for accepting the job as the town's new Police Chief can be explained in one word—Julia. He wants her back and will do whatever is necessary to achieve his goal, even knowing his biggest hurdle is the woman he still loves.

As they begin to reconnect, a terrible scandal breaks loose with Julia and Adam at the center.

Will the threat to their lives and reputations destroy their fledgling romance? Can Adam identify and eliminate the danger to Julia before he's had a chance to reclaim her love?

Our Kind of Love – Book Two
Kerrigans of Peregrine Bay – Contemporary Romance Series

Set in the beautiful lake country of Idaho, Peregrine Bay stories follow the lives of the five Kerrigan sisters and their family.

Read about Selena and Linc in book two. Releasing 2015